THE CAMBRIDGE EMPIRE

CHRIS KIRBY-RYAN

'It is the mid-forties: a family stands to lose everything they have worked for, ruthlessness and deceit are in the wings as a cinema empire is born, a trap is laid, and the drama unfolds.'

To my sisters,
Nola, Cheryl and Denise —
For all those fun days we spent
growing up in the Sunshine Picture Theatre.

And to John,
Again, and always

A Note from the Author

Whilst this book is a work of fiction, it is inspired by my family. The Sunshine Picture Theatre did start out of an old grain store in Sunshine and my grandfather, George Kirby, did remodel the New Sunshine Picture Theatre. The old grain store still remained standing until the early fifties. My father, Kingsley Kirby and my Aunty Lucy were talented artists and did paint the posters for the movies, you can see one of Dad's beautiful illustrations on the front cover of this book and further sketches at the end of this book.

We did build a theatre at Maidstone, The Roxy, and purchase a theatre at Altona, as well as Bacchus Marsh and others. I have managed to find some old press cuttings which are included at the end of this book.

There are other little gems of information that I have borrowed from my past, but all the characters and the story itself come purely from my imagination. I would like to apologise in advance, for any discriminatory and unwelcome or snide remarks about race, nationality and sexuality. This book is based in the forties and I am using the colloquialisms and expressing the thoughts of many people of that era. These are far from my personal thoughts and opinions.

A Note from the Author

Also, I thought you might find the following newspaper article interesting, seeing as that little grain store you are about to read about did turn into an empire which is now known as the Village Roadshow Group.

Enjoy the article. Enjoy the book.

In 1925, as F. Scott Fitzgerald was putting the finishing touches to the novel that would become an American classic, The Great Gatsby, an old grain store in the Melbourne suburb of Sunshine was converted into the first cinema in the area.

A few years later, the little single-screen Sunshine Picture Theatre was taken over by a fellow named George Kirby. All these decades later, the Kirby family's relationship with the cinema has led from Sunshine to the Australian movie director Baz Luhrmann's Hollywood version of The Great Gatsby, filmed in Sydney.

Old George Kirby's grandsons, Robert G. Kirby and John R. Kirby, are still in the picture business, though they have moved a fair distance from Sunshine.

Their father, George's son Roc Kirby, founded Village Roadshow. Having started sweeping floors and selling ice-creams at his father's picture shows, Roc opened the first Village Drive-in at Croydon in 1954. By the time he died in 2008, Roc Kirby's Village Roadshow owned a film production division, cinemas throughout Australia, theme parks on the Gold Coast and a stake in the radio company Austereo.

Roc's sons Robert and John are now respectively chairman and deputy chairman of Village Roadshow Ltd.

Village Roadshow Pictures, through a long-time relationship with Warner Bros, sank many tens of millions of dollars into the production of The Great Gatsby. Now there's a dynasty.

And so the world turns: F. Scott Fitzgerald writes a novel about the death of the American dream; an old grain store becomes a picture theatre in Sunshine, Victoria; an Australian family hands down a love of moving pictures through generations; and an Australian director turns Fitzgerald's American masterpiece into a film spectacular.

Of Dodgers and Dynasties
Tony Wright, Sydney Morning Herald
June 1, 2013
http://www.smh.com.au/national/of-dodgers-and-dynasties-20130531-
2nh7q.html

Chapter One

THE SETTING SUN cast long shadows through the stand of poplar trees that ran along the long lane leading down to the old Nissen army hut. It was no more than a slap-up building, a dome of corrugated iron on a large plot of land that ran directly adjacent to the railway line, but it wasn't unusual for 1945. The man who approached it was young in years, in his early twenties, with dark curly black hair that was a little too long for his father's liking. He was dressed casually in pleated trousers and plaid vest. He strode with a certainty that exuded confidence and purpose. He wasn't an overly tall man, but more than average at around five-foot-ten. He often turned women's heads, but that was probably more to do with his air of determination, rather than his looks, which were perfectly fine but perhaps not take-a-second-look handsome.

He opened the door of the army hut.

Anyone watching may have expected to see the door open into the typical grain storage shed that its exterior indicated. Instead, as the door opened it allowed a beam of light to fall onto an astonishing array of flowers, set in an enormous urn perched on a round, marble-like pedestal that was centred in a rather elaborate foyer. The foyer was small, given the limitations of the army hut, but elegant with its red velvet flocked wallpaper and gold embossed window frames. It was large enough to boast a modest kiosk stocking everything from peanuts to ice-creams to popular chocolate bars and the ladies' favourite chocolate boxes. To the right of this was a solid oak door, quite intimidating by comparison to the rest of the surrounds.

Without a hint of warning the floral arrangement sent irises flurrying and white petals fell from the roses as the figure of a tiny woman appeared from behind the enormous urn. She was perched on a ladder in order to reach the blooms over which she had total control, placing them carefully into the most artistic display.

'So, you're finally here,' she spoke when seeing the man who had entered the foyer. 'Dad's been in there with him for ages.'

'That's a bad sign.'

'Honestly Hudson, I don't know what you have against Mr Maxwell, he is a respected businessman around town.'

'Yeah, well I don't trust him,' Hudson retorted to his sister.

'Well maybe it's about time you started, because I think Dad is about to do a deal with him.' Hudson didn't like hearing his sister's opinion. He thought his father could do far better than wheel and deal with the man who was currently in his office. He rubbed his hand through his thick wavy locks and walked towards his father's office. Halted by the sound of his father's voice, he thought twice about bursting uninvited into a meeting his father had organised without his knowledge.

His sister glared at him. She may have been little in height, but she was strong on determination and sheer spunk. Her name was Cecilia, but everyone lovingly called her Cissy. Her artistic flair showed in her colourful clothes and wild head of hair. Perhaps her hair was not all that was wild, but being just eighteen years of age, Cissy was still largely under her father's thumb — struggling though she may be to free herself of that.

Hudson stood at the office door staring, straining to hear as the conversation of two men drifted out.

Beyond the door was not the type of office you would expect to find in old army hut with its expensive cedar panels and leather topped desk. There were three telephones, each of them cumbersome black models with heavy handsets. Like many of his peers, Carleton Cambridge liked to reserve different phones for different reasons. It always gave a man an edge to know who he was dealing with before he picked up the phone. Carleton Cambridge was a distinguished man. Formerly a land baron who had suffered the severe effects of year upon year of drought, only to be finally wiped out by a savage bush fire in Leongatha, where for so many years generations of Cambridges had lived off the rich grazing country the region in Southern Gippsland, Victoria had always been renowned for. When his wife succumbed to TB, Carleton had lost a lot of his fight, and moved his family of two sons and a daughter, down to the city.

He'd chosen to settle in a small town that was beginning to grow. An industry-centred community, the town was known as Sunshine and the population was growing rapidly due to the large number of workers required to run the factories. It was just the type of town Carleton Cambridge was looking for. A place of promise, where industry was growing and bringing young families looking for work. What was even better were the towns that were springing up around Sunshine, places Carleton knew would support the planned expansion of his theatre empire. Infrastructure and amenities were already being built to connect and cater for neighbouring towns and the farming communities which already existed nearby, as Sunshine bordered on the western outskirts of the city of Melbourne.

He'd located the old grain storage shed by accident. Before the move to the city Carleton had ventured down with his younger son, Seymour. They had been looking for a home. Carleton had not yet decided on his line of business, but he'd heard a lot about the movie industry and how cinemas were beginning to grow. He'd been to a couple of picture nights that had been shown in the Leongatha town hall. He'd thought even then how great it would be to build a picture theatre and let the people enjoy. He considered the possibility of turning this venture into a profitable business and the more he thought about it the more it excited him.

Why not? Cinema was the way of the future. It was what everyone was talking about. In the cities it was what everyone was doing on a Friday and Saturday night. Now that he was here, driving around this pleasant town, he could see his vision becoming a reality. And that was when he saw it.

It was a humble army hut, currently being used as a grain shed on a very large plot of land. The sign read 'FOR SALE' and Carleton's mind began to churn. It could be a start. The town currently had no picture theatre and very little in the way of entertainment. If he set up a make-shift theatre in the grain store now, then settled his family into their new home — later down the track he could build the theatre of his dreams.

His boys would help him, he knew that. And his daughter Cecilia, she was as talented as they came with an artist's brush and a decorator's eye. He imagined they could create their own movie posters, even his son, Hudson, had talent in that area and what's more — he could play the piano like no other — what great entertainment that would make during intervals and when the patrons were waiting for the show to commence. He was confident he and his family could make a real go of this.

He thought of all of the popular movies with the big stars that were pouring out of Hollywood, not to mention the Australian movies that were favourites amongst local audiences. And so, Carleton's dream began, right there on an overgrown plot of land, home to a meagre old grain hut. His family all pitched in, and it was during these early stages of building his dream that Carleton deeply felt the loss of his beloved wife, Margot. It was only the last winter on the farm that she'd succumbed to TB. Bitterly cold and in the grip of a drought, Margot had grown weaker throughout those horror months, trying to keep up with the chores bestowed on a farmer's wife while struggling to find energy to feed the family. When she took to her bed Carleton knew the worst lay ahead.

Still, the children had rallied when death came, they supported their father in all his decisions and when the move to the city was imminent, they were with him every step of the way, just as they had been to turn this old grain shed into something of which they could be proud.

Hudson and Seymour, hardly out of short pants, did all the heavy lifting, cleaning out the mess and giving the family a blank canvas on which to work. With paint brushes and timber and a variety of seating, the old army hut began to transform. They installed a kiosk, built a ticket box and a magnificent stage which would not only house the movie screen, but also have space enough for the odd live performance or two when the town needed somewhere to hold their celebrations.

Then there was the question of the projection room, and this was where Hudson shone. Very skilled at mechanics and engineering, what Hudson couldn't buy within their budget, he made. No tin can was wasted, no nut, no bolt, no piece of metal. Hudson soldered and clipped and screwed this and that together to the amazement of the rest of his family. He fashioned them a projection unit like no other, and before they recognised totally what was happening, the Cambridges had themselves a picture theatre in the middle of a close-knit community and growing industrial town. More than two years had now flown by, and Carleton was in the process of really firing up that dream. A brand-new Sunshine Picture Theatre was underway, it would be a regal picture theatre — no old grain shed — that the town could be proud of.

Like the man himself, Carleton's desk in his little grain shed office was organised in an efficient and logical manner. The desk blotter pad was filled with doodlings, jottings and phone numbers only the author could decipher. Important phone numbers were stored in the black Teledex, ready for handy access in alphabetical order. A globe of the world sat to the left of the desk and in prime central position sat a large bottle of Johnny Walker Black Label, Carleton's only vice.

As Carleton poured two glasses of the golden liquid, he looked across to the capacious gentleman seated on the visitor's side of the large desk, comfortable in the roomy leather visitor's chair and accepting the crystal tumbler as he listened with interest to the man who initiated the meeting.

'I want to expand Wilbur, the success I've experienced here is evidence of just how big this industry can become.'

'With all due respect CC, this is just a little makeshift picture house inside an old grain store for heaven's sake, what you're talking about goes way beyond that.' CC was the affectionate name for Carleton Cambridge meant only for his friends and close colleagues, however in a close-knit community and town as small as Sunshine, those friends and colleagues were many, and many who weren't so close, took liberties.

'Indeed it does, and I have to tell you that the foundations for the new Sunshine Picture Theatre will begin next week.' replied CC. 'Do you think I am going to sit here forever in this hut? Oh yes it has been a godsend in a way. What with the drought and then losing the whole farm to bushfires, I didn't think we'd ever recover.' Wilbur nodded knowingly, taking another sip of the smooth and agreeable Scotch.

Wilbur Maxwell was a roguish man and somewhat intimidating — a trait at which he worked to perfect. Coming from a family that was very lucky to survive the Great Depression of the nineteen-thirties, his determination to never want for anything had been his driver. His past may have been sketchy, but his future was on a steady path of capital growth. If he had to roll a few heads to get to there, so be it. No one had ever done him any favours, he'd worked long and hard to reach the enviable position he was in today, and it made him chuckle to now see men like Carlton Cambridge call on him for financial favours.

'With the money the insurance company paid out for the loss of the farm, and with the support of my kids, this little place has become a gold mine. We've shown every major film that has come out of Columbia, Paramount, MGM and Warner Brothers, not to mention our home-grown flicks. The locals went mad for *The Kokoda Front Line*.'

Wilbur leaned forward, placing his glass of Scotch onto CC's solid oak, leather topped desk. He switched to a more serious tone. 'Even so CC, you're proposing four major cinemas here. So, you're already well underway with the new Sunshine Picture Theatre, you're building another at Maidstone, purchasing Altona outright and have your sights set on Sorrento. It's a hell of a risk.'

'And one that I am more than willing to take. Look, I've done my research. These areas have the population, sure, they may be low-income areas, but what is there for the people to do other than to take in the latest movie at their local picture theatre for ten-pence a seat? I know we will have success here Wilbur,' CC responded confidently. He was a man who had placed his trust in other people for many years. Being on the land breeds a strong chain of camaraderie between landowners — people helping each other out in a crisis. Now in the city, CC believed that trust, honesty and openness were the only way to run a business, and through these virtues a man could build a solid business, one that he could be proud of and one day hand down to his sons.

He looked directly into Wilbur Maxwell's eyes. He could see that the man was intrigued with what he had to say. He understood Wilbur well enough to know that he hated to miss out on an opportunity. With an air of surety, he leant forward, picking up his glass in a salute as he summed up the conversation for Wilbur, 'And let me say this, I'll be doing this with or without you. And with or without you, Cambridge Theatres will make its mark and give my sons — and my daughter if it comes to that — a business that we can all be proud of.'

Outside the office Hudson shook his head. He knew his father had plans to further expand the theatres, but to lay your trust in someone like Wilbur Maxwell was definitely a bad move. Hudson moved quickly into the tiny ticket office, he was in search of a phone, and he needed privacy, somewhere where his conversation would not be overheard.

Chapter Two

WILBUR MAXWELL WAS glad to be home. Home in the house he had built to make a statement. Money, power, glory. He loved to drape his trophy wife, Dorothy, on his arm and head off to James' for dinner. James McCall was the richest man in Sunshine, having established a very successful Harvester Works which had basically put the town on the map and given it its start in the industrial amplification. There were no stylish restaurants or fancy hotels in this little community, and so dining out meant being invited to the homes of the more influential, and James was certainly top of the Who's Who in this community.

But right now, Wilbur was now relaxing in the bar of his large recreational room. As he sat on his leather padded barstool admiring his handsomely stocked shelves of liquor, he looked around the room. How he loved this room, his own special space. It was masculine, spacious and domineering in a powerful sort of way with its full-sized billiard table, heavy drapes and panelled walls. Wilbur could not stop thinking about CC's proposal. He knew CC had the brains and the combined talent within his family to make this empire he talked of work. He was not opposed to loaning CC the money at a profitable interest rate, but he just had a strong feeling that there was more that could be gained from CC's empire … and he was going to devise a way to get it — in fact he was going to devise a way to get it all.

Wilbur's son Godfrey arrived, and Wilbur was now in an intense conversation with him. Godfrey was the best thing his wife had ever done for him, other than being incredibly attractive. His son gave him the future he wanted, he and the boy, conquering the world together, building their fortune and ruling their world. He believed Godfrey had all the same intentions, and as he poured him a drink, he brought him in on the scheme that would make their next fortune. 'So, Son, I want you to keep a close eye their comings and goings. I mean you're mates with Hudson are you not?' Wilbur asked as he poured himself another Scotch.

'Define mates,' replied Godfrey. 'The guy rubs me up the wrong way to be honest. He's always got his head stuck in some sort of machine figuring out how it works, if he's not doing that he's getting totally absorbed in his art — painting portraits and pictures of movie stars. Why bother? Why not just have a life?'

Arrogant and ungrateful, his father knew his son was this way, but then he didn't believe in cowering to the masses either. His son was brought up with all the things that he had never had, so it was no wonder he took most of it for granted. Not quite of the silver-spoon set, but certainly picturing himself within it, Godfrey Maxwell was cunning for his age at 21. He believed he was too good for the town his father had chosen to live in and develop his business affairs. Why weren't they living south of the Yarra? Surely Toorak, South Yarra or even Brighton would have suited their success far more appropriately? He was disgruntled, and his entire demeanour showed it. Godfrey was simply bored with anything this hick town had to offer.

'Someone has to do these things Godfrey — where would we be without motor cars and … and movie projectors for that matter?' he commented, referring to Hudson's mechanical skills. 'Besides all of that, I've seen you with your eye on young Cecilia, now she's a bit of a prize.' Godfrey couldn't believe his father's ignorance and testosterone driven stupidity — at his age! God, his father really had no idea what he had been up to. Thinking ahead though, he took the inference on board and, not denying it, decided on a strategy.

'Who I go out with father is my business alone. You can't start dictating to me there.'

'Wouldn't dream of it my boy, but romance can have more than one motive if you think beyond your hormones. Just think about what I'm saying.'

Godfrey knew what his father was thinking and as much as he wanted to give him a piece of his mind, he liked the family money too much and did not want to see himself going it alone. His father had often threatened him with this growing up in the Maxwell household — always telling him to pull his weight like he had done all his life — or get out and see what it was like to make it on your own. Godfrey rolled his eyes and challenged his father just a little, 'Why does everything always have to be so calculated with you?'

'A little strategic planning never hurt anyone Godfrey. Look, you're off to the Palais tonight?' Godfrey nodded, wondering where this was leading. 'So, if you see Hudson say hello, buy him a drink, see what's going on at the Cambridge household.' Godfrey gave his father a long-suffering look, not amused at all. Wilbur reached out for his son, gently shaking his shoulder. 'Come on Son, if there's an empire about to be built, let's make sure we've got our finger on the pulse hey? Go on, live dangerously, remember what it's all about Son, work never takes a holiday … and if Hudson's sister, Cecilia, is there, buy her a drink, dance her off her feet.'

Pleased with himself, Wilbur rose from his barstool and approached the billiard table, 'Quick game — gonna let me whip your arse again?' Godfrey loathed his father's arrogance at times, even though he'd inherited that very trait. Really, it was like looking into a mirror when you had no idea that was what you were doing. He approached the billiard table picking up a cue, he would beat his father this time, he was just in a bad enough mood, and he needed a win.

'Rack 'em up. Let's see who the better man is,' Godfrey challenged, chalking his cue methodically.

Unlike the name, mornings in Sunshine could be very cool, and as the chilling wind whipped up a squall, taking with it sidewalk litter and sending fallen leaves and other debris on a journey towards roads and neighbouring paths, Hudson pulled into the kerb. He was a man on a mission and looked determined as he stepped out of his pride and joy — 1939 Ford Deluxe Convertible. He'd been the proud owner of the sporty red model for two months now. He couldn't believe his luck when his friend had told him the sports car was for sale at a car yard not too far away. After a lot of cajoling with his father, CC had finally agreed to the purchase and now Hudson felt on top of the world every time he got behind the steering wheel. A car wasn't everything, but it sure was a damned good start.

Despite the weather Hudson drove with the roof down, a spot of vanity — maybe, but the wind on his face made him feel happy and shrugging into his favourite lamb-skin jacket wasn't exactly a hardship either. Hudson didn't bother locking the car, anyone could get into it with the roof down, and in this town, nobody locked anything, it was a community of good citizens.

As he stood in front of the site of the new picture theatre, he surveyed the construction works. Hudson cast his eyes appreciatively over the progress of the building. The walls were on their way up and Hudson just couldn't wait for the opening, leaving the old grain hut picture theatre behind and running the movies in this amazing new cinema, but right now he had work to attend to in the old, converted grain shed. As he strolled down the poplar tree lined lane towards the Nissen army hut, his mind returned to the conversation he'd overheard the night before. Hudson believed that getting into debt with Wilbur Maxwell was a mistake, and he was about to tell his father exactly that.

The foyer of the picture theatre was deserted, Hudson went off in search of his father. 'Dad, Dad — are you around?' he shouted as he entered the double doors leading into the cinema. Beyond the door lay an aisle extending down to the stage and movie screen. Either side of the aisles were rows of theatre seats, purchased second-hand from a live theatre in Melbourne that had gone into receivership. Adequate as they were, they lacked the glamour of a regal cinema, and the old leather smell permeated the entire theatre space, which did not go unnoticed when patrons arrived.

There was no sign of his father and Hudson was just about to leave when he spied Cissy making some repairs to the red velvet stage curtains in front of the screen. 'Is our grand cinema falling apart around us hey?' Cissy looked up, recognising her brother's voice and happy to see him. 'Grand cinema indeed,' she said with a laugh in her voice. 'It will be so good when we have our new theatre built. What brings you into work at this time of the day?'

'I wanted to see Dad; do you know if he's here?'

'You'll probably find him in the projection box, I believe we just got some new movies in, direct from Hollywood,' Cissy informed her brother.

'Oh super, word has it we are expecting *Lassie Come Home* — that's just a huge favourite with kids and grown-ups.'

'Oh, I hate those dog movies — I always end up in tears.'

'Come on, you love them, and you know it.' Cissy turned her nose up at her brother's comeback. She loved Hudson, even though he was such a tease and a real devil for playing tricks on her. She thought he would have gotten over that, seeing as she was now eighteen and he a man of twenty-two. She was glad to have him here at home instead of off fighting the war like her brother, Seymour.

'Anyway, I'll go find Dad.' Hudson turned to walk away but just as he did so his movements were arrested by Cissy's curiosity. 'Say, who was that redhead I saw you eyeing-off last night?' Hudson turned back to his sister, smiling at her but revealing nothing. 'You know, at the Palais?' Typical sister, Hudson thought, always prying into his affairs and catching him out when he least expected it. Not to give anything away, Hudson simply shook his head at his sister and walked away. Cissy watched his retreat, itching to know what was really going on with her brother and the redhead.

Hudson opened the door that led to the projection box. The space itself was no more than a cupboard housing cans of film and a ladder that led up to a manhole that in turn led to a small mezzanine where the

35mm projector was whirring away. Hudson ascended the ladder to find his father engrossed in a can of 35mm film.

The room was tiny, with two film projectors side by side, one used as a back-up in case the main projector failed. Scattered around were cans of film and a stool for the projectionist to take the load off once the film was playing for the audience. The smell of celluloid was powerful but not unwelcome. The Cambridge family was very familiar with this unique scent, that and the warmth that the tiny projection room generated — it was sheer hell on a blistering hot summer's day.

Carleton was loading up a reel on the far projector. He looked up as his son appeared through the floor — out of the manhole entrance. Hudson looked around the dim, warm lighting of the projection room as the projector whirred into life producing a misty, magical effect in the close surrounding atmosphere, streaming rays from the projector that you could almost grab before they reached their final destination — the big screen. Cans of film scattered all around and the twin projectors were prominent, taking over most of the cramped space that provided the bread and butter that graced the Cambridge household's table and held great promises for the family's future.

'Dad,' Hudson greeted his father.'

'Good morning Hudson, how are you going son?' CC looked up from his current task of threading a reel.

'I bumped into Godfrey Maxwell last night. Tells me you've put the hard word on his father for a bit of financial help.'

'No one ever got far in this world trying to do it all on their own Son.'

'Look I understand you and Wilbur Maxwell have formed this special friendship, but what really worries me is — I don't know, there's something about his son — hell, if you want my opinion there's something up with Wilbur as well.'

'God's honest truth, I don't really want your opinion on this,' CC replied, being brutally frank and uncaring about his son's feelings. 'I run the financial side of the business and if anyone takes over those reins it is going to be your brother, Seymour. He has a head for figures, but you on the other hand, have your head in the clouds half the time.' Hudson glared at his father, tight mouthed, he'd heard it all before and he just couldn't stand it. CC looked at the dejected expression on his son's face and started to feel a little guilty. Hudson was a good son after all, just not maybe the world's best on the accounting side of things. He softened, backing down on his opinionated stance whilst in the process of threading the film through the sprocket.

'Look, don't get me wrong Son, you're a bit of a genius when it comes to engineering and the technical side of things — how ever would we have had this entire projection unit together without you? Sure, Seymour wouldn't know where to start when it comes to all this. So that's why it works so well, your brother on the management side and you on the creative side, running our little projection room and looking after all of our displays, billboards and advertising.'

'Really Dad? Are you sure I am not just being pushed into some useless corner because you think I am no good with money?'

'Hudson, I don't want to have this argument with you, we all have our strengths and together we are going to build an empire Son, it's all going to happen. But to do it, we need help, so trust me — and your brother — to lead this ship on a wave of success.'

Carleton now had the reel threaded and was about to roll the film, he looked towards the screen through one of the tiny projection windows and encouraged his son to do the same. 'Oh, look at this Son, it's the latest news. Apparently, there's a story in from Salonika, where your brother is currently fighting.'

The familiar 'Movietone News' theme music drowned out their conversation as father and son looked on. 20th Century Fox appeared to be followed by the Movietone News logo. The bold and bracing marching music introduced the latest footage from World War II. The reels had arrived at the Sunshine Picture Theatre that morning, which meant it would contain news around two weeks old. Radio and newspapers were a quicker way to receive the news, Carleton knew, but seeing the real thing up on the big screen always out-trumped listening to it on the radio. Often Carleton did not have time to read the newspaper, so he always looked forward to the latest from Movietone News.

Hudson and his father watched the war zone report through the projection box windows and were horrified at the intensity of the war-ravaged scenes in front of them. It was horrific, there was disaster everywhere. It looked as though a bomb had exploded and there were injured people crying for help. They saw a soldier carrying a wounded teenage girl towards a medevac unit. She was crying, clinging to her rescuer who barely looked able to walk himself. Carleton examined the hero closer and recognised his own son.

'Oh, Holy Mother, look, look Hudson, it's Seymour — if only I could pause this for a second, make the film stop right there, get a better look. Yes, that's Seymour, helping that poor girl.' The camera moved into a close up of Seymour, showing his distress in this war-ravaged environment. Carleton and Hudson looked on grimly. 'I wish this godforsaken war was over.' Hudson looked at his father then turned back to watch the report, wondering where his brother could be right now.

Chapter Three

HUDSON TOOK great delight in teasing his sister, Cissy. When she was little he would pull her plaits and chase her around the farmyard. He would hide from her and spring out when she was least expecting it, causing the poor girl a near fit of apoplexy. As she got older, he would play tricks on her girlfriends, then her boyfriends. The jokes became less funny as they grew up and he toned his tricks down, but he still couldn't resist the odd prank or two.

The Carletons lived in a rather lavish home, not quite the mansion that Wilbur Maxwell had built, but a spacious and beautiful home none the less. It was a tasteful home of the mid-twenties. The home of a former landowner, it boasted cedar panelling in the main dining room and wall to ceiling windows in the pleasant sunroom CC had added when he bought the place, along with two more bedrooms and an extra bathroom. This meant the boys each had their own bedroom and Cissy her own wing, with bedroom, bathroom and a guest bedroom.

The loungeroom was designed for comfort with club couches, an enormous open fireplace and an ultra-modern walnut veneer radio the pride of place. The bedrooms each had their own personality — Cissy's room was adorned in pastel wallpaper and pretty curtains, floral and frilled with matching bedspreads. Hudson and Seymour had separate bedrooms, each adding their own signature with trophies and keepsakes.

Hudson's trophies consisted mainly of his sketches, hung proudly around his walls. Lately they had been of movie stars. There were often quiet moments in the projection room, when the movie was rolling and everything was under control, Hudson would take out his sketch pad and begin to capture on paper, the actor on screen. Not only was this a great talent, it was a useful one. He and sister Cissy created most of the movie posters displaying the coming attractions. It helped keep the costs down and it was a responsibility which Hudson and Cissy took seriously — enjoying every moment of it.

Today was poster day and Hudson had retreated to their studio which was a refurbished shed at the rear of the back garden. Cissy just adored animals, she had cats everywhere, a beautiful big aquarium of tropical fish and a cute little dachshund dog who, for some unknown reason had taken a liking to Hudson and seemed to follow him adoringly — now being no exception.

In a moment of mischievousness, Hudson scooped up little Chipolata and held him over his head, twirling him around like a spinning top. 'Put him down,' cried Cissy as she entered the room.

'Why? He loves it. Can't you see that he loves it?'

'You're a beast Hudson, an absolute beast. You're frightening the poor little thing.'

Hudson laughed gaily as he continued to twirl the pooch. 'Come on Hudson, poor little Chipolata.' Hudson's expression softened. He would never hurt an animal and little Chipolata was never in any danger. He gave in and handed the dog to an over-anxious Cissy. She soothed it lovingly, glaring at her brother for playing yet another nasty trick on her and her beloved pet.

In an effort to put a smile on her face Hudson changed the subject. 'Say, are you off to the Palais tonight?'

'I am, I'm going with Veronica.' Hudson was not so sure about Cissy's new-found friend. Having met her at the Palais only a month earlier, the girl was a bit too bold for Hudson's liking. Perhaps people were just different in the city, and he should give her the benefit of the doubt and be glad that his sister was making new friends. But he just couldn't seem to budge that nagging feeling, there was something about this girl.

'Why do you hang around with that woman? She's just out for all she can get. You know that.'

'Come on, she's not so bad,' Cissy retorted. 'Besides, who else am I going to go out with?'

'What about your friend, Miriam?'

'I really like Miriam, but she can never really do anything because she is always looking after her sick mother — and you're an old stick in the mud, working all the time.'

'Says who? You don't see me missing out any fun. As a matter of fact, I'm off to the Palais again tonight.'

'How can you? You have to work, it's Saturday night.'

'We're running an Ellery Queen double remember? The Spanish Cape Mystery and The Mandarin Mystery. Both nice and short — I'll be well out of there by ten and at the Palais by ten-thirty — plenty of time to get into trouble.'

'You need to take it easy Hudson.'

'And you little Miss Bossy Britches, need to mind your own business.'

Veronica Pritchard was determined. Dressed to impress in flaming red, the satin dress clung to her like a second skin. Her jet-black hair glistened, and she had styled it into side-rolls that emphasised her high cheekbones and long dark lashes. She could feel a sea of eyes on her as she entered the Palais, and she loved every minute of it. She blessed the day that Cissy befriended her, not that she hadn't been scheming to make that happen. Poor, befuddled Cecilia, she had no idea what really went on in this world — living a charmed life with her brothers and the budding little Cambridge Empire. She couldn't comprehend what it was like to have your mother walk out on you when you were just four and have to suffer a drunk for a father. One who did nothing to help you but expected everything from you. She was glad when her father died.

No one could understand it, leaving a young girl of fourteen alone —an orphan—surely the devastation would be too much to bear. But not for Veronica. No one knew that she had contributed to his death. That she had loaded his drink with pills she hoped would do the trick. That he passed out into such a deep coma that all she had to do was to hold a pillow over his face until he gasped his last breath. Too comatose to fight and so drunk that everyone just presumed he died of alcohol induced causes.

That was the last time he would touch her body in anyway whatsoever. She swore that the next man to share her bed would be filthy rich, she would beguile him until he was like putty in her hands and then she would own him. Tonight was just the beginning. She had gained Cissy's friendship, now to move in on her circle of friends. Godfrey Maxwell, he may not be the richest man in Melbourne but he — or at least his father — was reputedly wealthy; and if there was one thing Veronica had it was vision, and she could see the future that lay at Godfrey's feet, with her on board his future would be brighter, bolder and richer than ever for her.

She walked into the dance hall of the Palais, never tiring of the stunning art deco style with its elaborate ceiling panels, wall niches and decorative cornices. Through the ornate columns you could see the Glenn Miller look alike band that owned the stage. They were immaculately presented in their slick suits and college haircuts. *In the Mood* had dancers on the floor moving rhythmically to the modern swing that had taken the world by storm. She looked around, Cissy in her wake like a faithful puppy, 'There's a table over there, let's grab it.' They snaked their way through the crowd to snag what seemed like the last vacant table.

Veronica looked around. Surveying the scene was an important tactic. Who was here, where they were situated? She spied her target. Godfrey Maxwell was at the bar, she watched him, intrigued by his charming manner and almost womanish way in which he held his cigarette between his index and middle finger. Tailor-made filter-tips too, no common roll-your-owns for Godfrey, she liked that. Time to strike, she strode off in his direction, telling Cissy she would get them a drink.

Seeing her bold approach, Godfrey appeared to shrink at the very sight of her, trying to pretend he hadn't seen her. He turned and ordered another drink, fooling himself that if he ignored her, she would go away.

'Well look who I found,' Veronica crooned as she sidled up to Godfrey. 'Who are you here with?'

'No one, I just got here.' Godfrey could have kicked himself for such a stupid answer. Pretty skilled at lying his way out of difficult situations he couldn't believe he had just given her a huge opportunity to ruin his night, he certainly didn't want to be stuck with the likes of Veronica Pritchard all night.

'Well then I insist you join us,' Veronica schmoozed.

Why was he surprised? He had a feeling she had an ulterior motive in there somewhere and feared that motive was him. 'You said us?'

'Yes, I'm here with Cissy Cambridge.' That caught Godfrey's interest, he turned to see Cissy through the crowd, seated at a table, she waved at him.

'Oh yes, I'd love to join you,' he said, instantly changing his mind as he remembered his father's words. 'What are you drinking? I'll get them.'

Cissy was a little peeved when Veronica brought Godfrey back to the table, she had been waiting on her friend Miriam to arrive and wasn't really in the mood for Godfrey's small talk and Veronica's blatant pursuit of the man. Miriam was working at the picture theatre that night and had a neighbour in to look after her mother. Hudson had said he would give her a lift into the Palais when they had finished for the evening. Miriam Worthing was a simple girl with a genuine nature, Cissy liked that. It didn't matter to Cissy that Miriam neither knew about nor cared for the finer things in life, she worked as a nurse at a public clinic during the day then took what night work she could get from the Cambridges. It all helped to pay for the care her mother needed, she had been diagnosed with TB and now suffered severely. Tuberculosis was an infectious and degenerative disease that caused the lungs to eventually collapse. Miriam knew her mother did not have a lot of time left and she was dedicated to making her as comfortable and happy as possible.

'Cat got your tongue?' asked Godfrey as Cissy was seemingly staring off into space.

'No, just wondering how long Hudson and Miriam would be.'

'Oh, what do you waste your time on that bore for? Forget about her and let's have fun,' wheedled Veronica.

'I think Cissy's entitled to choose who her friends are Veronica, she does not need you to run her life for her.' Recoiling at Godfrey's comment, Veronica disregarded the slight and decided to change the subject. She didn't like the attention he was paying to Cissy and thought it was high time she dug her claws in a little deeper.

'Oh, come on Godfrey, let's dance.' Godfrey was reluctant, he really couldn't stomach Veronica, but he didn't want to scare Cissy off by making it too obvious he was really there for her.

'If you insist,' he half groaned, turning to wink at Cissy. 'It will be your turn next, get those dancing shoes ready.'

And so, onto the dance floor they glided, leaving Cissy wondering what Veronica was up to. Was she really after Godfrey? She'd only just met him and somehow he just didn't appear to be her type, but then, what was her type? Cissy was only getting to know the girl herself and, in a way, she felt that could be a major exercise all on its own.

The familiar whir of the projection unit hummed beneath the movie soundtrack. Hudson wondered why no one had invented a way to embed the soundtrack into the movie so that it didn't have to run on a separate reel. Syncing them was always tricky but he was grateful tonight's Ellery Queen double had gone off without a hitch. He peered out at the audience through the tiny projection box window. As he squinted through the misty effect of the projector, he noticed Jack Sotheby, the staunch and formidable man employed as usher and all-rounder. He was only in his late twenties but seemed very regulated and believed in rules. He reigned over the little theatre like it was his own and made sure nobody misbehaved during the screening of a film. Shining his torch on a youth who had dared to stand up during the show, he ordered him to retake his seat or leave the theatre. The boy looked at the intimidating man and lowered his fist which he had been shaking at the screen as a suited detective arrested a young boy in the murder mystery that was playing out in front of the audience.

'Young man, sit down immediately,' Sotheby whispered sternly. The young man reluctantly obeyed, to the sniggers of his mates.

Hudson smiled to himself as he noticed the film coming to an end. Jack Sotheby kept an eagle eye on all of the attendants at the theatre, Hudson himself was wary of him and treated him with utmost respect. It wasn't a job he envied, keeping everyone in-line throughout the evening's entertainment. Some of the films could be quite exhilarating, particularly the westerns, and it was easy for the young men to become excited and show reaction, throwing Jaffas down the aisle and generally creating a ruckus — but Jack Sotheby had it all under control. He wouldn't think twice about escorting a rowdy patron from the premises.

As the words THE END were followed by the familiar anthem, God Save the King, the little picture theatre was emptying rapidly. Hudson had to pack up for the night. He was anxious to get to the Palais.

CC was ensconced in his office. On his desk, plans were laid out. He stood over them like a doctor examining a patient. He looked up as Hudson entered his office. 'All done for the night then son?'

'Yes, I've canned the film ready for despatch. I say, are they the plans for the new theatre at Maidstone?'

'Yes, come and have a look, give me your opinion.'

'Wow, sure beats the old grain shed, hey dad?' Hudson perused the plans. The theatre itself looked huge — an enormous stage and row up on row of seating. 'Impressive. How many does it seat? Five hundred?'

'Matter of fact it is going to seat exactly nine hundred.'

'Holy cow! Nine hundred! A bit of an improvement on the current one hundred and sixty in the old grain hut.'

'Yes, and the new Sunshine Picture Theatre we're building here takes six hundred — nine hundred — hmmm, yes, a lot of seats to fill.'

'Do you think we'll ever fill it?'

'Son, with some of these shows that are coming out of Hollywood I think we'll have to get out the camp chairs and put them in the aisles.'

Hudson chuckled. 'When do you think we will be able to start this one?'

'It's already started m'boy. Well, I've got the plans into council so I call that a start; and with chaps like Wilbur Maxwell on the permits approval board, we should have the go-ahead through in no time.'

'Are you sure about Wilbur, jumping into bed with him so fast? I mean what do we really know about him?'

'Sometimes you're too sensitive Hudson. Wilbur's a good man — a strong businessman — look at all he has done for this town. Besides, he will only be a minor shareholder, when everything is up and running we can buy his share back in no time.'

Despite his father's confidence, Hudson still looked worried. 'I'm telling you Son, don't worry. We'll be opening the new six-hundred-seater Sunshine Picture Theatre by the end of the year, and when we open the doors to the magnificent new Roxy at Maidstone, people are going to come from miles.' CC sat back in his chair, picking up his glass of scotch and taking a long, satisfying sip.

As Hudson left his father's office, he noticed Miriam Worthing still replenishing stock in the kiosk. 'Hey Miriam, I thought you'd be long gone by now.' She turned, shy in a way but a determined girl just the same.

'Actually, I was waiting for you, if you are off to the Palais I was hoping you could give me a lift.'

'Of course, Cissy told me you wanted to come along tonight. But what about your mum, don't you have to look after her tonight?'

'Actually, our neighbour has offered to stay over, said I needed a break. So, what do you say?' Hudson looked at Miriam, she was a homely sort of a girl, and he felt a little sorry for her — perhaps with the right hairdo and make-up, but then it wasn't his place to comment.

'I say let's go.' Miriam gave a giggle, she had never been in Hudson's new convertible and hoped he would have the roof down, she had imagined what it would be like to have the wind in her hair, even if it was a little cold, she didn't mind, how could it be anything but perfect with Hudson at the wheel.

As they walked towards Hudson's car, Miriam commented on the new theatre that was currently a work in progress. 'So, it looks like it's getting close to being finished. It must be an exciting time for your family.'

'It sure is,' answered Hudson. 'The roof structure will be completed soon; it *is* an exciting time for us.' In fact, the whole community was excited. The new Sunshine Picture Theatre would be a place where everyone could relax and enjoy a good night out in comfort.

Hudson admired the large windows at the front of the building, already seeing his posters displayed there. Rosalind Russell, Cary Grant, Lawrence Olivier, Barbara Stanwyck, Ingrid Bergman — he could see it all now. He imagined the patrons milling around the large entry doors and people hustling to get their treats from the kiosk before the bell went for the main show to begin.

'Good show tonight Huddo,' a familiar voice yelled as Hudson was helping Miriam into her seat. He looked across the road to Peter the Greek's hamburger café, to see Tommy McFarlane, a local lad who often helped out with odd jobs around the picture theatre and the Cambridge home.

'Thanks Tommo,' Hudson acknowledged.

The Cambridge family was very well known and liked in Sunshine. The hamburger café attracted theatre goers before and after the show, as well as other times during the week. Hudson was friendly with many of the people who frequented the friendly café, particularly as a lot of them were around his own age.

He walked around to his own door. 'Looks like the new theatre isn't far away,' Tommy added.

'Not long now Tommy.'

'We're looking forward to that,' Tommy said, speaking for himself and his mates.

'Aren't we all Tommy, aren't we all?' With that Hudson hit the accelerator and took off quite a bit too fast, along Hampshire Road and in the direction of St. Kilda and the Palais.

Chapter Four

THE PALAIS WAS in full swing when Hudson and Miriam arrived. Even though Hudson had a bit of catching up to do, he believed this was the best time of the night, when the alcohol had released inhibitions, a pretty lady was happy to dance with you and if you were charming enough, perhaps a kiss or two in a dark corner or even the honour of driving the lady home. He spied Cissy and Veronica seated at a table with Godfrey Maxwell. Taking Miriam by the elbow he led her in that direction, Miriam obeyed like a besotted puppy.

As Miriam sat down, Hudson proceeded to introduce her to Godfrey, but steering Godfrey's attention away from Cissy was not an easy task. This fascinated Hudson, he gave up with the introduction and thought he would talk to Veronica instead, until he noticed her visibly peeved at the lack of attention she was receiving from Godfrey. What had he walked in on here?

Veronica was inwardly seething. She couldn't believe Godfrey would prefer to shower his attention on Cissy rather than her. Surely she was way better looking and way more desirable than Cissy. Sure, Cissy may have been a bit of an imp, but hardly a woman yet. Wouldn't Godfrey want a real woman, Veronica knew how to be a real woman, she'd had plenty of practice with her loathsome father. Not since, but she knew the game. To hell with Godfrey for all his ignorance, now that Hudson had arrived, she had new prey. She knew Hudson would be an excellent catch and so she turned directly to him, 'Hudson, I'm so glad you could make it. Busy night at the theatre?'

Hudson had never been a fan of Cissy's new-found friend. To be frank he would rather talk to Miriam than her, but she had harnessed his attention and the last thing he was, was impolite. Hudson talked about the Ellery Queen double feature, but as he did so his attention was drawn across the dance floor. Cissy noticed her brother distracted from the conversation with Veronica and followed his eyeline. It was the redhead Cissy saw her brother admiring the other night. This amused her, her brother had a crush, she was going to milk it for all it was worth.

'Say, that's her, isn't it?' Cissy teased, elbowing her brother in the ribs. Veronica turned to glare at the redhead sitting on the other side of the dance floor — her stunning red hair fell in billowing waves around the creamy skin of her shoulders. It was enough to make Veronica scream, she wanted Hudson's attention.

'So, tell me about Ellery Queen, he writes mysteries, doesn't he?'

'Ellery Queen is not a writer, he is the character in Frederic Dannay's novels — many of which have now been turned into movies.'

Veronica thought she was so clever, engaging Hudson in conversation. 'I have never seen one of the movies — or read a book for that matter.' Hudson resisted a smart impart while Cissy, seeing the irked look on Hudson's face, decided to help her brother out.

'Come on Hudson — why don't you just ask the lady to dance?'

Hudson blinked, knowing his sister had caught him staring at the redhead again, the same redhead she was goading him about earlier in the day. 'Why hide it?' he thought, she was going to know about his attraction sooner or later, because sooner, rather than later, he was going to have this woman in his arms.

'I just might, in time. Right now, I need a drink.' As Hudson gathered everyone's drink orders, fume began to rise out of Veronica, first Cissy diverted Godfrey's attention away from her and now Hudson was off chasing after some redhead nobody knew the first thing about, there must be a way to nip this in the bud before Hudson became any more bewitched with this redhead.

'Let me give you a hand,' said Veronica rising from her chair to follow Hudson to the bar, 'You may be strong and masculine, but you can't carry all that.' Hudson was not surprised at Veronica's intrusion, she was so annoying.

'Ever heard of trays Veronica? I'll be fine.' Not deterred, Veronica tagged along behind him to the bar.

When Hudson arrived back at the table, Cissy, Miriam and Godfrey were sharing some light conversation. Godfrey really had a hard time seeing what Cissy saw in Miriam as a friend, where were the benefits? She had little to offer, and her presentation needed a lot of work. However, his private school education had drilled manners into him, so he politely entertained them with some meaningless banter. Glad of the diversion when Hudson returned with the drinks, Godfrey commented, 'Hudson, what's a nice bloke like you doing in a place like this anyway?'

'A nice bloke could be asking you the same thing.'

'Just looking for a beautiful woman to complete my life.' He looked at Cissy. 'What do you say Cissy? Shall we take the leap?' Cissy allowed a little smile to sneak through. Godfrey was, after all, quite good looking and, as she had overheard her father saying, well on the way to making his own fortune, following in his father's footsteps. As she accepted Godfrey's attention, Veronica fumed, two eligible bachelors at the table and neither appeared to be paying her any attention.

Like a gentleman personified, Godfrey stood, extending his hand to Cissy, she decided that a dance was innocent enough, and took him up on the offer, leaving Veronica open-mouthed. Turning her attention back to Hudson, she became even more aggravated when she saw him once again eyeing off the redhead. 'Say, will you ladies excuse me?' he said, addressing Miriam and Veronica as he rose from the table, 'Please let Cissy know I am not going anywhere, I'll be around to drive her home — and you too Miriam,' he told her, purposely not including

Veronica. He knew that if she could not organise herself a lift from some bloke she had never met before, then he would be obliged to drive her home too, but he couldn't resist the taunt and hoped she'd at least be a little civil towards Miriam as he left the two ladies alone, taking off in the direction of the exit — in pursuit of the redhead.

Cissy was quite enjoying the slow waltz in Godfrey's arms. She hadn't had that much experience with men except for the one boy back in Leongatha who was always trying to get her to *do it*. She probably would have if she had really liked him, but the truth was he was too podgy for her liking and he had bad breath. Really, why she even used to sneak around with him she didn't really know, maybe because he would never leave her alone.

She wondered about Godfrey; he didn't have a bad breath and he wasn't podgy. In fact, he really was quite a good-looking chap. She'd never thought about him romantically before, but now, being in his arms, something started to stir inside of her. Could he really be interested in her — that way? With her head pressed against his shoulder, little did she notice that his attention was elsewhere. Godfrey had caught the eye of a young man at the bar and the two of them were sending message-filled looks across the dance floor. Godfrey performing the dance-steps through habit rather than desire.

The man who held Godfrey's attention raised his eyebrows and dropped the corners of his mouth, as if to say, 'Who's the girl?' When Godfrey shrugged his shoulders in answer, it upset the smooth rhythm they held in the waltz and Cissy's attention was drawn back to him. 'Is there anything wrong?'

'Actually, I've just seen someone I know,' replied Godfrey, looking at the man in question who laughed with a sardonic grin and nodded his head mockingly. Cissy was stunned as Godfrey released her, leaving her standing in the middle of the dance floor surrounded by throngs of dancers, yet as lonely as if she were stranded on a desert island. In the background a broad and satisfied smirk spread across Veronica's well-painted face.

The carpark was quiet at that time of night, approaching midnight and the Palais still in full swing. The patrons inside enjoying themselves, not wanting to leave as the night drew to a close. Eleanor Lansing wanted to get ahead of the rush. Taxis were hard to come by when so many others were vying for them after closing. She'd really had enough for one night anyway. She headed towards the sidewalk, hoping to flag down a passing cab, when suddenly she was grabbed from behind. The arms spun her around and she found herself facing two young men. Fear rose immediately.

'Let me go, just who do you think you are?'

'Come on love,' one of the thugs answered, 'we know exactly who we are, and we know exactly what we are going to do with you. Get the car Mick,' the dark-headed one said to his accomplice, 'I've got hold of her.' As Mick scurried off for the car, Hudson came into the carpark, he had seen this redhead leaving and was determined to at least introduce himself before the night was through.

'What's going on here?' Hudson demanded as he approached the man who had a firm grip on Eleanor's arms. He had heard her shouting at the man, and it was pretty easy to figure out that whatever was going on here it was not what this very attractive lady wanted. 'Is this man bothering you?'

By this time Eleanor was extremely incensed and with the distraction caused by Hudson's appearance she took the opportunity to stamp her stiletto heel directly into the offender's foot. Wincing in pain he released his hold on Eleanor and began hopping, trying to hold his foot. Hudson was quite amused by the young woman's spunk and decided a swift upper cut to this good-for-nothing's jaw would also be in order. The young man staggered just as his mate arrived with the car. 'What's this all about?' the mate demanded, then seeing the state of his buddy and the anger on Hudson's face, he decided to leave it alone. The injured thug jumped into the car, and they disappeared into the night.

'Are you okay?'

'Yes,' gasped Eleanor, 'Thank you so much for coming along when you did. I honestly don't know what they would have done to me.'

'Well, I don't think they were planning on wining and dining you. What are you doing alone in the carpark anyway?'

'I just thought I would get a head start on the cabs before everyone starts swarming out of the Palais.'

'Would you like to come back in, maybe get a drink, calm down a little?'

'No, no. It's all right really, I'd rather just get home and have a nice cup of tea.' Just then a cab pulled to a halt at the kerb. Eleanor looked at Hudson, liking what she saw, the kind face, the dark curls and the sincerity in his eyes. 'Thank you, really, I must go.' Hudson opened the car door for her and watched as the cab drove away. Blue eyes, no, more sapphire than blue. Deep, sparkling blue, eyes the likes of which he had never seen. How quickly can love hit you? Hudson stood there as the cab faded into the distance.

Chapter Five

THE JULY MORNING WAS CHILLY, but it meant nothing to little Chipolata who snoozed comfortably on the porch of the Cambridge home, enjoying his special doggy-bed — a contraption built out of pallet boards by Hudson and fashioned into soft, velvety comfort by Cissy. The dachshund was suddenly awoken from his slumber as he heard the tell-tale whistle of the approaching mailman. Chipolata charged off the porch, happily leaping and barking with joy to finally have something to amuse him. The postman had arrived at the Cambridge mailbox, a bunch of mail in hand. Cissy also heard the whistle, as well as the barking commotion the dog had stirred up. She berated the dog as she walked over to the front gate to collect the mail, admiring the colourful show of pansies surrounding the beautiful front garden.

'Thanks Billy!' she shouted to the postman, 'Hope it's all good news today!' Cissy thumbed through the mail and suddenly her expression changed to one of great anticipation and excitement as she came across the letter she had been waiting weeks for. She headed into the house, dog on her tail.

Cissy rushed through the hallway of her home, looking for Hudson. She found him on the back verandah positioned in front of an easel, adding touches to a movie poster he has just painted. The famous face of Ginger Rogers was coming to life on canvas. Hudson, lost in his work, did not notice Cissy as she approached him. 'Looks like one of your best yet,' she said as she smiled, looking approvingly at his work.

Hudson turned to see Cissy standing there, a letter in hand. He grinned at the compliment. 'So, what have you got there?'

'It's the letter I've been waiting for.'

'Well, aren't you going to open it?' Cissy still stood there, holding the envelope in her right hand and smacking it nervously onto her left hand.

'Why? Why ruin a beautiful thing? I'm happy here, the way things are.'

'Come on, open it,' encouraged Hudson.

Reluctantly Cissy opened the envelope, silently she read the contents. Very solemnly she handed it over to Hudson, who read it after her. A huge smile crossed his face, and he took his sister in his arms, sweeping her off the floor and spinning her around and around. 'I knew you could do it sis, I knew you could do it. Paris here you come!'

Cissy squealed with delight at her brother's antics but not for long. Her mood changed and Hudson, sensing the shift in the atmosphere, put her down. 'What's the use Hudson? Father will never let me go.'

'He has to Cissy, he just has to. Not everyone gets an invitation to study art at the School of Paris. Oh, come on Cissy, you're so talented, he has to see that.'

'But you are talented too, Hudson.'

'Me, I'm just a hack — you are a fine artist Cissy, and you deserve the very best the world has to offer.'

'Oh, it would be so wonderful. But Paris is at war, Father will never, ever let me go. Hell in a handbasket, I wish Mummy were still alive.'

She looked off pensively into the neighbouring houses — gazing across the iron roofs, yet not registering them at all. Hudson sensed her change of mood, knowing how much she missed her mother. He tried to change the subject, hoping it might also change her mood, but it was not that easy. 'What's the other mail you've got there?' Cissy handed the rest of the mail to Hudson and then turned dejectedly, walking back into the house.

'I have to go, I have flowers to arrange, and Miss Wright-Smith is in today, I don't want her breathing down my neck.' Cissy declared as she left. Hudson thumbed through the mail. He picked out an envelope bearing the Australian Armed Forces logo. The letter was addressed to his father, he stared at it long and hard.

Sylvia Wright-Smith was a large buxom woman in her late forties. She was very officious and put the fear of God into all who came into contact with her, except for Carleton Cambridge. Miss Wright-Smith had been his secretary since his little empire began. Even more than that, she helped the widower around his home, fussing, cleaning and cooking. Anyone would think she was determined to snare this man who arrived in Sunshine just over two years ago, ready to make his mark on the community and build his empire.

The Cambridge offspring found Miss Wright-Smith too bossy for their liking, but they recognised the help she gave to their father. She was a companion to CC in general and he seemed to take her into his confidence, even more than he did his own children at times. She was very assertive and always acted like she was in charge. As she stepped into the foyer of the picture theatre, Cissy was once again sorting the enormous floral arrangement when this dowager-like woman passed through, creating the usual tornado effect.

'Good morning, Miss Wright-Smith,' Cissy politely greeted her.

'Cissy. Don't be wasting too much time on those flowers, there's the kiosk that needs re-stocking.'

'Yes Miss Wright-Smith,' Cissy replied, with just the hint of sarcasm in her tone. Then even more so, under her breath, 'Two bags full Miss Wright-Smith.' She hopped down off her ladder and headed towards the kiosk just as Sylvia Wright Smith entered CC's office.

CC was pacing. He knew something like this would happen. Decisions to be made and Margot no longer around to help. Life was sometimes just too lonely as a widower, sometimes CC seemed to be at such a loss that he felt as though he had nowhere to turn. This was one of those times.

'What's wrong CC, you look like the weight of the world is upon you,' Sylvia Wright-Smith said as she entered his office.

'Sometimes Sylvia my dear, I feel as though it is.'

'Whatever's wrong, sit down and tell me all about it.'

'Cissy's been invited to study at the School of Art in Paris.'

'Good heavens. You cannot let someone so young and foolish loose in Paris,' Wright-Smith commented. 'Besides that, in case you hadn't heard CC, there's a war over there.' CC rose from his chair again, irritated as only this woman could make him.

'Of course I know there's a damned war over there. I've had a son fighting there for nearly two years.'

'Oh, don't be ridiculous, obviously I know that.'

'Look Cissy doesn't even know that I know yet, Hudson let me in on the secret but insisted that I say nothing until Cissy comes to me. When she does, what I am I going to say to her?'

'Well you can't let her go CC.'

'Yes, you're right.' Carleton stared down at the letter on his desk, the one he had been reticent in opening, 'Which is the other thing — this letter arrived today.' CC held up the letter from the Armed Forces. Miss Wright-Smith saw it and immediately her face now went from indignant to concerned.

'Well open it, Carleton.'

'It's probably nothing …' Carleton pondered reluctantly. Just then there was a knock at the door. A young man stood in the office doorway. He was a bright looking chap just barely out of boyhood at age nineteen. He was neatly dressed, even if he had applied the Brylcreem too thickly as his overly slick hair seemed literally glued to his head. His eyes were bright and brown, and he was about six foot in height, a bit gangly, still waiting to fill out from his youth. CC looked at him, wondering what on earth he was doing appearing in such a way at his office door, especially when he was in the middle of highly sensitive family matters. CC peered past the chap to see the cavern of the empty foyer behind him.

'Sorry, there was no one around and I had a 2 o'clock appointment, with a Miss Wright-Smith.' The lad was nervous. Suddenly Miss Wright-Smith looked up, remembering her commitment.

'Yes, yes, quite right. Please wait in the foyer, I'll be with you in a minute.' The lad left, giving CC and Wright-Smith a second to talk.

'He's the young man I told you about. Highly recommended. You're going to need more help eventually, with the planned expansion you'll be left ragged. He's got a good head on his shoulders, just out of high school with very good grades.' CC nodded.

'OK, if you say so. Let's see what he's made of.'

'I'll ask him to come in, shall I?'

'Better yet, let's talk to him while we take him on a tour. Relax the lad, see what he's really made of.' As CC and Wright-Smith left the office to join Roger Rourke in the foyer, the Armed Forces letter was left lying unopened on CC's desk.

The library was big and overwhelmingly impressive with books, typical of a rich man's mansion. Wilbur Maxwell had spared no expense stocking the shelves with the right reading matter, even if he rarely lifted a book off the shelves. His daughter, however, was quite a different story. Heather Maxwell had been absorbed in books since the day she learned to read, at this very moment she was relaxing in a lounge chair, fully engrossed in a thick bound book, when her brother, Godfrey, entered.

'I don't know where you think all of this reading and studying will get you?' he snapped at her in a demeaning way. He glared at Heather and she glared back, dropping the book to her lap. Her brother was so annoying. 'You will just end up like all of the rest of the girls around here, married with countless babies dragging at your skirts.'

Heather ignored him, her brother wearied her. He was just like so many other chauvinistic men. Heather however, believed there was a life beyond the typing pools and raising children. She was currently working as a secretary in a law firm but secretly desired to get into law and help further the emancipation of women. There had been a lot of movement since the war, with women not only being asked to join the ranks, but to also take over in the workforce and keep the factories running, all of course while they were performing their domestic duties and keeping their families fed on war rations.

'You should be learning how to cook, that will do you a lot more good than this.' He picked up the book, 'What is this? The principles of common law — who do you think you are?' Heather grabbed for the book.

'Give it to me Godfrey and just leave me alone.'

'Get real Heather.' He turned towards her, book still in hand. He touched her hair, holding it between thumb and forefinger in a teasing, nasty-brother way. 'Why don't you try and make yourself a little more attractive? All of my mates think you are a frump — whatever are you wearing today?'

He pulled at her dress; she ran from the library upset. At that moment the doorbell rang. Godfrey walked through the expansive hallway and to the front door. He was surprised to see the beautiful redhead standing there looking somewhat familiar, but he couldn't quite place her. 'Is Heather here? You must be her brother, Godfrey is it?' she asked, wondering if this man was ever going to close his mouth or just let his chin continue to drag on the floor.

Godfrey was intrigued and pulled himself together, wondering what on earth a girl like her would want with his sister. 'That's right. And who, pray tell, might you be?'

Realising her error of failing to introduce herself the young lady apologised,

'Oh sorry, I'm Eleanor Lansing. A college friend of Heather's.' At the mention of college, Godfrey ceased to be impressed.

'Oh, another one of those. Come in, I'll see if I can find her.' With that, Godfrey yelled for his sister.

Heather was sick to death of her brother and his antics. She was lying on her bed, face down, her head stuck into her pillow. The room was very calming in varying shades of blue and featured framed certificates of Heather's academic achievements, however she had allowed herself one movie poster of Clarke Gable and Vanessa Leigh in *Gone with the*

Wind. She was longing for the film to come to the Sunshine Picture Theatre and swore she would attend every session. Just then she heard her brother yelling, 'Heather, you have a visitor!'

Heather raised her head, her eyes reddened from the tears she did not want to shed. Stupid tears for a stupid brother. She remembered that Eleanor was going to call and quickly she wiped her eyes, moving across to the mirror to check herself. Then, straightening up her skirt, she walked to her bedroom door and descended the staircase.

'Eleanor, I'm so sorry. I got side-tracked and almost forgot you were coming.' Eleanor looked at Heather thinking that she looked a little off-colour, almost as though she had been crying.

'That's all right, look, if this is a bad time ...'

'No, not at all,' said Heather, further composing herself. 'Say, why don't we grab a milkshake down at the corner hamburger shop? They have the best blue heaven milkshakes ever, butterscotch is good too.'

'Sounds like a fine idea.' With that the two ladies departed, leaving Godfrey standing there, wondering what it was all about, he rarely saw Heather with any friends, and especially not with a stunner like Eleanor Lansing.

Picture theatres, movies, fairy tales, sagas and works of fiction — it may have seemed romantic, but the truth was there was a lot of work that went into running a picture theatre. Cissy and Jack Sotheby were sweeping the rows and aisle before the Saturday matinee was to commence in two hours' time. CC, Miss Wright-Smith and the interviewee, Roger Rourke surveyed the theatre.

'So, it may seem fairly humble now ...' CC pontificated as, unbeknownst to him, Hudson appeared at the top of the aisle, '... but we have some pretty solid expansion plans. We are close to completing the new Sunshine Picture Theatre, you probably saw it all going on out front,' CC explained, 'and we have some land just a few miles up the road at Maidstone. Got our eye on a couple of existing theatres as well.'

'Sounds promising, sounds like you're really moving ahead,' said Roger, genuinely interested. He had succeeded in landing the job at the picture theatre and it was with a man whom he found more exciting the more he spoke. Roger wanted to go places, he wanted to release the binds of deprivation and make something of himself. He admired CC and even now was beginning to look upon him as a role model.

'Yes, we are. Time waits for no man,' said CC, committing himself to the words. Roger nodded at CC's words. 'Big things from small beginnings, that's what I always say. I'd like you to start helping out in the kiosk and generally assisting where necessary, but once you get to know the business who knows where it could lead. You're obviously a bright lad, you have come highly recommended, so let's get you started Son, and see where it leads to.'

In the background Hudson's lips were pursed tight, he was furious that his father was bringing in an outsider to help with the expansion, he was even calling him *son*!

'But what about your sons — you have two I believe?' queried Rourke.

'Don't worry about them lad — they have plenty to get on with. When Seymour gets back from the war he will be straight into running the financial side of the business, Hudson is tied up with running the movies and painting up those posters, we're still going to need a project manager and you may just turn out to be the right candidate, but let's get you to work first.' As they walked towards the front exit of the theatre, Hudson stayed where he was, he did not want to see his father, he was trying to hide his fury.

As he sat there stewing, Cissy noticed him, not realising the mood he was in she called on him for help. 'Come on Hudson, give us a hand,' she said, holding out the broom. As grumpy as he was, Hudson was always up for a bit of banter with his sister.

'Ah, but my leg is so sore today.'

'Not that old chestnut again Hudson.'

'Hey, come on, do you walk around on a broken leg all day?'

'Turn it up Hudson, that was ages ago. I've seen you run like the wind, and it doesn't stop you from whirling a pretty girl around the dance floor.'

'It takes skill, great skill and practice, my leg still aches.'

'Does it really Hudson?' she asks, more concerned.

'Good days and bad, kept me out of the army though didn't it. Reckon that old horse getting ornery with me might have really done me a favour.'

'Was it the horse, or was it the rider?'

Just then Jack Sotheby stopped his sweeping and turned to the siblings. 'So, what did happen, if you don't mind me asking?' he asked Hudson, always wondering why one brother had joined the army and not the other.

'Oh, we were just getting ready for shearing. Searing hot day and I had taken one of the mares out to look for a couple of stragglers when it happened. I noticed a few stray sheep around a clump of trees, stinking hot afternoon and I really thought the poor things would expire. I needed to round them up, but I didn't want to freak the buggers out, so I was about to dismount and core blimey if there wasn't a bloody snake, the thing rears up and scares the horse. The horse reared up as well, didn't it, throwing me right onto a huge boulder, the size of Ayers Rock, I swear.' Jack was fascinated, Cissy shook her head, she had heard it all before and it became bigger every time. 'Shattered my leg, I was a long time in a cast. I was due to register for the army the following fortnight, needless to say I am still here, and Seymour is off fighting for the good guys.'

'Seymour — your brother hey? Where's he stationed?'

'Salonika. Just hope he comes back in one piece. Dad's got some big plans for him about running the expansion.'

'I'd have thought you'd be in-line for that. First born son and all.'

'Nah, Dad reckons I'm better on the creative side,' Hudson said sarcastically, making talking marks in the air with his fingers on the words *creative side*.

'But you're here, finger on the pulse and all that.'

'Yeah, well the war won't last forever, will it?'

Suddenly their conversation was distracted by a male voice calling out from the foyer. Hudson and Cissy both turned in the direction the voice was coming from.

The hamburger café was quiet this time of day. Heather and Eleanor were seated at a booth, sipping milkshakes through straws from thick, stumpy stemmed milk-shake glasses, the metal shaker mug beside each one. The pale grey Laminex tables matched in with the lilac walls featuring posters of the ever-popular Frank Sinatra, Billie Holiday, the Ink Spots and Glenn Miller amongst other number-one chart-toppers. The juke box sat as testament to their fame, belting out tunes like Chattanooga Choo-Choo and God Bless the Child.

'Well I'd call it really lucky, your dad buying you your own hairdressing salon,' Heather commented enviously to Eleanor.

'I know, I should be more grateful. It's just that it's so far across town. I like it out this side and I really want to stay around here, but there's no way Dad will let me move into a flat on my own.' Eleanor's father had made his money from land. Previously a market gardener, he had owned half of Mentone — a middle-class suburb across the other side of town, near Melbourne's south-eastern bayside beaches.

With his market gardens failing as larger enterprises forced their way into the distribution channels, Bruce Lansing saw the right time to give the game away, subdivide the land off into housing and commercial lots and sell it up. He did however retain many blocks on which he proceeded to build and sell homes — a practice he was still busy with as well as a number of other projects.

He loved his daughter and would do anything for her. When she decided to enter hairdressing, he could not have been more delighted. He didn't, however, want her working for some male boss he knew nothing about, and so decided she should have her own salon. After much searching, a reasonably affordable salon became available at Footscray, the price was right, and Bruce Lansing snapped it up. That Footscray was a long way from Mentone didn't really worry Bruce, the suburb was growing rapidly, and he knew his daughter could turn this into her dream business — and make a nice profit doing so.

'So that means I'm faced with a two hour journey every morning and night,' Eleanor continued. 'This morning I had to get a bus to Cheltenham station, a train from there and then change trains in the city to get to Footscray. I'm over it by the time I get to work.'

'Well, if that's all you're worried about I have an easy solution,' Heather answered catching Eleanor's interest.

'You do?'

'Simple, you can move into our house.'

'I couldn't do that.'

'Give me one good reason why not?'

'Well because … I just couldn't.'

'You could so. You've seen the size of our house. There's plenty of room. We actually have three spare bedrooms not being used — you can take your pick.' Eleanor started to think about it.

'What would your father say … and your mother?'

'Dad? He won't mind — he's hardly ever there anyway. When he is, he is in his den, don't see a lot of him. As for Mummy, I reckon she'd love it — having a bit more girl-power around.'

'Well, it would certainly save me a lot of travelling time, Footscray is only three train stops from Sunshine, how quick would that be?'

'There you go then — it's settled. I'll talk to Mum tonight, and I'll give you a call after that.'

Chapter Six

WHEN A SHOW WASN'T RUNNING, a picture theatre took on an aura of its own. A real and echoing emptiness, longing for the throngs of people who crowd the foyer during intervals, jostling for their place at the kiosk to grab a drink or a romantic box of chocolates for their sweetheart. But in the absence of an audience a picture theatre reverberates the emptiness like a huge sigh in a long and cavernous tunnel. Even this tiny little grain hut theatre felt hollow, vacuous and void of any feeling.

Godfrey stood alone in the empty foyer, his voice bouncing off the panelled walls. 'Hello!' he repeated, 'Is anyone around?' Cissy and Hudson emerged through the entry doors to the auditorium, surprised by Godfrey's unusual visit.

'Ah, Godfrey me old mate, what's all this shouting about?' asked Hudson.

'Well, a fella comes in here and the place looks deserted.' Cissy looked at Godfrey remembering his ungracious exit from the dance floor the previous evening, she was a fool to think that he may have been interested in her, and as for her even thinking she might have been falling for him! What a joke, he could stick with Veronica — she was way more his style.

'So, what's up anyway?' inquired Hudson, believing Godfrey's visit would be directed at him.

'Actually, I wanted to talk to Cissy.'

'Oh, oooh,' said Hudson, the penny dropping as to the real purpose of Godfrey's visit. 'Well, that's fine, I have stuff to do.' Godfrey and Cissy stared at Hudson, willing him to leave. Cissy's lips turned to string; she couldn't wait to give this lummox a piece of her mind. Hudson looked from one to the other and then finally, taking the hint, he turned to head back into the auditorium.

'So, I don't see what you could possibly say to me that I haven't already thought?' said Cissy, wanting to take a piece out of him and get it over and done with. She could feel her temper rising, remembering the humiliation of returning to the table alone, with Veronica looking at her with false sympathy and Miriam too stunned to believe that anyone would have the nerve to leave Cissy alone on the dance floor.

Godfrey, having suffered the wrath of his father all morning for not securing a further date with Cissy, knew it was time to start taking his mission seriously, 'Look, I think it would be a really good idea if you and I had dinner.'

'Whatever for? So, you can leave me at the table eating dinner on my own?'

'Come on Cissy, don't be like that. I'm not such a bad chap am I?' He looked at her with doe eyes.

'I don't understand why you just walked off last night, at least you could have escorted me back to my table,' her glare could have downed a troop of combat soldiers.

'Look, I'm really sorry,' said Godfrey, reciting his well-practised explanation. 'I saw an old buddy from college, I have been trying to catch up with him for ages. He must have moved house because I just haven't been able to contact him. He is part of a very important business deal Dad is working on, I thought if I lost him that night, I might never see him again. Look, I'm really, really sorry.' He looked at her again with those eyes, he could see her softening. 'Give a guy another chance?'

'Well, it's not a really great way to ask a girl out.'

At her words Godfrey crossed two hands over his heart, 'Cecelia Cambridge, would you do me the incredible honour of allowing me to take you out to a sumptuous dinner.'

'Well, seeing as you put it like that,' Cissy giggled at the absurdity of it all, maybe he was not such a bad guy after all.

The vacant block of land was huge, fully cleared except for a plethora of weeds and a few scraggly bushes. On the eastern side was a Shell service station, distinctive because of its huge yellow Shell logo displayed as a lightbox on a pole. CC and Sylvia Wright Smith stood on the street surveying the land. CC as always was easily recognised in his well-tailored suit and his signature bowler hat, which he always, always wore outdoors, even when driving his gleaming black Humber Super Snipe. He turned to Sylvia, 'It's a huge block of land, and right on this main road. Lots of passing traffic.'

'This is such an up-and-coming area here too,' replied Sylvia, 'they say the population here will quadruple over the next five years.'

'Yes, the new factory precinct is going to contribute to that, plenty of employment.'

'Bringing in plenty of people. They are building a new state school just a block away.'

'That's what we want, hey. I wonder where Wilbur is, we have to get to the architect's.'

'What do you mean? Wilbur Maxwell, what's he got to do with anything?'

'If Cambridge Theatres is to expand like what I've got in mind, then we are going to need investors,' CC explained to Sylvia in a slightly apologetic tone. Miss Wright-Smith rubbed him up the wrong way at times. She took way too much for granted in CC's mind. Almost as though she thought she had rights over him.

There were times when he suspected she wished he would propose marriage — the furthest thing from CC's mind. He had loved his wife Margot so much, and still loved her memory. He was a man on a mission to build an empire, to honour his late wife — how exciting she would have found all of this, how proud she would have been. Marrying again really was the last thing on CC's mind, he had things to do — and besides, Sylvia Wright-Smith was hardly the woman of his dreams with her buxom figure, bun-style hairdo and dowdy clothes. If he was ever going to marry again it would be to someone far more appealing. Still, she was a good secretary and a good companion, he valued her opinion.

'Yes, but Wilbur Maxwell. He's a bit common isn't he — running the city's waste disposal?' CC flinched at Wright-Smith's words; he hated snobbery. All men were created equal, some were luckier than others and some chose different paths. Wilbur's business was a community necessity, he saw nothing wrong with running the local garbage collection.

'Don't knock it my dear, plenty of money has been made council contracting … and he runs the local ice-works — plenty of money in that too.'

'I suppose money's money no matter where it comes from,' she said a little too condescendingly.

'His is as good as anyone else's,' CC replied, checking his watch. 'Where is he? I have so much to do.' Sylvia gave him a slightly offended look. 'Of course, I haven't forgotten the dinner at Wilbur's, are you still happy to accompany me?'

'Yes CC, what else would I do?'

'Then I'll pick you up at 5.30 — oh, here's a cab, why don't you head off and I'll wait here for Wilbur.' CC bustled a somewhat indignant Sylvia Wright-Smith into the car. She really would rather have waited to see exactly what was discussed between CC and Wilbur, but when CC made up his mind she knew her limitations, she would see what she could glean over dinner tonight.

'I can't talk now Son, I'm running late for an appointment with CC,' Wilbur was in his office, pacing, phone to his ear. 'What's so urgent it couldn't wait?'

Godfrey leaned against the interior glass wall of a bright red phone box. The hamburger café in the background was busy with a group of youths ordering milkshakes and hamburgers while across the road, the new Sunshine Picture Theatre was coming together superbly. The roofing structure was well underway — the builders and labourers busily scurrying back and forth, eager to get the day's work completed just as a truck arrived with more roofing materials. Its humble predecessor, the little grain hut picture theatre, sat to the rear among the poplar trees, waiting for its next big audience to bring it to life.

'I just wanted to let you know that I am officially on a dinner date with Cecelia Cambridge tonight.'

'Well done Son, glad to see you have taken my advice. I'll have a talk to you before then.'

Happy with himself, Godfrey hung up the phone. He glanced at the phone box and decided to press the reject button, you just never could predict your luck. To his delight his three pennies dropped back out of the return slot. Godfrey chuckled to himself, pocketed the pennies and whistled a tune as he walked towards his brand-new Roadster, gleaming red it shone like a beacon. Godfrey leapt over the door and into the seat, making the extra effort to show off in front of the group of youths now gathered at the front of the hamburger shop, and the team of workers constructing the new picture theatre, all of whom now looked longingly at the car like they'd never seen an automobile before in their lives.

That's what life was all about, take what you could get, be ahead of the pack and leave people open mouthed in your wake. He hit the accelerator pedal hard and laughed as his tyres squealed and he zoomed away from all the envious eyes.

Dorothy Maxwell was quite a smart woman and a real homemaker. While she followed the old-fashioned rule of doing what her husband asked, she also was quite independent when it came to running her household and Wilbur was happy to leave most of those decisions up to her. However, she knew her place and just how far she could go, otherwise the wrath of Wilbur could become quite unbearable. It was no wonder then, that when Heather came to her with the request of Eleanor moving in, she was a little reticent.

The kitchen was bright and modern with green wallpaper featuring a pattern of fresh-looking vegetables. The latest glass-panelled overhead cupboards adorned one wall above a long green Laminex bench. The modern refrigerator, a recent addition, stood proudly. With its built-in icebox it rocketed the Maxwells into the wealthy set and Dorothy was delighted to be able to offer her family home-made ice-cream.

She loved these moments of sharing a pot of tea with her daughter. Dorothy was a very attractive woman. Her jet-black hair kept that way through regular hair-dresser visits. Her make-up always perfect and her clothes looked like something from George's fashion emporium which was nestled in the Parisian atmosphere of Melbourne's famous Collins Street — and they usually were.

'How's your day going Mummy?'

'Oh honey, I don't know. Your father's got me running all over town trying to organise this fancy dinner he has happening tonight, I'm really not good at all of this.'

'Yes, you are Mummy. You underestimate yourself, the last one you put together was just a sensation. People are still talking about it.'

'Luck, it was just all luck, plus I had Mrs Collins help me with the desserts, she's a genius when it comes to baking and sweet making.'

'Well do that again Mummy, I am sure she would be grateful for the work … and the money. It's not too late, give her a call.'

'Yes, I think that's a good idea,' replied her mother, nodding.

'Great, now that that's settled, can I talk to you about something else?'

'Of course you can sweetie.'

'You know my friend, Eleanor …' Heather said, laying the groundwork for her big request.

'Daughter of that land developer over in Mentone? I read about him in *The Age*,' stated Dorothy, referring to the Melbourne's largest metropolitan newspaper.

'That's right.'

'Lovely girl,' continued Dorothy, smiling at her daughter's good judgement in friends.

'Well, her father bought her a little hairdressing salon in Footscray.'

'Lucky girl, but a long way from Mentone.'

'Well, that's why I wanted to talk to you.' They looked at each other, her mother anticipating what was coming and Heather hoping she had laid the groundwork carefully enough. 'I told Heather she could come and live with us; her father won't let her live alone in a flat.'

'Well why would he? She is a young woman, only nineteen years old. No decent father would allow his daughter just to take off on her own.'

'So, will it be all right, can she come? She'll pay board and everything.'

'Oh, I don't know honey, what will your father say. He's very busy, he doesn't like to be disturbed.'

'She won't disturb him Mummy, you won't even know she's here. She'll be at the salon most of the time — even Saturdays.'

Dorothy thought for a minute as Heather looked at her anxiously. 'I will talk to your father, I'll bring him round, don't worry.' Heather's face brightened, she looked as though she was about to jump for joy. 'Go on, go and phone your friend, you can tell her it will be fine to move in.' Heather clapped her hands in glee, running from the room, just as Godfrey was leaving the living room, and by the look on his face he had quite possibly overheard everything they had just said.

'What — you been eavesdropping dear brother, listening to everything we have been talking about?' Heather accused, knowing her brother better than he sometimes knew himself.

'Why would I want to listen to your drivel? I have far better things to amuse myself,' he said in an attempt to clear himself of the accusation. As Heather shook her head in disbelief, Godfrey headed towards the front door. Heather shrugged, what did it matter anyway? Eleanor was coming to stay, he'd know soon enough. Heather walked towards the phone, situated on a little phone table in the hallway right by the staircase.

Carleton anxiously checked his watch once more, as Wilbur finally pulled up in front of the vacant block. He leaned out of the window of his gleaming black, brand-new Jaguar Mark 1V. Noticing CC's agitation, he stepped out of the vehicle in his usual pompous manner — like royalty, a cigar in his mouth completing the picture. Carleton's temper was suffering badly.

'Glad you could spare the time Wilbur,' he stated sarcastically.

'Sorry old man, a million things to do and only so many hours in the day,' Wilbur said, surveying the land in front of him.

'So, I wanted you to see the land, the position, the opportunity — before we paid a visit to the architect. He'll be there now waiting for us; he's got the plans all drawn up.'

'OK, well I don't see a lot of benefit in gazing at a vacant block of land. Let's get over to the architect's and see what he's got on the drawing board.' In his typical arrogant manner Wilbur was determined to get the upper hand on the tense situation. He tossed his cigar aside, using his heel to stub it out on the pavement, then walked back towards his car.

It was times like this that made CC wonder why he was dealing with this overbearing power freak. Carleton walked to his car, shaking his head, 'One of these days ...' he muttered under his breath.

The architect's office was light and airy, a break-away from the conservative wood-panelled offices chosen by most professionals. Adorning the space was a modern teak desk and designer chairs. Vincenzo Rossi stood by a tall easel on which plans were laid. Behind him, a huge window announced that the day was drawing to a close as the sun set spectacularly over Port Phillip Bay.

Vincenzo Rossi moved to Australia, from Italy, twenty years ago when he was just twenty-two. He was now one of the most successful architects in Melbourne, having worked on some of the biggest commercial projects and with many credits to his name.

A knock sounded.

Rossi opened the door to CC and Wilbur. On entering, CC removed his bowler hat, taking notice of the sunset. 'Well, it's worth the trip to the other side of town just to see this sunset.'

'Yes, you've sure got some view here,' added Wilbur, his jealousy showing.

Vincenzo's office was housed in his home on Beach Road, Brighton, it was the sort of view you pay handsomely for and that was exactly what Vincenzo had done. He had come to Australia as the son of Italian immigrants and his parents had worked hard to eke out a good living from their fruit and vegetable business at the Queen Victoria Market. They put Vincenzo through Melbourne University and now he was one of Melbourne's most successful architects. Vincenzo gestured towards the plans.

'Ahh, you have done a lot of work since our last meeting,' said CC, impressed with what he saw. Vincenzo nodded in agreement and then guided them over to the other side of the room, where a model sat on a glass top table. Even Wilbur had a hard time hiding his reaction as the splendid piece of architecture was revealed. The model was cleverly lit from the inside which highlighted the detail glowingly.

The two men walked closer to it. 'This will be the foyer. You see the chandelier and the decorative cornices ...' As Vincenzo talked CC imagined just what this cinema would be like once built. The excitement of the chattering crowd, all looking glamorous as they gathered in the foyer of a stunning art deco picture theatre on opening night. Everyone would be dressed as if for the opera, long cigarette holders and champagne glasses abundant. In the background was a sweeping circular stairway, on which well-to-do people would stand, chatting and surveying the crowd.

Vincenzo pointed out the magnificent auditorium — with the most ornate walls and ceiling; circular seats were raised and in sections with stalls, lounge and onwards up to the height of the dress circle, with private balcony boxes off to the sides.

'Splendid Vincenzo, absolutely splendid,' said a delighted CC. 'I knew I hired the right man for the job.' He looked at his prospective investor, 'What do you think Wilbur?'

'I must admit, I'm a bit overwhelmed. If we can achieve this, we will attract people from all over town.'

'And further afield my dear fellow. With a cinema like this, I'll be ready to invite the big boys out for a look-see.'

Wilbur didn't quite get CC's meaning and looked at him enquiringly. CC understood the puzzlement, answering with, 'Hollywood old chap, we'll be going straight to the source.'

Chapter Seven

THE TRAIN TRIP to Footscray from Mentone was long and boring. Eleanor looked out of the window as the train finally rumbled into the Footscray Station. As she rose from her seat and moved to the door, she thought how much simpler life would be if she could live closer to her salon. Heather's offer to move into her house was so generous, but she doubted Heather's parents would approve, today she would start looking for some boarding style accommodation, perhaps her father would be more comfortable with that.

When she arrived at her new salon she looked around with a satisfied sigh. She already loved this place. It needed work, but she didn't mind fixing it up. She had bought some leafy wallpaper for the salon's back wall. The three basins were all in reasonable condition, perhaps the hoses could do with replacing but she'd do that once she started to make some money. She was going to frame the mirrors in green to match the wallpaper and she would spend a little money buying some green chairs to put in the waiting area. She had scheduled to open next week so there was a lot of work to be done. Eleanor decided to start with the wallpaper.

Just then the phone rang, giving Eleanor a bit of a shock. The PMG man had only installed the phone yesterday and nobody had the phone number yet — except of course for her parents and Heather.

'Eleanor, where have you been? I've been phoning you — I tried to phone you last night, but the phone was constantly engaged.' It was Heather.

'Sorry, Dad's always on the phone and I'm a bit late in today. Lots to do with the salon opening next week and it was such a slow trip in this morning.'

'Well, you won't have to worry about that anymore, it's all systems go.'

'What do you mean?'

'You, here, moving in. I checked it with Mum and she's fine with it.'

Eleanor was so delighted with the news she let out a little shriek, 'Really, that's fantastic.'

'I know,' Heather shrieked back, 'So when can you move in?'

'Well, that's up to you.'

'What about tomorrow?'

'Tomorrow … wow.'

'Yeah, what do you say?'

'I say — why not? That'll give me a chance to get settled before the salon opens. Tomorrow it is.' If phone lines could burst, they probably would have, with the two young ladies shrieking with delight and jumping up and down, unaware that the other was doing exactly the same, phone in one hand and pumping the air with the other.

The modern medical centre where Miriam worked was just recently built and now there were clinics like this opening up all over Melbourne. It was a good alternative to visiting the emergency wards at the big hospitals, as the clinics had doctors and nurses on staff, ready to cope with day-to-day medical issues and minor emergencies. Miriam was in her starched white nurse's uniform and hat. It had been a busy day and she was well and truly ready to call it a day.

'So, will there be anything else Doctor?' He was a mature age doctor with a kind face.

'No, you run along dear. By the way, how's your mother doing?'

'Oh, I don't know Dr Wallace, she seems to be worsening. She is more or less bed-ridden now and it is very hard for her when I am away all day.'

'Don't give up my dear, there are new treatments being studied and tested as we speak. We are all praying for a cure.'

'Well I truly hope so Doctor, I will tell her that when I get home.'

'You run along now and wish your mother all the best from me.' Miriam gathered up her bag along with the groceries she had managed to pick up at lunchtime. The night was beginning to descend, and she wanted to get home before it was too dark, so that she could turn the lights on for her mother.

When she finally did arrive home her mother was pale and sick looking. Once a very attractive woman, she was now wizened, her body shrunken. She sat in her flimsy nightie by an old kerosene heater, grey hair so thin you could see her scalp. As she saw Miriam come in the door, her effort to say hello turned into an extremely bad, hacking cough.

The front door led straight into a living room of sorts, with its bare boards and draughty atmosphere. Miriam's mother sat at a wooden table, beyond which lay a wooden kitchen bench and an old cast iron sink. Wrestling with the door key and her groceries, Miriam saw her mother and immediately became annoyed and worried, all at the same time. Miriam put down her bags and began fussing as she berated her mother. 'Mum, I told you not to get out of bed, you're going to catch your death of cold in this flimsy nighty.'

'Well good, perhaps I can get out of this life a little earlier, I'm sick of living like this,' her poor mother complained.

'Oh Mum, you don't want to give up. Doctor Wallace said there was hope. He said researchers are discovering new treatments all the time.'

'Inventing new treatment? Who the hell does he think is going to pay for these … treatments?' On the word, treatments, Miriam's mother used the two fingers of each hand to make air quotation marks. She then broke into another round of hacking coughing, using her well-worn handkerchief to reveal blood. Miriam looked on worried and sympathetic.

'You don't even know what's involved yet … but if you keep behaving like this you won't live long enough to know whether there's help out there.'

'Help — pah — nobody wants to help the likes of us,' her mother replied sarcastically. 'Oh sure, you're young. Still got stars in your eyes. But they'll fade my girl, nothing is surer. You will see.' Miriam stared into the eyes of her mother, she'd had such a hard life. Her mother was the only person she had in the world. She had lost her father in a freak drowning in 1938, when they had been camping on the Murray River. She remembered the day, it had been perfect. A glorious summer's day in early March and they had taken the long weekend to go camping on the banks of the Victorian side of the Murray.

The rambling river was a popular destination, and they were lucky to have found a quiet spot away from the many other holidaymakers seeking an escape from the city. Miriam loved to pay cricket with her father and had hit the ball hard, sending it all the way into the river. Her father didn't hesitate, diving into the cool water the rescue the ball.

Only he didn't come out.

Suddenly he seemed in difficulty. He yelled for help. He appeared to be snagged on something beneath the water. He had the ball in his hand, but something was dragging him under.

Miriam's mother couldn't swim and was fiercely holding Miriam back from going to his rescue as she yelled for help. When nearby campers finally arrived on the scene Miriam's father was nowhere to be seen. Only the ball remained bobbing on the surface as three rescuers went to his aid, but nothing could be done. Miriam had never entered the water again since that day, she not only had a fear of water — she loathed it.

Mrs Worthing had battled on, raising Miriam on her own, and now it was Miriam who was struggling to keep her mother going. Miriam wanted to give her mother hope, but it was so difficult when all that she got back from her was disillusionment and disdain.

The dining room of Melbourne's Windsor hotel was busy as usual. Cissy had never been anywhere so elegant before and was feeling a little out of place. Even though she had worn her very smart black dress with the polka-dot bodice, she couldn't help but notice some of the other women with their fur stoles, elegant evening dresses and sparkling diamonds. The waiter wore an immaculate dinner suit and addressed Godfrey as sir, Cissy wondered what on earth to order as most of the menu was in French, and all the meals looked very complicated.

'We'll have the champagne thank you, the Veuve Clicquot, thanks, and some water too.' Godfrey seemed so relaxed, Cissy wondered how many women he wined and dined in places like this.

'Have you been here before?'

'Once or twice. Mum and Dad come here often, I occasionally tag along.' Cissy nodded. 'Do you like it, or is it too formal for you? We can just have a drink and go somewhere else if you like.'

'No, no. It's beautiful really, but it's a first for me.'

'Splendid. I'm glad I'm your first, and I'm looking forward to many other firsts with you Cissy.' Cissy wasn't sure what he meant but the way his eyes drilled into hers she found herself blushing furiously.

The waiter returned with the champagne and gracefully poured the sparkling liquid into the delicate crystal champagne saucers. Cissy observed his every movement and noticed that Godfrey was doing the same. As the waiter left the table Cissy watched Godfrey's eyes following him as he walked away. She had lifted her glass, but he had yet to do the same. 'What shall we toast to?' she inquired in an attempt to gain his attention, which it did. Godfrey realised he had been staring at the retreating waiter and immediately focused his attention back on Cissy.

'To us I think, what better than to toast to us and a lovely evening together.' Cissy agreed, and they clinked glasses.

'Do you know him or something?'

'Sorry, who ... know who?'

'The waiter, the way you were looking at him, like you knew him or something.'

'No, no, just ... well he does remind me of someone I knew — but I don't think it's him. So, tell me about life in the Cambridge household.'

'Oh, not much to tell really. We probably all spend most of our time at the picture theatre, work, work, work. But of course, I have to do the housework as well, being the only girl — and that's all pretty boring.'

'Yes, indeed, you'd think these housewives would get really bored,' Godfrey replied derogatorily.

'Oh, there's plenty to do running a household, don't worry about that.'

'Is that what you want to do one day Cissy? Run a household?' Godfrey questioned her with an amused edge of belittlement.

'Well no, actually. I'd like to paint. Study fine art.'

'Hmmm,' came Godfrey, still with that disparaging edge, 'well how about that? Do you have the talent?'

'Actually, I've just received an invitation to study at the School of Art in Paris.'

Godfrey's jaw dropped, 'Really?' The waiter was back, ready to take their orders. Godfrey addressed him, 'Now what do you think of this young man? This little lady here has just been invited to study at the School of Art in Paris.'

When the waiter replied both Cissy and Godfrey were stunned by his broad Aussie accent, having expected a far more refined voice coming from this elegant waiter. 'I'd say it would be bloody dangerous to go anywhere near Europe at the moment,' and then remembering his demeanour he quickly refined his accent, '... er ... sir, but an amazing opportunity for the young lady.'

Godfrey looked a bit shocked at him being so forthright and Cissy could do nothing else but look away, embarrassed. Godfrey collected himself, remembering his mission to snare the lovely Miss Cissy, and so he raised his glass, as the waiter stood, order pad in hand. 'Here's to you Cissy — wherever life may lead you.' Cissy accepted the toast and Godfrey proceeded to give the waiter their order. She watched Godfrey's over-friendly interaction with the waiter, something was niggling her, but she just couldn't quite put her finger on it.

The weather in Melbourne was usually cool in July, however the chill had escaped them this evening and people were out, enjoying the moonlight and stars. A group of youths were outside the hamburger shop admiring a brand-new Harley Davidson. Across the road, CC's black Humber Super-Snipe pulled up in front of the near-completed new picture theatre. Wearing his trade-mark bowler hat, CC got out of the vehicle looking harried and checked his watch. There was something he'd left in his office, and he hurried down through the poplar lined path and into the little grain hut picture theatre, removing his hat as he entered.

First things first, CC lifted the telephone receiver and dialled. Seeing the stack of mail, he picked it up, tapping it against the desktop as he waited for the phone to be answered at the other end. Finally, it was. 'Yes, yes Sylvia I'm sorry to do this to you but do you think you could get a cab over to Wilbur's, I'll be there in about 15 minutes,' he spoke rather tersely into the phone.

'Oh CC, whatever's wrong?' inquired Sylvia.

'Nothing my dear, nothing's wrong, just had a busy day and running a little behind.'

'All right then CC, I'll call a taxi right now.'

'Good, good, I must go.' With that he hung up the phone, picked up the mail and reached for his hat. As he did so the phone rang, thinking it would be Sylvia again he silently cursed, but decided to pick up the phone anyway.

'Carleton Cambridge speaking.' The voice came through with a slight crackle, CC strained to hear. 'I'm sorry, who is this, speak up, I am not hearing you very well. Suddenly he collapsed into the chair, dropping the stack of mail down as the Australian Armed Forces envelope fell to the floor.

Dorothy Maxwell was entertaining guests in the main dining room of their home. It was a formal occasion, eleven people seated around a large dining table, all that was missing was CC. Tapestries adorned the walls, candelabras — the table. The guests were formally dressed and chatting civilly among themselves. Sylvia Wright-Smith was a bit annoyed that CC was not there, but she was determined not to let it ruffle her feathers. Wilbur's annoyance however was quite apparent as he kept checking his watch every few minutes. 'Yes, well I don't think we can wait for CC any longer, let's begin, shall we.'

Just then the doorbell chimed.

Wilbur had hired a butler for the evening and the dinner-suited older man proceeded to open the front door. CC entered looking flustered as he handed the butler his coat and hat. All eyes turned to CC as he entered the dining room. The look on his face spelt out some sort of pending disaster. Sylvia noticed it first and became extremely concerned, remembering the letter from the Armed Forces. The rest of the guests followed, their eyes glued to CC.

CC looked around the room at all the faces, still in some sort of shock, finally he spoke. 'It's Seymour.' Gasps were heard around the room. Sylvia's hand flew to her chest, fearing the worst. With WWII occupying everyone's thoughts now for so many years, people feared the worst when news arrived. Now the faces staring at CC became more expectant, waiting with dread of the words he was about to deliver. 'He's coming home!' As the faces of the dinner guests began to change all the concern left CC's face and he broke into a huge smile, 'Tomorrow!!'

The dinner party breathed a collective sigh of relief. Then the cheers went up. CC approached Sylvia and they embraced heartily. Everyone was elated, even Wilbur lined up to give CC a matey hug.

The guests took their seats again, the conversation was whirring with excitement and vibrancy as the entrées were brought in. Wilbur raised his glass and proposed a toast to CC and Seymour, the rest of the guests responded. In all of the excitement CC had totally forgotten about the letter from the Armed Forces, which lay unopened on his office floor.

Chapter Eight

WILBUR WAS NURSING the sore head of a hangover when his wife entered his office. 'I didn't get a chance to talk to you last night with the stress of the dinner party, and then I forgot all about it.'

'What? Forgot all about what?' Wilbur responded grumpily, just wishing everyone would leave him alone.

'Heather asked me if her young friend could come and live with us for a while.'

'Why? What's wrong with her own home?'

'Well, her father just bought her a hairdressing salon in Footscray and her family lives way over in Mentone. You know the man, Bruce Lansing.'

'He's that property developer.' As hungover as he was, the wheels started to churn in Wilbur's head. He'd heard quite a bit about Bruce Lansing, and he had often thought he wouldn't mind an introduction, he was sure there was some business to be done there. 'That's a hell of a long way for a young lady to travel each day,' said Wilbur.

'Yes exactly, and we have plenty of room,' replied Dorothy.

Wilbur thought about it and could see nothing but benefits to him, having Bruce Lansing's daughter lodge with them. 'Go ahead and give the girls my blessing, I'm hardly at home anyway so I don't see what a great deal of difference it is going to make to me,' he said rather nobly. 'When is she going to arrive anyway?'

Dorothy looked a little perplexed, 'Today actually, Heather couldn't wait to have her here.'

'Good God above — well you had better get your skates on then, close the door on your way out, I must try and get some work done.'

As Dorothy closed the door, she thought the only household member she had to contend with now was Godfrey, not knowing of course that he had already overheard their conversation and was well aware of their new lodger.

Hudson loved to play the piano. He had watched the film about the life of the famous pianist and composer, Frederick Chopin, over and over. In A Song to Remember, Chopin had written the Polonaise in A Flat and Hudson thought it was one of the most beautiful pieces he had ever heard. He had never been taught music, no time on the farm for that, however he played superbly by ear and also by studying the keyboard so many times as Cornel Wilde performed the Polonaise. Now the piece was indoctrinated into his memory, and he played it like an expert, so much so that Cissy was drawn into the room. She began to dance and had the movements of an angel.

'I love the Polonaise, I love Chopin.'

Hudson spoke as he played, 'Have you told Dad yet?'

'Told Dad what?' she responded as she danced.

'About the School of Arts, the letter.'

'Oh no, not today, he is that rapt in Seymour's arrival I just think it's best to leave it today.'

'Maybe you're right. Hey, what time is he due in?'

'The train gets into Spencer Street at two o'clock this afternoon.'

Hudson checked his watch, it was already close to one o'clock. The large city terminal for interstate and country trains was eight miles away in the heart of Melbourne. 'Well, we had better get a move on then.'

Just as Hudson, Cissy and CC were leaving their home to pick up Seymour, Eleanor was arriving at the Maxwell's. It was quite foreign to move out of home. Her father had offered to drive her, and she jumped at the gesture, given that she had way more stuff to take to Heather's than she thought. She hadn't yet had time to organise a work uniform, so she had to have a different outfit for each day of the week. She also wanted some casual clothing as well as dresses to wear out. After cramming everything into two trunks she then looked at the rest of the things in her room.

Some of the photos she could not live without, so they had to accompany her. There was her make-up and her vast array of toiletries. Heather had said she would have her own bathroom, so she was not afraid to pile them all into a bag. She took a couple of the stuffed toys from her childhood and surveyed the room. She hated to leave really, but on the other hand was excited about her new beginning. Living with Heather would be fun, she was sure, she just hoped the rest of the Maxwell household would be so welcoming.

Now, as she knocked on the door of the Maxwell's, her nerves were beginning to fray. She heard Heather yell from within, 'I'll get it!' Eleanor's father was approaching the door, battling with the two trunks. Just then the door opened, and Heather stood, all smiles and welcoming hugs. Wilbur Maxwell appeared in the background, anxious to get an introduction to Bruce Lansing. 'Here, let me help with those,' he said looking at the trunks, 'Heather, you show this young lady to her room.'

'Wilbur Maxwell ...' he said to Bruce offering his hand, 'pleased to meet you.'

'Oh, the pleasure is all mine,' replied Bruce, moving a trunk in Wilbur's direction, 'I can't thank you enough for what you are doing for my daughter. Saving her that long trip every day — it really is magnanimous of you.'

'Ah, it's nothing at all really, we have plenty of room.' As he spoke, Godfrey arrived. 'Ah, here's Godfrey. Be a good chap and takes these up to our new guest's room. Let's you and I have a small sip and get to know each other a little better,' he said to Bruce, inviting him into the bar.

'Don't mind if I do,' responded Bruce, thinking what a gentleman Wilbur was and feeling very comfortable to leave his daughter in the man's care. In the background Godfrey swore under his breath as he was left to lug the heavy trunks up the stairs.

Spencer Street Station was alive with people bustling everywhere. Men in uniforms dominant — Australian Armed Forces, the Navy and American Military. CC, Hudson and Cissy stood on the platform, anxiously awaiting the arrival of the modern steam train, Spirit of Progress and of course, Seymour.

'Did he say why he was coming home Dad?' asked Hudson of his father.

'No, not really, it was a bad line, lots of crackling noise and I couldn't really hear him very well. He said he'd explain when he saw me.'

The announcement came over, The Spirit of Progress was about to pull into the station. CC, Hudson and Cissy strained their necks to look down the track, finally the big steam train rounded the bend. Slowly it pulled into the station puffing clouds of steam and spurting wet geysers over those who stood too close. The crowds milled about anxiously, watching for their loved ones as the passengers alighted the train.

'Where is he dad? Can you see him?' Hudson asked impatiently.

'No sign of him yet Son, just be patient.'

The crowds started to thin, there were very few passengers left on the train and CC was rubbing his jaw with worry. Where was Seymour? 'Perhaps you got the date wrong dad?' Cissy stated, but it was more of a question.

'He definitely said this train on this day.'

And then they saw it. A wheelchair was being lifted from the very end carriage. The Cambridge trio watched — a little horrified, very excited. When the chair was lowered to the ground the occupant spun to face them. Yes, it was Seymour, finally.

Cissy was first to take off, rushing towards her brother. Hudson and CC took a little longer to absorb what was happening. They looked at each other before embarking on a swift journey towards Seymour who now had Cissy in his arms and practically on his lap. 'Step back girl, step back. Your brother is hurt, can't you see that.'

'Oh, it's all right Dad,' Seymour replied happily, 'it feels just great to be hugging my little sister again.'

'What happened son? How are you?' CC said all at once before awkwardly embracing his son.

'What? Didn't they send you the letter?' CC looked puzzled at first, then remembered the unopened letter from the Australian Armed Forces. He didn't answer his son, embarrassment getting the better of him. Seymour continued, 'It's a long story Dad,' Seymour replied looking at Hudson, 'but it looks like I am going to join the ranks of the gammy leg,' he commented, the inference being at Hudson's own injury. Hudson laughed at his brother making humour of his own, obviously dire situation.

'Don't worry mate, the girls just love a good sob story.' With that the brothers embraced, and they all turned to leave the platform as The Spirit of Progress hissed once more, blowing out its last puffs of steam before taking a rest.

Later that same evening CC, Seymour and Hudson were in the living room, enjoying a glass of smooth Scotch. Seymour was telling them of the battles he had fought and how his leg injury had occurred. 'So, you see, I wasn't shot after all. A land mine had exploded beneath our jeep and sent us all skyrocketing. I came off the best of them actually, even though I was trapped under the jeep.' CC and Hudson listened intently to the story.

'One poor chap has lost his sight — nearly lost his head if the truth be known, and it's doubtful if the other two officers will ever walk again.'

'But you will regain use of your legs, right Seymour?' asked his father.

'Absolutely. The right one is pretty good, it's the left that is causing me most grief,' he explained. 'They have me booked in at the Royal

Melbourne Hospital for repatriation, I am going to have to visit three times a week to start with.'

'No problem, I will take you in,' offered Hudson, thinking the trip into Melbourne's leading repatriation hospital would otherwise be impossible, 'wait till you see my new Ford.'

'Not necessary, but thanks anyway Huddo, the Army will send a car for me, all part of the service,' he explained, using his nickname for Hudson since boyhood, 'but I would love to see your new car. Let's go take a look.'

'Aren't you tired after your long journey Son, wouldn't you like to rest,' asked CC.

'I'll sleep when I'm dead dad, right now what I want to do is live, and Huddo's new car sounds like a good place to start.'

Hudson was glad to have his brother back. He missed the camaraderie and his brother's humorous wit. It was good to have him home and anything he could do to help with his recovery he would. Seymour said he would be up and around in no time, and knowing his brother as he did, Hudson believed every word of it.

Chapter Nine

'HOW COME you don't go out much Heather? I see your brother Godfrey at the Palais every now and again, why don't you go in with him?' Eleanor enquired of her friend. They were in Eleanor's bedroom, Heather sitting on the bed while her friend unpacked and got the room organised. Eleanor loved the lilac walls and clean layout of the room. It was like having a blank canvas to work with and she was going to spend a little time making it her own.

'I don't know,' replied Heather, 'I guess Godfrey's the reason I don't go to the Palais. He can be such a cow of a brother; you don't know what it's like.'

'Believe me, I do, I have three brothers and they are all beasts. Jacky even threw a spider on me the other day, I really thought I was going to have a heart attack.'

'Oh my God I would have, I hate the horrid hairy beasts.'

'That's brothers — I suppose they're all alike.'

'Some girls are lucky, like Cissy Cambridge.'

'Who?' asked Eleanor, wondering where she had heard the name before.

'Cissy Cambridge,' explained Heather, 'she has a really good brother, quite a bit of a dish actually.'

'Hmm, so are you sweet on him?'

'Me, no. I don't think I'd stand a chance. You would though, you look like his type.'

'So where do I meet this brother?' she asked cannily. Heather picked up on her piqued interest.

'He comes here sometimes to meet Godfrey — and he goes to the Palais too, I know that for a fact, but if you really want to meet him then we should go to the pictures.'

'The pictures, whatever for?'

'Because his father owns the local picture theatre — and I hear they're planning to build more, so the family's obviously got money.'

'That's where I've heard the name. There was a Mr Cambridge enquiring about land, from my father, I think he wants to build a picture theatre out at Cheltenham.'

'There, you see it's a small world, let's go to the pictures on Saturday night and see if we can bump into Mr Handsome Hudson.'

Eleanor giggled, it would be a fun thing to do, even though she was pretty sure the only man she wanted to meet up with was the one who had saved her from some horrible fate, two nights ago at the Palais. She pictured him in her mind — dark curly hair, the body of a well-muscled man, just the right height and lovely eyes. She would love to know what his name was.

Wilbur was surprised to hear of Bruce Lansing's business dealings with Carleton Cambridge. 'I didn't know he was looking for land around Cheltenham. I know he has already secured land at Maidstone, and he has the land in Sunshine, where the new Sunshine Picture Theatre is just about completed.'

'That's interesting,' responded Bruce, 'the man's obviously building himself a little empire.'

'That's exactly what he is doing. Asked me to get into bed with him on the financial side.'

'Well how about that Wilbur, hey? Do you think this man is a good risk?'

'I think that whatever he sets his mind to he will achieve. Hell, he is already talking about bringing out the big guns from Hollywood to show them exactly what he is doing. He currently screens all of the big box office hits from Hollywood and Australia — even though his current picture theatre is just a little makeshift joke in a grain shed. The new Sunshine Picture Theatre is really looking quite grand — I don't think anything would stop Carleton Cambridge from achieving what he has set out to.'

'Right. That sounds like the sort of chap one should become involved with. I might just give him a call about that land.'

'You do that Bruce — and let me know how you get on.'

Bruce stood to leave, explaining that he had quite a drive ahead of him. As Wilbur saw him out, he couldn't help but become more excited about the prospect of investing with CC. He could see how big this theatre empire could become and he didn't just want a small piece of it, one day he would like to own the lot. Time to start planning how this could take place. Wilbur returned to his office to make a call, right now he had another acquisition in the wings and he needed to make sure everything was going according to plan.

'Sammy, is it taken care of?' Wilbur enquired when the phone was lifted at the other end. The voice that resounded back through the phone was the hoarse, throaty voice of a slippery reprobate.

'Yeah boss-man, I did just like you told me.'

'No evidence, nothing left behind?'

'No, like I said, I did just like you told me.'

'Okay, now you can start the blackmail, just like I told you,' said Wilbur mimicking his words. 'I don't want you to let up until we have what we want.'

'Yeah boss-man, yeah sure. I start the black-mail and don't let up until he gives it over.'

'That's the way. Tomorrow Sammy, start tomorrow. We'll see how quickly he starts cooperating.'

'Don't worry boss-man, he'll cooperate with old Sammy on the job, just you wait and see.'

'Just take it easy Sammy and do it like I told you.'

Yeah boss-man yeah, just like you told me.'

Wilbur replaced the receiver and picked up his glass of Scotch, downing it in one satisfying gulp. Just then Godfrey entered.

'Hey Dad, what's with the little miss's father in here with you for so long?'

'Just having a drink Son, getting to know the father of the young lady whose daughter will be living under our roof.'

'But why, it's unlike you to worry about getting to know anyone unless there's something in it for you.'

'Ahhh the cynicism Son, you are learning from your old man after all,' Wilbur smiled. 'The thing is, there could just be something in it for me.'

'Enlighten me.'

'Did you know old Bruce Lansing is a very big landowner.' Godfrey looked, nodding at this father, willing him to tell him more. 'Owns a lot of land over Cheltenham/Mentone way.'

'Oookaay.'

'And he has been talking to one Carleton Cambridge about selling him some land to build a theatre at Cheltenham.'

'But that is not in the plans that CC gave you.'

'Exactly Son, exactly. And I reckon if we can get our hands on that land before CC does, then we will have ourselves some real bargaining power to get a big slice of that empire he is about to build.' Godfrey was still nodding. 'And I know a sure-fire way to make that all happen.'

'Planning another blackmail dad?'

'Now, now Son, what do you take me for? No need for underhanded tactics, the land will be enough to sway the odds in my favour. CC will see it my way.'

'Speaking of the Cambridges — how are you shaping up with Cissy?'

'Eating out of my hand father — literally and figuratively.' Now Wilbur was the one nodding his approval. 'I took her into the Windsor for dinner two nights ago, charmed the pants off her.'

'Son, you didn't?'

'Figuratively speaking only, this time father.'

'Hmmmm. Good job though Son, when are you seeing her again?'

'I might just pop over there tomorrow, see what she's up to.'

'What do you think of her son?'

'She's a pretty little thing and all, but not really my type.'

'Good God Son, exactly what is your type?'

'Oh, I don't know, I haven't met the right person yet.'

'No, and you probably never will. Just forget about *the right type* and use marriage for what it is, a contract that will help you lead a better life in a variety of ways. Look at your mother and I — she is a great entertainer, impresses the best of them, she looks good on my arm and is a great asset in a number of ways.'

'Asset? What about love?'

'Pah, love is a load of nonsense. Happiness is all about never having to worry about where your next quid or next meal is coming from.' Wilbur poured his son a glass of Scotch and refilled his own.

'I left home before I was your age Godfrey. I got away from my abusive bastard of a father and made my way in the world. I started with nothing and now I have all this. I will never go back to having nothing and I do what it takes to keep me on top. You stick with me Son and you'll never have to know what it's like to feel hungry, humiliated, and belittled.' Godfrey picked up his glass as he listened to his father.

'And finding the right woman is a big part of that, so go and romance little Miss Cecelia and let's see just how much we can milk from your relationship with her.' They chinked glasses and drank to the lucrative courtship on which Godfrey was about to embark.

Chapter Ten

IT MAY NOT HAVE BEEN a metropolis yet, but the little town of Sunshine was growing. With the harvester works now attracting more and more workers to the suburb, other factories were making their mark. More shops were opening, and the local residents were enjoying the choice the diversity was offering them.

Loretta Spalding worked on the Starlight make-up counter in Coles and maybe that was where she got the beguiling stars in her eyes. Brilliantly violet, people were always telling her how much she looked like Elizabeth Taylor, the budding young film star in National Velvet. Loretta was not really that impressed, she didn't mind being compared to a Hollywood actress — but not a child, she would rather look like Ava Gardner or Veronica Lake.

Loretta liked working on the make-up counter. Coles was the only department store in Sunshine and had long rows of counters, each assigned to different product lines. There was sewing with an area for a vast array of fabrics and sewing patterns; there was hardware, variety, haberdashery and of course, the irresistible sweets counter with lollies and chocolates of all shapes and sizes. And then there was the cosmetics department.

Many pretty women visited the store, and she would study their make-up and mimic it at night when the rest of the family had all gone to bed. Being the eldest of eight children was an ordeal. Her parents barely had enough money to put food on the table so hence she had been working at Coles since she was fourteen. She was a smart girl and wanted a lot more from life. She had gone from junior shop assistant to counter manager, at just 18. Her parents were very proud of her, the way she looked after her siblings and helped out financially. Without her their situation would be much worse.

Of course, this pressure didn't help Loretta. She wanted to live the life she dreamed of in a beautiful home with a handsome man who loved her. So far, she had only met men who were after one thing. The fact that she came from the wrong side of the tracks meant that they all thought she was an easy girl, the type who wouldn't mind giving them what they were after.

The fact was that Loretta was waiting for that right man to enter her life. She wasn't interested in kissing or even making conversation with the types of boys in her neighbourhood. They were beginning to call her a snob now. Her dress sense had really improved since working at Coles, she knew how to style her hair glamorously, and her make-up was applied just right, not too much but enough to enhance her beautiful features.

Today was like any other day, until *he* arrived. She couldn't say what it was, his handsome moustache or the twinkle in his eye, but when that man pushed the other up to her counter in the wheelchair, her heart fluttered as it never had before.

'Where can I buy some after-shave?' he asked.

'Haven't you heard there's a war on?' she replied with a pretty grin. 'You'll be lucky to find after-shave anywhere, unless you're looking for Old Spice, we have some of that on counter six.'

'Of course I know there's a war on my pretty one, how do you think I got to be in this wheelchair?'

Loretta felt so embarrassed, she should have guessed that his injuries had come about because of this horrible war. 'Oh, I am so sorry, I didn't realise.'

'That's all right, you weren't to know. Counter six you say?'

'Yes, around to the right.' Feeling a little more game, she ventured, 'So who's the lucky girl then?'

'What?' responded Seymour, 'What lucky girl?'

'The after-shave, who are you trying to impress?'

'You never know Miss, it could even be you.' Seymour laughed as Hudson wheeled him towards counter six, leaving the young shop assistant open-mouthed with a hand on her heart.

'You are such a tease, Seymour, leaving that poor girl pining after you,' Hudson commented, laughing at the innocent antics of his brother and remembering the fun they always had together.

'She was a bit of a looker though, wasn't she?'

'I couldn't disagree there brother, I couldn't disagree at all.'

Eleanor's salon was looking splendid. The leafy wallpaper now perfectly adhered to the rear wall and the mirrors all shining in the bright green frames. Now all she needed was customers. She proudly hung out her shingle:

ELEANOR'S

Pin Curls, Pompadours

Permanent Waves

Dyes and Tints

Tomorrow the *Footscray Mail* would be delivered to all local homes in the area. She had placed an ad in the *Early General News* and just hoped it worked. She'd also placed one in the *Sunshine Advocate* and that was due to be delivered the same day. After that she'd hoped word of mouth would bring the customers in. She dreamed of having an apprentice to help her sweep up, wash hair and do other chores around the place. She wanted to be rushed off her feet with no time to think about those mundane tasks, but at the moment she didn't mind, she would do it all on her own for now — she was determined to make a success of this business.

She thought about her new home. Heather's brother was a bit strange. She had caught him going through her toiletries in the bathroom. He apologised in a fashion, saying he was just curious. She thought it weird that he had sprayed a little of her perfume onto his neck, she could smell it when he walked by, the fact that perfume was so hard to come by in the war-rationed years made it worse. But why would a young man want to use a woman's perfume anyway? She noticed some of her pots of creams had been tampered with as well. Her brothers may have been annoying, but they would never touch her girlie stuff, that was strictly for ladies only.

Then there was Mrs Maxwell. She seemed like a slave to Mr Maxwell, even Godfrey seemed to have her under his thumb. She was always running after the men, meeting their every demand. Mr Maxwell had even installed an office intercom system that ran from his office into the kitchen, where Mrs Maxwell spent most of her time. He would make demands, from coffee to a bucket of ice to a sandwich. He would make sure she was on track to cater to any important clients he may have been visiting and remind her about any clothing he needed especially prepared, such as starched shirts or pressed trousers.

A version of the same treatment also came from Godfrey. Even though he did not run an office from home, he would demand coffee and sandwiches. He would become upset if the right clothes weren't ready for him and Eleanor just could not understand how Mrs Maxwell could put up with this style of treatment. In the Lansing household women were treated with respect. Her father adored her mother and was always giving her little hugs and looks of endearment. Even though her brothers joked with Eleanor, they would never abuse her. They loved her and looked out for her, in fact over-protective would be a better term. And as for their mum, they idolised her and helped wherever they could, did what she asked of them from carrying in the firewood to taking out the garbage to lifting the washing out to the line.

So, Eleanor wondered why Mrs Maxwell was treated so poorly yet acted as though she was the luckiest woman in world. She always looked immaculate, never a hair out of place and her clothes perfect, even her nails were manicured, polished and flawless. How did she manage it with the household to run and so much to do? She did have help two days a week, a lady to help with the general cleaning. Eleanor noticed when the cleaning woman was there, Mrs Maxwell's persona changed into the boss-lady rather than the submissive lamb she was in front her husband and Godfrey.

Eleanor had brought the subject up with Heather. Heather's face dropped in what Eleanor took to be embarrassment and she wished she had never mentioned it. However, Heather apologised. Saying the Maxwell men could be bullies and she just ignored them, hoping Eleanor would do the same. Heather spent most of her time at home in her room or in the library, that way keeping pretty much to herself. Eleanor thought most of her time would be spent at her salon, so she was sure she could dodge any unwelcome treatment from the Maxwell men.

Eleanor left her musings behind as she locked the salon and headed for the train, she didn't want to be late for dinner on her third night in the household, Mrs Maxwell had said Wednesday night was steak night, and that was a real treat with meat so hard to come by.

Chapter Eleven

GEORGE ROBERTS COULDN'T BELIEVE that he had been so stupid. How could he let himself be misled by that dreadful woman? He should have realised that any woman who even thought of entering the saloon bar of the Derrimut Hotel was no good, just a cheap whore out for anything she could get. Why had he been so stupid? And now here were the photos as proof of his stupidity. He'd been set up, he was sure of it. Trouble was, by whom? Sure, every businessman had enemies but overall, he believed he was pretty well-liked in the community. And his wife, his poor wife.

George hung his head in his hands. What would Frances do? Something like this would kill her, and the swines were threatening to go to the local paper with the photos. 'Local Businessman Involved in Sex Scandal.' He could see the headlines now. He would be ruined, unable to show his face in society again. And poor Francie — oh, what could he do?

Three thousand pounds. That's what they were asking. It was a small fortune and one he didn't have. He had already taken a loan out on his business to pay for the upgrade at the dairy. The building itself had a second mortgage. He had no way of raising that sort of money. What would his kids think? What would anyone think when the liquidators moved in and took his business away? When the headlines screamed local dairy owner in sex scandal and his life and that of his family lay in tatters?

There must be a way of raising the money, all he needed to do was think. He picked up the phone, surely with his connections around town he could find someone to help him. Carleton Cambridge would be a good start.

'George my man, I haven't spoken to you in what seems like eons. How are things?'

'Well, to be honest CC, I am in a spot of bother and need a bit of a helping hand.'

'That sounds ominous. What's happened?'

'Oh, nothing a bit of money won't fix.' CC frowned, he really hoped George wasn't going to ask him for money. He was stretched himself at the moment, what with the expansion and all. Perhaps it wasn't as bad as George thought and there would be another solution.

'Look, why don't you come by a bit later this afternoon, we'll catch up and have a chat about exactly what it is you need.'

'Thank you CC, I knew I could rely on you, you're a real friend, an honest citizen and a gentleman.' CC thought it was a bit of overkill and wondered just what strife George had got himself into. He hoped he could solve it some other way rather than just money.

Dinner had been served in the Maxwell household and Eleanor and Heather were upstairs in Eleanor's room. 'Sorry about my dad, he can be a bit unfriendly.'

'Don't apologise, men will be men. I guess he enjoys talking to his son more than us women. It's not a problem.'

The dinner conversation had been strictly limited to Mr Maxwell and Godfrey, talking mainly about the new picture theatres the Cambridges were planning. Eleanor thought it sounded exciting but didn't dare interrupt the men's conversation, this being her first dinner with the entire family present. The name of the family involved in the theatres was Cambridge, Heather had told her that before. Wilbur didn't make mention of the proposed Cheltenham picture theatre, although Eleanor knew he had spoken about this with her father. Godfrey mentioned the eldest son was calling by tonight for a game of billiards, wasn't that the fellow Heather was saying was a dreamboat?

'Who is this Cambridge family anyway?'

'They moved here a few years ago,' replied Heather. 'I believe they lived up Leongatha way, got wiped out when the bushfires hit.'

'Oh, that's sad.'

'Yes, but they're doing good here, making a new life for themselves with their picture theatres.'

'Sounds exciting.'

'Doesn't it? All those connections with the movie world, Hollywood. Aaaah ...' Heather sighs, gathering up a pillow to her chest and lazing back on Eleanor's bed. 'Let's do something.'

'What, what can we do?'

'Oh, I don't know, I am so stuffed after dinner why don't we go for a walk to get rid of some of that steak.'

'Where to?'

'There are some nice gardens just by the harvester works, we could walk through there, it is not far.'

'Okay, sure thing.'

As the girls descended the staircase, Godfrey was leading Hudson into the billiard room. Hudson caught a flash of red hair and immediately pictured the mysterious redhead from the Palais, but knew it couldn't possibly be her. 'Say, who was that with your sister?'

'Oh, didn't I tell you? We now have a border. Miss Eleanor Lansing.'

'Hmmm, any relation to Bruce Lansing.'

'The very one, his daughter in fact.'

'Oh, interesting. Very interesting,' said Hudson, picking up a billiard cue, still completely unaware that the redhead of his dreams was now part of his own neighbourhood.

'Look, I'll extend you the money you need CC, but you are going to have to cut me in. I want a fair share.' The two businessmen were in the office of the Sunshine Picture Theatre, the usual Johnny Walker Black Label on the desk, two glasses half full.

'I'm happy to cut you a share Wilbur, it's the right thing to do. I'll have my solicitor draw up a contract for five percent.' Wilbur shifted arrogantly in his chair.

'Five percent. Heavens above CC, what do you take me for, some kind of chump? I'm financing this thing and I expect my fair share.' CC became a little unsettled.

'You're financing some of it. Wilbur.' Wilbur looked surprised; he was under the impression CC had no other way of raising the money other than through him. 'I spoke to the bank last week; besides the advance I already have in place for the new and very soon to be completed, Sunshine Picture Theatre, they are happy to look at extending the funds for the Roxy in Maidstone. The bank manager there has seen the crowds we are drawing in and believes this will be a very good investment. The bank will get their interest rate and the town will get a brand-new picture theatre.' CC smiled then, 'And besides that, I threw in a lifetime pass to the movies for him and all his family. Old Martin was tickled pink.'

Wilbur was silently fuming. Was this deal slipping away from him? He was sure he had CC right where he wanted him, but now CC had found finance elsewhere — hadn't even mentioned it to Wilbur. 'So where does that leave me?'

'Nothing much has changed, I am still looking at the theatre at Altona, and since our last chat an opportunity has become available at a quaint little country town called Bacchus Marsh, out west of here.'

'Forever on the look-out hey? Grabbing opportunities left, right and centre.'

'Mad not to Wilbur, so are you still interested? What sort of figure did you have in mind?' CC asked, picking up his Scotch.

'I don't see why I shouldn't hold fifty percent. Fifty-fifty partners.'

'Absolutely not. My sons and I will retain the majority share otherwise I will keep looking for the further funds,' CC said getting agitated.

'All right, all right. Calm down. There's no need to do that. We must be able to work something out.'

'Ten percent, I'm willing to give you ten percent of Altona and Bacchus Marsh only.' Wilbur rubbed the palm of hand across his face. He was not going to settle for ten percent of just two theatres — one sounded like it was in the middle of nowhere. He'd heard of Bacchus Marsh, but it really was only good for a Sunday drive and a picnic — not something that appealed to Wilbur at all.

'It's not just about the money CC,' Wilbur started cajoling. 'I want to come on this journey with you, back you up. Help in the expansion, bring some important people in, make sure you have everything you need. Two intelligent men are better than one. We can do this together CC and I will be here to help you every step of the way. What do you say to forty percent?'

CC wasn't ready to give away forty percent of his dream. He needed the money but there were other avenues he had yet to explore. If it took him a little longer to build his theatres then so be it, Sunshine was almost finished and once it was open that would take up a lot of their energy. When it was all said and done, he wanted to own them. It wasn't as if he was a control freak, he just wanted to build the vision he had dreamt of and not have it ripped out from under him.

He'd seen it all too often, on the land and in the cities. People worked hard to carve out something for themselves. A farm, the corner store, a profitable business, only to be called up by the banks, have a bigger enterprise take the customers or swallow them up completely. Con men waiting in the corners or shysters ready to pull the rug out from under you.

Wilbur's urgency and need for a bigger share put a bad taste in CC's mouth. He wanted this right from the beginning. He wanted to go in with a solid foundation. Work hard with his family and build his empire. Stepping back now could be a wise move, go over everything again and make sure bringing Wilbur in on the deal was the right thing to do.

'Let me sleep on it, Wilbur. In fact, give me a couple of weeks to just let the dust settle. I've got the new build here at Sunshine to concentrate on and plans aren't even through council yet on the Roxy. Let's not rush it. You've got a lot to think about and so do I. I'm sure we can figure out something we will both be happy with.'

CC rose with those last words, indicating that the conversation was closed. He held out his hand to Wilbur and Wilbur decided not to fight it, although his brain was clicking over at a hundred miles an hour. He would get CC to sign on the dotted line and he would get what he wanted, there was more than one way to achieve the right outcome.

Just as he was about to leave his office CC heard Sylvia Wright-Smith talking to someone in the foyer, it was only then that he remembered his appointment with George Roberts. Sylvia popped her head around the door.

'CC, George Roberts is here, said you told him to pop by.'

'Yes of course Sylvia, please show him in.' Wilbur left, acknowledging George on the way out, and wondering to himself what George was going to talk to CC about. He wiped his brow, suddenly he seemed to be in a sweat.

The two men exchanged pleasantries and CC could tell that George was very nervous by the way he was rotating the brim of his hat that he held in his hands in front of him. 'Take a seat George, take a seat,' he gestured towards the still warm seat that Wilbur had just vacated. 'So, what's all this about?'

As George explained his sorry predicament, CC felt deeply sorry for him. He may have acted the fool, but nobody deserves to be blackmailed. 'There must be another way to fix this George, have you been to the police?'

'I just can't risk it, CC. If Francie gets wind of this or it gets out in the papers, I am ruined. I just want to get the money together and get this mongrel paid off.'

The two men exchanged a long, hard and meaningful stare. 'Look, I know I can repay it,' George went on. 'We have just upgraded the dairy with the most modern equipment available. I've expanded my local run to Albion and Braybrook, and we are now supplying most of the restaurants, cafés and hotels from Deer Park to just this side of Footscray.'

'That's great news George, it really is,' encouraged CC as he listened to George's expansion through the neighbouring suburbs, 'and I wish I could help you with a loan, but I am absolutely up against if myself at the moment — what with the new theatre just about finished we are going to need every penny to bring in more stock, not to mention staff.'

George looked crest fallen. CC could see his agitation and really wanted to help him. 'I have an idea,' he said. George now looked up at him, hopeful. 'Why don't you pay a visit to Wilbur Maxwell, tell him your story. Hell, we've all got ourselves into a predicament from time to time — and knowing Wilbur he would certainly be no exception.'

'I don't know the man that well,' said George. 'Never had much in common.'

'That's not so, you're both local businessmen, members of the community.' He could see George was still reluctant. 'Look, why don't I give him a call for you? You saw him just leaving my office — he should be home by now with a bit of luck.'

'Well, if you say so CC. Beggars can't be choosers and all that,' reasoned George.

'I'll do it right now,' concluded George.

Wilbur was just entering his front door when the phone rang in his office. It was nearly six o'clock at night and he wondered who it could be. He hurried in, quickly hanging his hat and coat before hastening to his office. 'Maxwell,' he announced arrogantly into the phone.

'Oh good, you're there,' came CC's voice from the other end. 'Listen, I don't know whether you know George Roberts, the dairy owner?'

Wilbur's face broke into menacing smile. He painted the picture quickly. George had gone to CC for help and CC being short of cash had suggested that perhaps Wilbur, being the kind-hearted man and upstanding citizen that he was, might be able to help him. Everything was going according to plan.

'Well vaguely. I saw him going into your office, I don't know him personally,' explained Wilbur, 'but yes, I am aware that he owns the dairy.'

'Look, the chap's got himself into a spot of bother, needs a little financial assistance which I'm in no position to give him at the moment.'

'Financial assistance, this is all sounding very ominous CC.'

'Come on, we're all men here Wilbur, seems some low life has managed to take some inappropriate pictures of him in a compromising situation and is now threatening to show them to his wife.'

'Oh, I see — he has been a silly boy, hasn't he?'

There was a stretch of silence. CC knew the best strategy was to let the information filter through Wilbur's thought channels. 'I tell you what CC, George Roberts and I may be able to help each other. What's say you send him around tomorrow? I have some time available at around 11am.'

'I'll see that he's there Wilbur, I'm sure he will be. And I haven't forgotten about our other conversation — I'll get back to you soon.'

Wilbur hung up the phone, delighted. Gleefully rubbing his palms together, he thought about how he now had George Roberts right where he wanted him. The new refurbished dairy was a veritable gold-mine and good old CC thought he was an angel of generosity, rescuing those in need. What a laugh — but it should also help to make snaring CC that much easier as well.

George left CC's office with a little less weight on his shoulders. He understood perfectly well why CC couldn't help him out and he had done all he could by engaging the help of Wilbur Maxwell. He had heard good and bad things about Maxwell over the years. Still. Desperate times call for desperate measures and he would be there at eleven o'clock in the morning to hopefully enlist Wilbur's help.

Chapter Twelve

FOUR WEEKS HAD GONE BY, and Seymour was becoming increasingly depressed. The rehabilitation was a drag and he just wanted to be able to get off the damned crutches and be able to walk again, run, kick a footy — whatever. He was well and truly over being an invalid and everyone was starting to notice.

They were in the courtyard of the Cambridge home. It was a pretty place, with palms and other large leafed plants. The court itself was paved in different shades of sandstone and slate — crazy paving that travelled up a bench seat, one on which Hudson now sat, as Seymour attempted to pace on his crutches, venting his frustrations.

'Come on Seymour, you're doing so well,' Hudson told him.

'What would you know? You're walking around doing as you please.' Hudson looked at his brother, the look reminding Seymour that Hudson had been through a very similar recuperation when he came off the horse a few years back. 'Look I'm sorry, if anyone knows what I am going through it is you. How is your leg?'

'Well, I have to say it still causes me grief, particularly in the colder weather — but hey, I'm doing what I want, that's the most important thing. I can still take a girl for a spin around the dance floor at the Palais.'

'The Palais, boy I have missed that place. Why don't we go there tonight? It's Friday and Dad said you could have the night off, brothers just hanging out.'

'The Palais, I don't know Seymour, don't you think it's a little too soon? ...'

'Come on Huddo, just to get out of the house. I don't even have to dance ... hell I can't dance! But I can have a few drinks, eye-off all the pretty girls.'

'What pretty girls?' came a female voice. The brothers looked up to see Cissy coming through the French doors, closely followed by Godfrey. Hudson was a little peeved at Cissy's relationship with Godfrey, even though he and Godfrey were mates, he didn't really trust the man and worried where this relationship with his sister was going.

He tried to tell her once, but she became very agitated and told him to keep his opinions to himself. From that time Hudson had swallowed his words, just waiting to see where the relationship went. Since their fathers had been working on the expansion deal, Godfrey seemed to be spending a lot more time with Cissy, and that worried Hudson for reasons he was unsure of.

'Seymour wants to go to the Palais,' Hudson said to Cissy.

'Good for you Seymour,' responded Cissy, 'about time you started having a bit of fun.'

Hudson looked perturbed. 'Don't you think it's too soon, what if he falls and breaks something?'

'You're just being the over-protective older brother like always Hudson,' said Cissy. 'Give the guy a break. Let's all go.'

'Great idea,' piped in Godfrey. 'And if Seymour's got girls on the brain, have I got a stunner for him?'

'Yeah, and who's that?'

'Eleanor Lansing, a ravishing redhead currently living in the Maxwell household.'

Hudson laughed — remembering the flash of red hair when he last visited Godfrey. It made him remember the stunning redhead at the Palais. He began to think it may be a good idea to head off in there tonight after all.

'Okay why not? Let's go,' he said to Godfrey. 'I'll bring the wheels, you bring the redhead.' With that they all laughed, looking forward to a good night out.

It was interval at the Sunshine Picture Theatre. The foyer was a throng of people battling their way to the kiosk. Dixie ice-cream cups, Fantales, Scorched Almonds and Passiona soft drinks were in big demand. Miriam was run ragged while the underling, Roger Rourke, battled to keep up with the patrons jostling for position at the counter.

Jack Sotheby had finished sweeping the aisle and rows and was now coming out to lend a hand. He admired Miriam and her work ethic. Her determination to keep her mother at home was commendable, heaven knew she was nearly run off her feet with it all though.

He thought about that. For a man in his late twenties he had not really achieved that much in his life and often pondered about settling down with a good woman. He wasn't much for the night life really and was looking for an opportunity that could lead him into a more successful career. Up until working for the Cambridges he had been working at the offices of the local council. Being a quiet sort of a chap, he had managed to save quite a bit of his salary and plodded along from day to day.

Unsure of what had come over him, one day he just decided to quit. He did the right thing and put in his notice. His manager was worried for Jack, without another job to go to he could become destitute. But Jack had had enough. He would never really know what urged him to do it, but he gave his two weeks' notice and on the day of his leaving he walked into the Sunshine Picture Theatre and applied for the job as Assistant Manager.

Funny, the job wasn't all he'd imagined (his own office, secretary), instead he was sweeping floors and overseeing the patrons' behaviour during the movies — but he was becoming more and involved in the operations of the theatre and the future planning of the Cambridge expansion.

That was what he found exciting and felt sure he was headed in the right direction. He was in on the ground floor, he respected the Cambridge family and would do all he could to ensure their success, at the same time hopefully ensuring his own. He looked across to Miriam, she wiped her brow as the bell started ringing for the main feature to commence. The patrons began filing back into the cinema as Jack stood on the door collecting pass-outs.

He wondered about Miriam, what it would be like to ask her out. He knew she was twenty-three and still single, spending all her energy looking after her mother. There wasn't that much of an age difference, and besides, an older man could look after her properly. He'd think about it, there was no rush.

Hudson, Cissy and Seymour were enjoying the spaciousness of the front bench seat of Hudson's Ford Deluxe Convertible. 'You've done well Huddo,' announced his brother. 'Wait till I'm off these crutches, I'll upstage you with a grandiose vehicle of my own.' Hudson laughed at his brother's rivalry.

'You go right ahead brother, then we can have a race and see who the better man is.'

'Do you two ever stop trying to upstage each other?' said Cissy, neatly tucked in between her two brothers. 'Sometimes you both drive me insane. You've only just got out of your wheelchair, Seymour.'

The conversation came to a halt as they pulled up in front of the Maxwells. 'Hop out Seymour, I'll show you the engine.'

'What do I want to look at an engine for? The thing goes, that's all that matters.'

'I know you're an ignoramus when it comes to all things mechanical but let me show you what really makes this little baby special.' Hudson was under the hood of his car when Godfrey appeared with Heather and Eleanor in tow.

'So, this is the illustrious Seymour, fresh from the battlefields,' he announced to the ladies. 'Seymour, meet my sister Heather and her friend Eleanor Lansing.' Seymour laughed at Godfrey's antics and tipped his cap to the two ladies. Eleanor Lansing certainly was a looker and he wished fervently that he was off the crutches and a man capable of taking a lady for a stroll or a whirl around the dance floor.

Just then Hudson decided Seymour wasn't getting out of the car and so he closed the bonnet, only to meet Eleanor's eyes. It was a moment of recognition. Hudson's jaw dropped at exactly the same time as Eleanor's did. 'Well, if it isn't the damsel in distress.'

'And if it isn't my brave hero.' Cissy, Seymour, Godfrey and Heather looked on, befuddled. What was this all about?

'So, you two have obviously met,' said Seymour.

'Oh, I don't know whether you'd actually call it "met",' Hudson started to explain.

'Yes, we've met,' cut in Eleanor. 'This brave chap came to my rescue when I was accosted by some unsavoury types in the carpark at the Palais a few weeks back.'

'You never told me about that,' said Heather.

'And Eleanor's not the only one keeping secrets,' cut in Cissy, vaguely recognising Eleanor as the redhead Hudson had been so interested in at the Palais. 'You never told us anything about it, brother.'

'A fellow doesn't have to tell his little sister everything.'

'Quite, quite,' put in Seymour, still a little mystified as to what was actually happening here. His brother seemed very interested in this fascinating lady. Godfrey stepped in to get the party rolling again.

'Okay, well what say we all get in the car and get on our way.'

Eleanor looked across at Hudson, 'So I assume you're Hudson, the one I've heard so much about.'

'You have assumed my name correctly, the rest of it I have no idea.'

'Yes, well maybe that's for me to find out.' She gave Hudson a look that sent shivers right up his spine, he couldn't believe that the woman who had been monopolising his dreams had been living under Godfrey's roof for more than a month and he'd had no idea, pining for the moment he would see her again, and there she was, well within reach.

Swing was the big thing and Godfrey and Cissy had been on the dance floor for nearly an hour when the announcement came over. 'Ladies and gentlemen,' a silence fell over the dance hall at this unusual interruption. All eyes were suddenly upon the bandleader, who stood in anticipation, ready to make the big announcement, 'I have just had word that the war is officially over.' A huge cheer went up in the Palais and excitement broke out. 'The allies have won, and the troops are on their way home!'

The band struck up, *Don't Sit Under the Apple Tree*, and the crowd were on their feet dancing and celebrating the enormous news. Many were thinking of their family members and loved ones who would be returning home, others were just excited that this long, long war was over, and life had a chance of returning to normal. No more rations, no more news of death on the battlefields, prison camps and horrific injuries. No fear of family members being spirited away to join the ranks. Godfrey grabbed Cissy's hand and joined the over-crowded dance floor.

Perhaps it was the electric atmosphere that was circulating the dance hall, everyone felt charged, like it was a new beginning. Godfrey looked into Cissy's eyes and the moment overwhelmed him. 'Marry me,' he said in what was probably a moment of madness. Cissy looked at him in disbelief.

'W-what?' she stammered.

'Marry me,' he announced louder, and then shouting. 'I asked you would you marry me?' The dancers swishing past them were now all staring at Cissy, she hesitated but the fervour had got to her too.

'Yes … yes,' she answered nodding her head. 'Yes, all right I'll marry you.' Those nearby dancers who had heard the proposal congratulated them as the newly betrothed couple decided to rush back to their table, no time like the present to let everyone in on the good news.

If not overjoyed at the startling news, Seymour and Hudson were happy for them, they shook Godfrey's hand, welcoming him as a brother and each gave Cissy a big bear hug. Heather however was a little surprised, she gave Cissy a tender hug and welcomed her as a sister. She turned to her brother, Godfrey, and gave him a rather emotionless peck on the cheek and a pat on the shoulder wishing him all the best. 'So, when is the big day, brother?'

Godfrey looked at Cissy, she shrugged. 'There is so much planning to do now, we will have to work things out. Besides, there is an engagement party to be dealt with first.' At the word 'party', everyone relaxed back into the excited atmosphere going on all around them. Glasses were raised and a toast was made to the happy couple. As the chatter continued Heather looked at her brother, who didn't seem to notice. What was he up to? Something just didn't feel right to Heather, after all, she known her brother all of her life and to her way of thinking he'd never seemed smitten with Cissy, never spoke of her to any great extent — there was more to this, and she was going to make it her mission to get to the bottom of it.

Eleanor was elated for Cissy, not that she knew either of them very well. She felt the adrenalin of the new love pact envelop her and looked at Hudson as he was over at the bar replenishing the drinks. Was he ever going to ask her to dance? Okay, she may have had American soldier after American soldier spinning her around the dance floor — but what was she meant to do? Just sit there like a wallflower until Hudson decided to escort her onto the dance floor? Maybe she had misread the whole chemistry thing and Hudson was not into her at all?

As the Palais drew to a close for the evening the excitement was still in the air. Out in the carpark Godfrey announced that they should party on — go to a late-night club. Hudson could see the weariness on his brother's face and said that he should get him home. Eleanor and Heather chose to go home with them, while Cissy thought it could be fun to visit a club, she had never been to one but had heard all about them.

'Cissy my darling,' Godfrey said, placing his hands on her waist, 'why don't you go on home with your brothers, get some rest? We have a big day tomorrow, making plans.' Cissy grabbed either end of the scarf around Godfrey's neck, staring into her fiancé's eyes, pouting sexily but it seemed to do little to change his mind. 'Come on my pretty, I want you fresh and ready tomorrow to put your best thinking cap on. I'm just going to go and unwind for an hour, catch up with some of the fellas.' Cissy thought about it, she really was tired, and the night was chilly. A warm car ride home and a cosy bed may be just what she needed and if it was an all-boys club then she would feel hugely out of place. She agreed, and as Godfrey went off to hail a cab, his sister's eyes followed him.

The St Kilda bar was overcrowded. News of the war's end had broken out and everyone was celebrating. Godfrey elbowed his way through the smoky atmosphere. The men wore suits, others sported expensive cashmere jumpers over their shirt and tie. The patrons appeared well heeled, mostly men, with the occasional glamorous woman seen smoking from long cigarette holders.

It was a club Godfrey loved and frequented. The buzz was always vibrant, and he knew so many of the people who spent their nights here. A group of young men spotted him. One of them raised his hand in a manner just a little too delicate, and then prissily waved Godfrey over. Godfrey pushed through the crowd.

'Isn't it splendid?' said the chap, 'the nasty war is over, and we can all relax, our boys are coming home.' The three men raised their glasses while Godfrey ordered a cocktail. They chinked glasses to toast the end of the war and Godfrey threw an arm around each of the men's shoulders to his left and right. The laughter and banter grew thick, and Godfrey felt at ease, he relaxed into the atmosphere with which he was most comfortable. He unwound his scarf and loosened his collar. It was going to be a really good night after all.

Chapter Thirteen

ELEANOR WAS PLEASED WITH HERSELF, though not fully booked out, the salon was very busy. Word had spread about her great talent with the latest hairstyles and Thursday nights, Fridays and Saturdays were proving extremely busy. The young ladies wanted hairstyles that would take them through their weekends of dating or at least trying to catch a date. Her older clients, mostly married women, were entertaining guest after guest and needed to look the part. It was Saturday and Eleanor was just finishing up with her last perm. Business always ended at 12 noon on Saturdays, but she had stayed open an extra hour on this day in order to help this regular client who could not get there before midday.

As she twirled the last of the lady's curls, she couldn't help thinking about Hudson. She had been so surprised, so overwhelmed to finally meet her handsome stranger last night. She had often pondered about bumping into him at the Palais again but had never contemplated that they could have been moving in the same circle of friends.

She wondered what he was thinking. He seemed so flabbergasted when they were introduced, but then took little interest in her at the Palais. Perhaps she had read him all wrong. 'Is everything all right dear?' Eleanor barely heard her client speak, as though coming out of a fugue, she realised she had been standing, comb in hand, staring into the mirror, but she might as well have been staring into space, her mind miles away.

She brought herself back to earth. She needed to finish up with Mrs Weathercock and close up the salon for the weekend. Although how she was going to use her free time she hadn't really yet decided.

Hudson was restless. He had been standing on Footscray train station for what now seemed like hours, waiting to surprise Eleanor, but there had been no sign of her. He had devised the plan last night. Unable to sleep after the big night at the Palais, he had smoked cigarette after cigarette.

What sort of fool was he? There she was, at his table, with his group of friends, all talking and laughing together. Why hadn't he spoken more to her, asked her to dance. Instead, he watched soldier after soldier spinning her around the dance floor. Had he been kidding himself? This gorgeous lady could have her pick of men, he was probably way out of her league. But then his attitude changed.

When he awoke on Saturday morning, after finally falling off to sleep at around 4am, he wondered whether it was time to take action. Waiting for something to happen was not getting him anywhere. He needed a plan, and as he started to think about what he could do, his brother walked into the kitchen.

His brother, the great strategist. As he stood alone on Footscray Station, he was beginning to think he was a jackass to take his brother's advice so quickly, to imagine it would be so easy. In fact, it was arrogant of him to think he could just ambush her at the station. Just wait here on the platform until she arrived to catch her train home after working at her salon. He had it all mapped out in his mind now. Seymour had said to just casually bump into her and then ask her out to dinner.

Perhaps he could have done all that if there had been any sign of her. She had probably been picked up by some good-looking guy in a flash car when the salon closed. Probably enjoying his company right now. 'Ah to heck with it,' he thought, and left the platform. He knew where he was going. If he didn't man-up now, find the woman and ask her out on a date, he believed he would never sleep again. She was so much in his head he couldn't even think straight.

To call it shock would be an understatement. When Hudson walked into the salon Eleanor nearly had her client's eye out with the tail comb. She composed herself quickly, 'Hudson, you after a haircut?' It was a silly thing to say, but it was the first thing that had popped into her head.

'Yes, no, I mean, why not?' Hudson stammered, searching for words.

'Well, I don't usually do men's hair and it is getting late,' she teased, thinking that perhaps a haircut was not why he was here, so why not give him a hard time? She had been way too forward for her liking at the Palais last night, but nothing had come of it, and she hadn't stopped berating herself. How could she be so stupid to think that he was interested in her? But now this sudden appearance changed things, she was certain, and it was her turn to pretend like she didn't care.

'Sit down,' she scolded, 'you really look as though you could do with a good trim. I'm just finishing up here with Mrs Weathercock.' Dutifully, Hudson did as he was told. He sat in the hairdresser's chair looking at himself in the mirror. What a mess he was, hair all over the place and he had missed a spot when shaving. How could he think he was worthy of her? He'd fretted all night about his stupidity and even his brother had backed him up on that one.

'Come on brother,' Seymour had said over breakfast, 'You're crazy about the girl, it is clear. Go and ask her out for God's sake.'

'I thought you were the one who wanted to ask her out. After all, Godfrey did line her up for you.'

'I agree she's a beauty, but the way you looked at her, man — I couldn't make a move on that. You're smitten brother.'

'Is it that obvious?' Hudson had asked in reply.

'Huddo, you ain't very good at hiding things. You were like a love-sick puppy last night. What gets me is you never even asked her to dance.'

'How could I? Every time I went to ask her there was some American in uniform, whipping her onto the dance floor before I even had a chance. And when the announcement came over the place was bedlam.'

'Hmmm, and yet you managed to dance with Heather a number of times.'

'Yeah, well.' Hudson felt a pang of guilt, hoping he hadn't led Heather on, she was more like a second sister than a date. He thought about it as he watched Eleanor taking Mrs Weathercock's payment, the woman now looking splendid with her new hairdo and smiling face. Eleanor would be attending to him soon and his nerves were at their pinnacle. He tried to get Seymour's voice out of his head.

'Look Huddo,' he had nagged, 'go and call on the girl, ask her out, what's the worst that could happen?'

'She could say no.'

'Exactly and put you out of your misery.'

'Oh, I don't know,' Hudson's confidence was really letting him down.

'Do it brother, do it today. It is Saturday — doesn't she work at the salon till twelve? That's good, she's away from the Maxwell household, go and meet her at Footscray station, take her by surprise.'

'You really think I should?' Hudson asked, gaining a little spunk.

'I know you should.'

And now here he was, and Eleanor was standing at his back, looking at him in the mirror as he sat in the hairdresser's chair. She draped a cape around his shoulders and then gently placed her hands on his shoulders and the electric jolt that ran through him was enough to knock him out. All he could do was look at her reflection in the mirror, he was speechless. 'So, what would the good sir like today? Just a trim or perhaps a permanent wave and a bit of colour?' she said, running her hands through his hair. Hudson thought he going to have apoplexy and remained speechless. 'Okay, a trim it is.'

She started to cut his hair and he was still lost for words. She seemed to have a look of amusement on her face and Hudson didn't really see the humour in it at all, he was still in shock. 'I'm afraid I don't have one of those neck trimmer things, don't get much call for them with ladies' hair, but I'll do my best.'

Suddenly Hudson felt silly, sitting here in a ladies' hairdressing salon surrounded by curlers and hairdryers, draped in a flowery green cape and having a beautiful woman attend to him. What was his problem, why couldn't he speak? In a force of energy, he grabbed Eleanor's hand that held the scissors and cupped it in his own. Eleanor got a bit of a shock, and her humour left her momentarily. 'Eleanor,' Hudson gasped, 'I didn't come here for a haircut.' He stared into her eyes, the courage to go on rising from within.

Before she could respond he blurted it out, 'Could I take you out … somewhere … anywhere. Like, what about dinner … or even just a walk in the park?' He was blowing it, he knew it, how could he be so stupid? Eleanor looked so composed he felt like the biggest jerk. She smiled, not an over-joyous smile, the kind of smile you might give a naughty child.

'Yes, yes, I'd like that. A walk in the park — or dinner, they both sound like fun.'

'Well then let's do them both,' Hudson said before his brain could connect to his mouth, 'like right now, we could go for a walk in the Footscray Gardens right now.' He was shell-shocked, totally unsure of what was going to happen next.

'Okay, I've never been to the Footscray Gardens,' she replied calmly, 'but first of all I am going to have to finish your hair now that I have started it. I can't leave you like this.' Hudson looked in the mirror and laughed, once side of his hair was short and the other unruly. He relaxed with the silliness of it all and let her hairdresser hands take over, but as her fingers ran through his hair the electricity it generated within him was unbearable, he'd never felt like this — ever.

CC arrived at Bruce Lansing's home at 12.30 that afternoon, briefcase in hand. Bruce had built himself a beautiful home overlooking the Mentone beach. 'How lovely it must be to live by the beach, always with that view,' CC thought. His active mind leading to thoughts of a cinema in a beachside holiday resort, something to think about for the future. Bruce welcomed him in, and they sat in the sunroom watching the waves roll in. 'Beautiful home you have here Bruce, been here long?'

'Building was finished three years ago. Moved straight in.'

'Family? Wife? Kids?' CC was making small talk, he didn't really know a lot about this man, but so far liked what he saw.

'My wife and two of my sons currently live here, one is married. As you know, Eleanor is now living over in Sunshine — with the Maxwells.'

'Yes of course, I believe she is a very beautiful and talented young lady, you must be very proud.'

'Certainly am, her salon is doing well and I'm pretty sure she's happy with the way everything is going.' CC decided to cut to the chase.

'So, have you thought any more about that land down in Balcombe Road?'

'I have, I have thought about it a lot. It's an exciting venture you are proposing.'

'Movies are the way of the future Bruce. People want to be entertained and now that the war is over, they are going to be looking for more entertainment, an escape from the misery everyone has been through. We're shedding our war-torn souls and looking for happiness. Movies are a big thing that will give the people some release, give them what they are looking for.'

'Ah, I do like to hear you talk CC. I believe your little grain store picture theatre over in Sunshine has done extremely well.'

'Packed out just about every night. I made the right move there Bruce and couldn't be more satisfied. Now I am looking to expand into Maidstone and Altona, as well as rebuilding the theatre at Sunshine, which is near completion now. Things are on the move — exciting times for all involved.'

'And I believe one of those involved is Wilbur Maxwell.'

'Correct.'

'He seems to have a good business head on his shoulders — after all, I wouldn't let my daughter live with just anyone.'

'No, no, I expect you wouldn't. Wilbur is a good man, I'm sure of it. My daughter is now engaged to his son, Godfrey, did you know that?'

'No, I didn't. Well congratulations, you must be very proud.'

'I'm very happy, it's good to see her going in the right direction.'

'Have they set a date?'

'No, not yet, we have the engagement party to get through first, of course, you must come over, with your daughter there and all.'

'Nancy and I would enjoy that very much. Now, about that land, what did you have in mind?'

'Well, financially Bruce, I'm strapped. With the planned expansion and the current building of Sunshine, all of my funds are pretty much allocated, but I see the opportunity here in Cheltenham and I don't want to miss out.' Bruce nodded, understanding CC's plight.

'That parcel of land such as yours is hard to come by, what a prime position. We could build a grand picture theatre and more.'

'What do you mean by more?'

'Well, when people come to the pictures they come for a night out. There's before the pictures, the intervals and after the show. People are always looking for somewhere to go. You know the little hamburger café across the road from our tiny picture theatre does a booming business on theatre nights. People gather there before and after the show as well as during intervals. Peter the Greek's never had it so good. So, I'm thinking that as well as a picture theatre we could build a milk bar, a café, a restaurant — hell, even a hotel. Give the people a destination, somewhere they will flock to.'

'When you say "we", CC, what are you getting at?'

'No man can do it all on his own,' CC explained. 'We need to surround ourselves with like-minded people, people who can help achieve the sort of success we are all looking for. Come in on this one with me Bruce, let's work out a deal.'

'You're a hard man to say "no" to, CC. And I like the sound of what you are talking about, but how much have you looked into this?'

'I have had feasibility studies conducted and this area is right on track to explode. People love the beach. The wealthy are buying up the beach front blocks — you should know, you've sold more than half of your land to them.' Bruce nodded knowingly.

'Beaumaris, Black Rock, Sandringham — they're all populating faster than you can build the houses and all of these people are looking for things to do.' CC tapped his brown leather briefcase, 'I have the reports right here. If you are interested, I can leave them, you look them over and then get back to me with your answer, but don't leave it too long Bruce. The longer we wait the more chance we are giving someone else to jump in ahead of us.'

Bruce looked at CC, he was interested, but he was a wise man, and he would take his time to look over every detail of CC's proposal.

When CC returned to the picture theatre that afternoon, the place was bedlam. Hudson was nowhere to be seen and Sylvia Wright-Smith was running around like a woman possessed. 'What's going on?' CC testily inquired.

'What's going on?' she repeated back to him. 'Wouldn't you like to know. Your eldest son hasn't turned up for the matinee. Jack Sotheby had to take over in the projection room and poor little Roger Rourke has been run ragged.'

'So, where's Hudson?'

'You tell me. I had to call Cissy in to handle the box-office and we have barely been able to cope.' Just then Hudson appeared with a huge grin on his face, Eleanor was with him, hand in hand. CC was so incensed he ignored the young lady, even though he knew who she was, and started in on Hudson.

'Where have you been?'

'I er, I …' even though he was being roused on, Hudson could not wipe the grin off his face.

'Get up to the projection room now and start getting organised for the intermediate session. And wipe that smirk off your face.'

Hudson knew when an order was an order. He dropped Eleanor's hand immediately. His grin gone, he strode angrily to the projection room, leaving Eleanor reeling, wondering what in heaven's name just happened. Cissy came to her rescue. 'Eleanor, where did you come from?' she turned to her father, understanding his anger but also annoyed at the fact that he had been so rude to this lovely lady.

'Dad, have you met Eleanor Lansing?'

CC, then remembering her to be Bruce's daughter, silently reprimanded himself for putting on such a display of temper in front of her and checked his emotions. He smiled, 'No, we haven't been formally introduced,' he held out his hand, 'Carleton Cambridge. How do you do? I know your father.'

Eleanor was a little overwhelmed at the sudden change of mood and didn't quite know how to react. 'Hello sir, I-I'm sorry about Hudson. I hadn't realised ... that is ... he didn't tell me he had to work. I would have ... I mean we would have ...'

'Please Eleanor, don't apologise. He doesn't need a nursemaid.' Eleanor was slightly offended at the remark; did he think she was a nursemaid? However, she held her tongue, it was not her place to comment. 'He knows his duties and he's old enough to know when and where he has to perform them.' CC started to calm down. He could see this young lady was feeling uncomfortable and he realised he should not have put her in this situation, it was not her fault that Hudson had shirked on his duties, and he didn't want Bruce thinking he was some sort of despot. 'I'm sorry, would you like a cup of tea, soft drink ...' he said gesturing towards the kiosk, 'ice-cream, anything at all?'

'No thank you Mr Cambridge, I am fine. I had better be getting home.'

'Let me call you a cab, my shout, it's the least I can do.'

'It's not necessary, I prefer to walk, really.'

'All right young lady, as you wish. I must get back to work myself. Say hello to your father for me.' As CC headed for his office and Eleanor bade Cissy farewell, Hudson's sister couldn't help but wonder what had happened between Hudson and Eleanor, leading up to this confrontation, she headed for the projection box.

'Okay big brother, tell me all,' she drilled Hudson as she entered the celluloid scented, filmy atmosphere of the projection box.

'There's nothing to tell, okay? Just leave me alone.' Hudson was still smarting from the verbal blow his father had delivered to him in front of all people, Eleanor. Just when he thought the world was wonderful his father had to go and tear it all down for him. Eleanor would probably never talk to him again.

'Come on Hudson, if you're worried about Eleanor she's all right.'

'Don't even mention her name,' he snapped. 'God, how embarrassing.'

'What happened, I mean how did you get to arrive ... hand-in-hand?' He glared at his sister and then, remembering his afternoon, he softened.

'I went to her salon. It was all a bit silly at first, but then ...'

Hudson told his sister all about their encounter. How he had made an idiot of himself at the salon and how she had given him a haircut. Then later, when they walked through the Footscray Gardens. They hadn't held hands at first, Hudson not knowing what to do and talking nervously the whole time. 'There are these beautiful green lawns there with undulating hills one could just lose all inhibitions and roll down. Eleanor grabbed my hand, and we ran down, almost toppling over.' His eyes went misty at the memory, Cissy knew love when she saw it. 'It was the most wonderful afternoon I have ever spent.'

Hudson didn't tell her about the misty rain that had started to fall and Eleanor grappling with her umbrella. He'd helped her put it up and as they stood under the tiny shelter watching the fine droplets surround them, they kissed. Hudson was truly swept off his feet. He'd lost all thought of time, of work, of reality. With the rain starting then to get heavier, they knew they should make a run for it and made a dash for Hudson's car.

Never had he been so grateful for, or proud of, his in-dash car heater. As the convertible started up the warm air rushed through, and Eleanor was delighted. 'Thank heavens for your heater,' she commented as she loosened her damp hair and tilted her head forward to dry it, her brilliant red locks spilling luxuriantly and filling the car with an exquisite lavender fragrance.

Hudson knew he wanted more from her. He suddenly felt as though his life could not continue without her. He wanted to introduce her to his father, to show her off to all around. He knew she wasn't his to present, maybe she never would be, but right now, in the magnificence of this moment, Hudson wanted to shout to the world, besides, she had said she had never been to the Sunshine Picture Theatre, so what better time to show her around than right now.

Cissy interrupted his thoughts, 'Don't worry about Dad, Hudson, he'll get over it. Right now, you had better get the intermediate movie ready to go. Look,' she said peering through the tiny window of the projection box, 'Our fans are already beginning to gather, I'll leave you to it.'

As Cissy climbed back down the ladder to the foyer, Hudson busied himself loading the reels, but try as hard as he did, he could not get Eleanor out of his mind. It was Sunday tomorrow, no movies on a Sunday, he would call on her and he hoped he could make amends.

'I know all of the children have shares in the business,' Wilbur explained to Godfrey as they sat at his bar.

'Even Cissy?' Godfrey was surprised, why give a woman a share in your business? Stupid and unnecessary. 'Are you sure?'

'Yes, even Cissy, I am positive. I don't know how much, but you need to find out. Once you are married those shares can become yours and that will be more in our pile. I am going to talk to Bruce Lansing tomorrow. I don't believe he has sold CC that parcel of land in Cheltenham yet, and if I can get my hands on it then I will have some more ammunition in my arsenal for CC.' Wilbur got down from his leather backed bar stool and went behind the counter to open another bottle of Scotch. 'Have you set a date yet?'

'Well, we're having the engagement party in about six weeks from now, in November. Cissy has now said she wants to get married in March. She doesn't want to get married when it's cold and wet, March usually turns on the best Melbourne weather and so she has chosen the long weekend, Moomba.'

'Pity it's not sooner, but there's plenty to be done between now and then.'

'How's it going with old George Roberts?'

'Funny you should ask; he is coming to papa as we speak. He went to see CC a couple of weeks ago, to ask for help.'

'And how do you know this?' asked Godfrey of his father.

'CC told me himself. He wanted money of course, even told CC what it was all about. CC felt sorry for him, said anyone can make a mistake and the blackmailer must be some low-life slimy bastard. He asked me if I could help him and so of course I said to send him over, I would see what I could do. I told him I was flat out for the next few days — just to let him sweat. I have an appointment with him here, tomorrow.'

'Hmmm, better tighten the screws a little more then.'

'Yes, don't worry. Sammy has been reminding him and he will be paying him a visit,' Wilbur looked at his watch, 'in a few hours from now as a matter of fact. Don't want the man getting too relaxed and forgetting his responsibilities now do we?' Godfrey nodded. To him it seemed a pretty easy way to build up your assets. How much more could they acquire by providing a good night out for a weak-willed gentleman and snapping a few photos? Godfrey dwelled on the possibilities.

The fog was lifting as the mist made way for the spring sun. The dairy was in full production mode. Pints of milk in thick glass bottles were capped and loaded onto the carts. The hard-working draft horses were harnessed and the milkman, in his starched white uniform, was ready for his rounds.

George watched as the last cart left the depot, he asked the apprentice to clean up the cobblestones and as the boy grabbed a broom, George walked back into the impressive red brick building. He hadn't noticed the man slip through the foggy shadows and when the hand came around his mouth, George froze in horror, fearing the worst. An arm went around his throat, and he was shuffled into a dark vestibule, none of his workers any the wiser, machinery and plant equipment making such a din, workers shouting to be heard over the noise.

'I need the money George, I need it today,' came the hoarse voice of his captor.

'I told you I'd get it; you have to give me more time.'

'I've been waiting too long now, George. I'm sick of your stalling tactics. Today George, I need it today,' the voice became more threatening.

'I don't know if that's possible.'

'It has to be possible George. I'll give you until 7pm, otherwise the local papers will be receiving some very juicy material for publication.' The captor's arm tightened around George's throat.

'All right, all right,' George struggled to get the words out, his throat so constricted. 'I'll get the money, I'll get your money.'

'As long as we understand each other, George. See you at 7pm.'

'Where will I meet you?'

'Don't worry about that George, I'll find you.'

Suddenly the grip on George's throat was released. George immediately rubbed his neck, catching his breath. He'd never seen the face of his blackmailer, he turned but it was too late, there was no one in the vestibule and as George rushed into the dairy, only the swishing of a coat could be seen disappearing into the fog.

Should he go to the police? He just couldn't entertain the idea of anyone finding out what he had done. How could he trust the police? What if they leaked the information or showed one of those dreadful photos around? It would destroy Francie. He had an appointment with Wilbur today and, like CC, he was sure he could trust this fellow businessman and was hopeful that Wilbur would understand his predicament and give him a short-term loan. He could have the money paid back within three months.

Chapter Fourteen

CISSY WAS HAVING a girl's meeting. Miriam had offered to do what she could to help her plan her engagement and Veronica was not missing out. If there was any scheming to be done, she would be at the forefront. Eleanor had also offered to help, given her growing involvement with Cissy's brother and Heather more or less was tagging along for the ride.

The hamburger café was a good place to meet, it was generally quiet at this time of the morning and not being a theatre day would probably remain so for quite some time. What was annoying though was the noise of the construction that was going on across the road as the new Sunshine Picture Theatre was taking shape.

'There must be a lot of excitement in your family,' said Heather to Cissy, 'with your engagement, your new theatre being built and plans for more.' Cissy was about to answer her when Peter the Greek, the café owner, shouted from behind the counter as he flipped the girls' hamburgers,

'Pah, all this construction! She's a-ruining my business,' he complained in his Greek accent. 'The people, they no coming anymore, my business she's a-going down the drain.'

'I hardly think that's the case,' Cissy responded. 'Our little grain store theatre brings you more customers than you ever had.'

'Yes, is too many, too many at once then no one during the week.'

'Don't worry Peter,' Cissy responded, 'when our new picture theatre is finished you will have that many people here you will not be able to cope with the rush.'

'Pah,' Peter barked, and got back to cooking his hamburgers.

'So, Dad wanted me to hire in professional party people,' Cissy said, 'but I think it would be much more fun to do it all ourselves. I'll get some help with the cooking, I can call on people like Mrs Collins, she needs the money, and she has some other ladies who will help.'

'So, what do you want us to do?' asked Eleanor.

'Well, you're so good with colours and decorating, look what you did with your salon, you can be in charge of decorations, maybe Veronica can help you.' Veronica looked a bit peeved. Truth be known she didn't really want to help with anything, but she guessed that by being around Cissy and Eleanor, she would also get to be around Seymour. She'd turned her eye to him since Hudson and Eleanor had become an item — it was a while since the big night out at the Palais and they had seen each other every chance they got. It was now obvious that Seymour was not going to be on crutches forever, so Veronica thought it might be a wise move to set her sights on the younger brother. Still, it was not as if Eleanor and Hudson were engaged or anything yet, so anything was a possibility.

Heather offered to take care of the hiring: the marquee, the tables and chairs, glasses, plates etc; while Miriam said she would organise the cake and help Cissy with the music. She had an old school friend who had a swing band that played at Footscray Town Hall occasionally, she was hoping she could hire them for the night.

'So, what is Godfrey doing to help with all this?' inquired Eleanor.

'He'll look after the drinks,' Cissy replied. 'He and my brothers are going to organise a couple of niners, as well as a selection of Pimm's, Vermouth and a range of spirits and mixers.'

'Well at least he's doing something,' retorted Heather, 'he doesn't seem that enthusiastic to me.'

Cissy hung her head. She felt it was true. For a man who was getting engaged and then about to be married, he certainly went around half-hearted about the whole thing. And really it was more than that. That first time on the dance floor, and a few other times after that, she had felt the tingle. She had felt the electricity bolt through her body when he touched her. But it was gone now.

She wondered if that happened to everyone. The only one she could really ask was Eleanor, given the other ladies had not been in serious relationships, but she was too embarrassed to ask Eleanor given she was going out with her brother. She knew Godfrey wanted to wait until they were married, and she respected him for respecting her, but he didn't seem that anxious to kiss her, or hold her or even spend time with her if the truth be known.

Thursday nights was their obligatory date night, which was pretty silly because not a lot happened on a Thursday night in Sunshine. They would go for a walk in the park or take a drive. Cissy always imagined they would go parking and get into a bit of heavy petting, but all they seemed to do was drive and drive and then come back again. Things would change though, she knew that. Once they were married their lovemaking would trump everything and they would build a lovely home together filled with babies.

'Are you all right Cissy?' Heather asked, jolting Cissy out of her musings. 'I didn't mean to imply he wasn't interested, it's just ... oh it's just Godfrey. Sorry Cissy, he's my brother and sometimes I think he could just shower a little more attention on you.' Cissy wanted to change the subject.

'I was just thinking Eleanor, they have some super things for decorations at Coles. Why don't you and Veronica go there this afternoon and pick up some balloons, streamers, whatever you can find. Hudson will drive you, I'm sure.' That got Veronica's attention, she would be around if Hudson was in proximity.

Coles was pretty busy that afternoon. Seymour had come along for the ride. He remembered the pretty girl behind the counter and had an inkling to see her again. He just wished that annoying Veronica wasn't around. If she wasn't throwing herself at Hudson, she was making eyes at him. What was with that woman? It was pretty clear where Hudson's affection lay, and as for him, well he had no interest in her whatsoever.

Seymour was only using the one crutch now. His right leg was healing well, his left leg still needed a bit of help. He looked around the store. 'You go off in search of your decorations,' he said to the others, 'I have something I need to look for, for myself.'

'Would you like me to help you?' asked Veronica.

'No, really, I am good, I know what I want.'

'Are you sure you don't need some help,' she repeated, her tone nagging.

'No, really, just give me some space, I know what I am doing,' Seymour answered quite tersely. Veronica got the hint and pouted slightly as she walked off with Eleanor and Hudson, them arm in arm and her tagging along.

Loretta Spalding was working on a new display. She should have had it finished this morning but there had been a crash out the back with a shelf coming down and a lot of the cosmetics shattering onto the floor. She was in charge of the clean-up and resurrection team and had not long got the job finished. Now she was on a ladder, battling with fitting a race hat to a mannequin on a stand. It was the Spring Racing Carnival in Melbourne, and with the Melbourne Cup about to be run on Tuesday week, Lorretta had a lot to contend with.

'Now there's a pretty sight if ever I saw one.' Loretta was used to the passes and smart remarks from customers, and she was sure this one would be no exception. However, she nearly fell of her ladder when she looked down to see that man's face staring up at her.

He had haunted her dreams since his last visit quite a few weeks back. She had battled to get him out of her head, but as time went by the images faded and she resigned herself to never seeing him again. Two ships that pass in the night — or actually in Coles, in this case. Seymour grabbed hold of the ladder to steady it, nearly losing balance himself as he let go of his crutch. 'I'm sorry, I didn't mean to frighten you.'

This man was not getting the better of her again. She would attend to his shopping needs and then get on with her work. She refused the hand he offered and descended the ladder. It was only then that she realised she had inconvenienced him. His crutch was the floor, and he was now finding it a little difficult to let go of the ladder.

Delicately she stepped around him and picked up the crutch. 'Are you all right sir,' she inquired, just as a good customer service person should.

'Much better for seeing you.' Loretta tried not to blush; she was beginning to think that this man was a bit of a womaniser with lines like that.

'So how can I help you?' As she asked that question a fancy lady wearing a little too much make-up approached the man from behind. Quietly she slipped her arm through his and asked him how much longer he would be. The colour rose in the man's face. Loretta wasn't sure whether it was from a reaction to her touch or embarrassment.

Seymour was furious, he didn't want to cause any more kerfuffle in the store or inconvenience to the shop assistant than he already had, however he did remove the lady's hand from his arm. He was at a loss now; he didn't know what to say. He had come to talk to the pretty shop attendant and Veronica had ruined it. Never had he felt more embarrassed.

'I'm fine actually, I was just browsing around the store.' He glared at Veronica, 'Don't you have something else to do?' Dejectedly, Veronica took the hint, she would keep an eye on this shop girl though, she wasn't letting another Cambridge man slip out of her clutches. Seymour looked at the shop assistant again. 'I'm sorry, I remembered you from when I was in the store a few weeks back. You were very helpful.' Loretta looked at him, unsure what to make of him.

'When I saw you up the ladder, I couldn't resist coming over to say hello.' Just when he thought he was getting somewhere, Eleanor and Hudson arrived, laden with goodies.

'Say, I remember you,' said Hudson. 'You helped us find that after-shave last time we were in here.' Loretta just smiled, not wanting to let on that she remembered them too. Hudson looked at Seymour like a satisfied shopper, *let's go* signals written all over his face.

'Right,' said Seymour, 'I guess that's it. Watch out for those wild mannequins,' he said to the shop assistant, trying to make light of a ruined opportunity. Hudson noticed his brother's attitude and sudden bells awakened his male chemistry.

He spoke to Loretta, 'Do you like the pictures?' Loretta was taken by surprise, Seymour was astounded, what was his brother doing? 'The movies, do you like the movies?'

'Sure, doesn't everyone?' replied Loretta.

Hudson dug into his pocket bringing out a ticket. 'Well, here's a free pass for Friday night, we're playing *Casablanca* with Humphrey Bogart and Ingrid Bergman. Absolutely fantastic film.'

'What do you mean we, you said we're playing *Casablanca*?'

'That's right, we're the Cambridge family, we own the Sunshine Picture Theatre. Come along on Friday night, we'll all be there.'

Loretta was stunned as they left. Crazy, crazy stuff. First of all, she had dreamt about some poor returning soldier in a wheelchair and now she finds out he's probably a mogul who owns a picture theatre and has women hanging off his arm all the time. Well, she'd be damned if she'd go along to their picture show and crawl to them.

Casablanca though. Sensational movie. She'd heard it had sold out every night, from the very first moment it was advertised at the theatre. Free ticket, it was tempting. Very tempting indeed.

'What did you do that for?' Seymour rounded on his brother as they left Coles.

'What? I just gave a pretty girl a free pass to the movies — we do it all the time.'

'Come on — you know what I mean?'

'Look my dear brother,' Hudson said, trying to calm his brother down a little, 'I saw the way you looked at her, I'm not blind. You weren't going to do anything, so I stepped in for you.'

Seymour was still agitated. He was receiving help with so many things, things he used to be perfectly capable of doing on his own, now his brother thinks he even has to fix him up with a date. 'I can handle my own affairs thank you very much, and I ask you to keep out of them in future.'

Eleanor and Veronica were silent and slightly embarrassed by the brothers' bickering. Veronica was so annoyed that Hudson had given that woman a free pass. She had never had a free pass and she knew the Cambridges way better than that shop assistant.

She would have to be there on Friday night, she would convince Cissy to sneak her in for free. The best way to stop this is to do it before it gets started. She had been patiently waiting for Seymour's leg to get better, but waiting any longer now, with Little Miss Coles on the scene, could prove to be her downfall.

No, she must get to *Casablanca* on Friday night.

Wilbur was ready to spring the trap, George had arrived at his office. Wilbur could see how tense the man was as he sat on the edge of Wilbur's Chesterfield couch. It had been a good strategy to make the man wait a while, he was now as nervous as a turkey on Christmas Eve and as desperate as it gets. Slowly and uneasily he began to explain his predicament to Wilbur.

'I don't know what else to do Wilbur, they want three thousand pounds by seven o'clock tonight, otherwise they are going to take the photos to the local papers. '

'Yes, well you have got yourself into a spot of bother haven't you George?'

'I was such a flaming idiot. How could I be so stupid?'

'Come on George, we all trip up from time to time, you just got yourself caught. That's the ... and I'm sorry to say it ... stupid thing that you did George.'

George looked at Wilbur, grateful that he understood, wondering what he meant by, 'we all trip up from time to time'? Had Wilbur been in a similar situation, or was he just a bit of a player? George had no time to worry about that now and the last thing he was going to do was to probe into Wilbur's private affairs. If this man could help him then he would be indebted to him, and as far as he was concerned that would make Wilbur an absolute top bloke.

'I can loan you the money George, I can.' George felt relief flood through his body. 'But we are going to have to work out some terms.' George wasn't worried about terms, he knew he could work something out and would agree with whatever proposal Wilbur came up with.

'I'm sure I can have you paid back within three months,' he blurted out, trying to curb his growing excitement at resolving this hairy situation in which he'd found himself.

'That won't be necessary George. Give yourself a break,' Wilbur said charmingly, 'six months will be fine, but I'll need a guarantee.'

'Guarantee?' queried George. 'What sort of guarantee?'

'Some collateral.' George was starting to look a little worried now. 'I'm going to need some collateral, just until the loan is paid off.'

'Oh, I'll pay it off Wilbur, you don't have to worry about that.'

'Yes, I'm sure you will. But all the same I'm a businessman George and three thousand pounds is a lot of money ... a lot of money George.'

'I know, I understand. What did you have in mind?'

'The easiest thing would be to put a lien on the dairy, which will be released the moment the loan is paid in full,' Wilbur explained, reclining in his high back leather chair like lord and master.

'A lien on the dairy?' George blew out a breath. 'That's worth a lot of money Wilbur, I just had it valued at forty-eight thousand pounds. It seems a bit extravagant to put a lien over the entire dairy just for three thousand pounds.' George watched Wilbur's expressionless face, he didn't want to risk the dairy, he was desperately trying to come up with alternatives.

'What about the trucks Wilbur? Brand new trucks. We're phasing out the draft horses, keeping up with the times.' Wilbur didn't look impressed, whether he used draft horses or trucks to deliver his milk, was not any of Wilbur's concern. George pushed on, trying to convince him. 'They cost me over one and a half thousand each, and they're only a month old.'

'Trucks George? Trucks?' Wilbur said, shaking his head. 'They lose their value the minute you take them out on the road. In six months' time who knows what they'll be worth. Look George, you need the money and I need some reassurance you will pay it back. That's all this is, a bit of reassurance. Let's put a lien on the dairy and I'll give you the three thousand pounds, right here, right now.'

George's shoulders sagged in defeat. What could he do? 'All right then Wilbur, let's do it your way. But I will pay you, I'll pay you back every cent.'

'Plus interest,' butted in Wilbur.

'Yes Wilbur, of course I will pay you interest.'

'Well then, let's get this organised shall we?'

George was surprised when Wilbur opened his desk drawer and pulled out the papers. Wilbur noticed the look of astonishment on George's face. 'I did get a phone call from CC, he explained your predicament to me and asked if I could help. So, I have been expecting your visit George, so I drew up these papers in anticipation.' George nodded, a feeling of discomfort was creeping through his body, but he was in a tight squeeze, what other option did he have?

When he saw the interest rate, George sucked in his breath. He didn't want to think about it anymore, he just wanted the money. He wanted to get the cash and get out of there and then sit down and figure out how to get this loan paid off quickly and get back on track with his business. He signed on the dotted line, Wilbur smiled and shook his hand, reaching once again into the draw to bring out the three thousand pounds in cash.

It was Friday night and the little picture theatre was bursting at the seams with patrons. *Casablanca* was showing and everyone in town wanted to see it. CC was busy being busy and Hudson was climbing up to the projection box to get the show on the road. Cissy had opened the kiosk early. They were lining up for their chocolates and peanuts and Seymour was now mobile enough to take the tickets on the door, even though he had a chair next to him in case he felt the need to sit down.

The bell sounded. The show was about to commence. Crowds swelled at the theatre door and Seymour was flat out taking everyone's ticket. The patrons were feeling the pressure to get seated before the show commenced. There was only one person who wasn't in a hurry, she hung back until the doors were just about to close and the theatre would be inaccessible until interval time. She approached Seymour.

The look on his face was priceless. Here she was again. The girl from Coles.

'Hello, you made it, fantastic.' They looked at each other saying nothing, saying everything. 'You had better get in, the movie's starting, and you need to be seated.' Loretta understood, she handed him her ticket, looking him over intensely as she did so.

He had lovely grey blue eyes, a sculptured face and neat black hair. His body was lean, from his time in the army Loretta guessed, and his height just slightly less than his brother's at around five foot ten. The music started in the theatre. It wasn't the main feature yet, there was the Movietone News to be played and of course the cartoons. But rules were rules, once the doors were closed entry was not permitted except under dire circumstances, theatre policy was to let the guests enjoy their night's entertainment and not be bothered by people coming in and out of the theatre. However, Seymour had the authority to escort Loretta to her seat.

As he led her, crutch steadying him under his right arm and torch held low in his left hand, he showed her to a row of seating in the very back, reserved for management and their guests. She looked at him questioningly. He nodded his head assuredly and she took her seat. Seymour left her there to enjoy the movie, would he dare to return later to sit beside her?

Chapter Fifteen

BRUCE LANSING BELIEVED in a bit of family time, get away from the business and be with the people you love. This Saturday was no exception and Bruce decided a trip over to his daughter's salon would be in order. He and Nancy could see what she'd done with the place and catch up on everything that was happening in her life. Bruce pulled his car into a parking spot in Barkly Street, Footscray. Being the gentleman as always, he stepped around to the passenger side of the car to open the door for his wife. Arm in arm they approached Eleanor's salon.

Eleanor was busy with two customers. As she was styling one lady's hair into pin-curls, Veronica was sitting under the dryer. Eleanor asked Veronica what she thought of *Casablanca*. 'Oh, it was so dreamy, that airport scene, I thought I would just die with the sadness of it all.'

'*Casablanca*? It is supposed to be great,' said the other customer. 'I hope I get to see it; I couldn't get into last night's session it was packed out, tonight's show is already sold out.'

'In Footscray you mean?' asked Eleanor.

'Yes, where else?'

'I saw it at Sunshine,' replied Veronica. 'I actually know the owners and I got a free pass.' Eleanor was just finishing up the customer's hair, she wished Veronica wouldn't go on about knowing the owners, it was so pompous. She led the woman to the counter and took her payment.

'Well, that was lucky for you then,' replied the customer. 'Thanks Eleanor, I'll see you next month.'

Eleanor turned to Veronica, 'You shouldn't go bragging about how you got a free pass to the cinema, you'll most likely get Hudson into trouble.'

'Why would Hudson get into trouble, *he* didn't give <u>me</u> a free pass?'

'That's right, and Cissy shouldn't have really let you in. The theatre was booked out and those were seats reserved for the family.'

'The family and Little Miss Coles, why should she get to sit there?'

'Because Hudson *did* give her a free pass, Cissy on the other hand can get into big trouble just letting people in willy-nilly.'

'Well, I don't care; the whole thing was a bit of a disaster anyway. I thought Seymour was going to bite my head off when he saw me sitting there, and then he went and sat right next to her.'

'How could he do that? He had work to do,' replied Eleanor, wondering.

'Yes, well he wasn't there for the whole movie, but he made sure he was there towards the end. He whispered something to that shop assistant, and I saw her hanging around waiting for him after the show. I was furious, I gave up and went home.'

'Why should you be furious?' questioned Eleanor. 'Seymour obviously likes the girl, good luck to them both.' Veronica glared at her. 'What, have you got a crush on Seymour or something?'

'No, it's nothing like that.' Eleanor knew that Veronica had gone after Godfrey, then Hudson and had obviously now set her eyes on Seymour. Eleanor saw her for the gold-digger that she was and vowed she would make sure Seymour did not end up in the arms of Veronica.

'That's good then, because it seems to me, he has his sights set on Loretta, and she seems a lovely person too, by the way.' Veronica harrumphed. Lovely person indeed, she hadn't given up yet, not by a long shot.

Just then Eleanor's parents arrived. Eleanor was surprised at their unexpected visit and greeted them both with hugs. She introduced them to Veronica who was glad of the interruption, she was sick of hearing about Little Miss Coles. Bruce and Nancy admired the work Eleanor had done on the salon. The wallpaper really seemed to give the place a lift and the touches of green everywhere were fresh and inviting. Bruce walked around surveying while Nancy admired Eleanor's talent as she swept Veronica's hair into a fashionable roll.

'What about these hoses?' Bruce inquired, turning on a tap to test the worn hoses. Water sprayed over his shirt as the hose sprang a leak. 'Good heavens girl, you can't be turning these on your customers.'

'I know Daddy, I've just had so much to do, and they were last on my list. I'll get around to replacing them next week.'

'Consider it done, my girl,' Bruce said, taking a notepad out of his pocket and writing down the specifications. 'I'll have someone drop them off to you early in the week.'

'You don't have to do that Dad.'

'I know, but I want to. If I can't help my daughter, then who can I help?'

Veronica seethed beneath her smiling exterior. Why was everyone's life better than hers? Nice parents, nice boyfriend, nice salon, nice everything. One way or another she would get what she wanted, Veronica wasn't going to end up in the gutter or married to some loser with a brood of kids hanging off her apron strings. She had a vision, and she was going to make sure it came true.

Eleanor finished Veronica's hair. Veronica was well and truly peeved when Eleanor took her money, she had expected her to do her hair for nothing, seeing as she knew her and all. Eleanor gave her a slight discount. Big deal. She left the salon; she had shopping to do in Footscray. She would check Forges for the shoes she wanted to go with her dress for Cissy's engagement party. They had some great things at affordable prices, and no one would know she hadn't bought them from Georges on Collins.

Eleanor turned to her parents, 'I'm going to close up, what are you both doing now?'

'Well, we were planning to spend a bit of time with you,' replied Bruce. 'Your mother was hoping to see where you lived, as long as you think the Maxwells wouldn't mind.'

'Oh no, I'm sure it will be fine. They really are very nice people.'

'Well come along then, the car's out the front.' Bruce escorted the ladies to his car, and they were on their way to the Maxwells.

Miriam's mother was getting worse. Dr Wallace had arrived, and he looked at Miriam gravely. 'The news is not good, I'm afraid,' the doctor explained. 'Her lungs are really failing her and the only thing we can do for her now is to make her more comfortable. Sunshine has a small hospital that can cater to her needs, we can relieve her pain with morphine, but from there I'm afraid the only thing is to let nature take its course.'

Miriam was devastated. How could she possibly afford to pay for a private hospital? She would have to miss out on work at the theatre today, given her mother's condition. Dr Wallace could see the concern on Miriam's face. 'Is there someone who can sit with your mother while you go into work, I know you always do Saturdays at the picture theatre.'

'Not really, Mrs Johnson has been so kind, but I can't keep asking her to come and help me.'

'You shouldn't be so hard on yourself Dear, I am sure Mrs Johnson will help you if she can. Why don't you go down and ask her and I'll sit here with your mother until you return?'

He was such a kind doctor, Miriam was so grateful for his help and compassion, as she walked to Mrs Johnson's she wondered just how she would cope with all this. 'Well, I was going to make a lamb stew and then bake some cookies, I've got my brother and his family coming for dinner tomorrow,' explained Mrs Johnson after Miriam had popped her head in the back door. 'But it's nothing I can't do just as easily down at your place.'

'Are you sure Mrs Johnson?' Miriam asked, wondering at the kindness of this woman. 'I mean I can call up work, tell them I won't be in.'

'Goodness me no. I know how much you need the money. Wouldn't be doing it otherwise, would you?'

'I just don't know how to thank you.'

'Now don't worry about that. You go on and get yourself back, get ready for work, I'll be along in about fifteen minutes, I'll just gather up all me things.'

As Miriam walked back to her house, she knew the time had come to place her mother in professional care. How she was going to pay for this she had no idea. She thought about the house they lived in. Her mother owned it outright, having used her husband's insurance money to pay it out when he died. She had been left with little else, but the house had been a godsend. Miriam struggled to keep up with the electricity, the rates and just the expenses of day-to-day living. Besides this there were the doctor's bills, medications and the nurse's visits.

It was all a drain on Miriam's resources. She thought the time had come to perhaps take a loan out on the house. She needed some advice from someone who knew about these things. She wondered if Mr Cambridge might steer her in the right direction. He was a kind man, and a smart businessman. He would know way more about this sort of thing than Miriam. She would see if she could talk to him sometime today.

When Eleanor showed her parents into the Maxwell's home, Dorothy was just cleaning up the lunch dishes. Wilbur and Godfrey had both been home for lunch as had Heather. She swiftly wiped her hands on her apron and untied it, welcoming Bruce and Nancy into her home. Hearing their voices, Wilbur also entered the kitchen, he was delighted to see Bruce Lansing once again and shook his hand.

'Dorothy, why don't you show Nancy around, and I'll show Bruce my billiard room, he hasn't even seen my bar yet.' Bruce smiled, it sounded like a good idea to him, and as the women headed up stairs to see Eleanor's new room, Wilbur escorted Bruce to the bar, his mind churning like a windmill in a rough storm.

'So, I was interested in this land you have in Cheltenham.' Wilbur didn't want to alert Bruce to the fact that he was after the very same land as CC, that could put suspicion into his mind.

'Which land was that Wilbur? I have quite a bit there you know.'

Wilbur didn't know whether the man was showing off or just being frank, still, it didn't worry him greatly either way.

'Large parcel in Balcombe Road, ready for development I believe,' Wilbur said nonchalantly, like they discussed land every day. Bruce pursed his lips and thought for a minute as Wilbur poured them both a Scotch. Bruce thought about the types of businesses that Wilbur operated, which were more industrial than retail, he came to the conclusion that CC must have told him about the parcel of land near Reserve Road that was up for development and was zoned for industrial, that made sense to Bruce.

'Down near Reserve Road, you mean?'

'Yes, that would be it.' Wilbur had no knowledge of the area at all, and it didn't register with him for one second that Bruce may have owned more than one large parcel of land in Balcombe Road.

'What's your interest Wilbur?' Wilbur couldn't possibly tell Bruce that he was planning on back-stabbing CC, forcing him to agree to his deal now that he would have the land CC was dead set on acquiring.

'I am looking at getting into the freight game.' It was true, Wilbur had been researching the feasibility of opening a freight service and parcel delivery business. Sunshine was a way better location given its proximity to the major highways that led to Sydney, Adelaide and Brisbane, but you couldn't overlook the Cheltenham location for the southern suburbs service as well and being close to Point Nepean Road, giving good access to the Mornington Peninsula and South Eastern Victoria.

Bruce was ready to sell this piece of land for the right price and the two began to talk figures. After their second glass of Scotch, heads were nodding and Wilbur was pretty satisfied that they had reached a deal. Bruce offered to come by later in the week. He just had a few details to sort out and then he would get the contract of sale drawn up.

They shook hands just as the women arrived, wondering what had kept the men busy for so long. 'We've been invited to Cissy's and Godfrey's engagement party next Saturday night,' Nancy told Bruce.

'Well do we have any other commitments?' he asked his wife.

'No, dinner at the Lakes was cancelled, she's not well, so we are free.' Bruce turned to Dorothy,

'Well then we accept and thank you for your kind invitation.'

'Then it's settled. And don't worry about coming Bruce — I will come to you later in the week and we can finalise that land deal.'

'Yes, well that would save me an extra trip over.'

'Oh, you men,' complained Dorothy, 'it's always about business.' Wilbur glared at her, and she knew to hold her tongue.

'Well it's what keeps you in all your finery dear,' retorted Wilbur, then quickly checking himself, not wanting to upset Bruce or Nancy.

'Well, I'll see you both next Saturday,' said Nancy. 'We're looking forward to it.'

Miriam knocked on CC's door, he invited her into his office, wondering what may have motivated this meek girl to visit his office without an appointment. 'Miriam, can I help you?'

'Umm, I was hoping you could, Mr Cambridge,' she said humbly, 'I need some advice.' CC softened. He knew about the girl's mother and wondered if this is what had sent her to his office.

'How is your mother?'

'Well, that's just it you see.' CC looked at her understandingly. 'She is much worse. The doctor was there today, and he says I have to put her in hospital.' Miriam was struggling to hold back the tears, 'That she is in a lot of pain and that she will be more comfortable there.' Miriam burst into tears, CC offered her his clean, starched white handkerchief. She accepted it and wiped at her nose.

'It is going to cost a lot of money, more than I can afford, and I was wondering if I should take out a mortgage on our house. I thought you might be able to give me some advice on that, Mr Cambridge.' CC wasn't so sure the doctor had given Miriam the right advice. He was well aware of people living out their final days at home. With the right care and medication people were often more comfortable in their own environment than being bundled off into a hospital. He buzzed Sylvia Wright-Smith to come into his office.

'Miss Wright-Smith,' he addressed her formally in front of his staff member, and he explained Miram's plight to the woman.

'There's nothing wrong with hospital care of course,' summarised

Wright-Smith, 'but when my mother passed, and mind you that was from consumption too, she spent every moment at home. We had a posse of people looking after her around the clock and my mother died contented, glad to be around the ones she knew.'

'A posse of people?' inquired Miriam through intermittent sobs.

'Yes, we had a roster. Let's see now, there was about six of us in all, and we all took our turn in caring for mother. It took the burden off just the one person and spread it across family and close friends.'

'But I don't have any other family, at least not close by. A couple of aunties — but they live on the other side of town.'

'Your mother's sisters I take it?' questioned Miss Wright-Smith.

'Yes Miss Wright-Smith, they are quite a distance away.'

'Well come and see me after the matinee is over, I am sure we can come to a better arrangement than just putting your mother into hospital.'

Miriam left CC's office with hope in her heart. She had always thought Miss Wright-Smith a very staunch person, but obviously she had a kind heart and that was coming to the surface now.

With the matinee over and a break before the intermediate session, Cissy decided to telephone Godfrey to see if he had done anything about ordering the drinks for the party. 'I don't know Godfrey, I just thought you could put in a little more effort than you are,' she said testily when she discovered he'd done nothing. 'This is your engagement too, after all.' Godfrey was completely put out that he had to do anything at all for the stupid engagement party. If it wasn't for his father forcing him into this, he would have nothing to do with Cissy at all. She was turning into a bit of a control freak.

'Look stop panicking like some sort of rabid dog, the booze will be there, the party will go on and all will be well. Just calm down and leave me alone.' Cissy was incensed, leave him alone? What was that supposed to mean?

'Leave you alone? Is that what you want Godfrey?' Cissy shouted, not caring who heard. Miss Wright-Smith rushed into the ticket office and hush-hushed Cissy, such noise was not allowed in the Sunshine Theatre. Cissy knew she should not be shouting and tried to calm down, breathing deeply waiting for a response from Godfrey.

Godfrey knew he had gone too far, time to pull things back into line. 'Look, we're all under pressure. Everything is going be all right my darling. What's say we go to the Palais tonight? Just you and me. The others are working late and you're off at eight?'

Cissy calmed down, she did love him, really, and a night at the Palais on their own, without everyone else butting in, could be just what they needed.

As usual, the Palais was crowded. Cissy found herself alone at their table, as Godfrey chatted to some men at the bar. She was getting a little irritated when he finally arrived back at the table with a large, blond man in tow. He introduced Ambros Zimmerman to Cissy, she was taken by the man's appearance, his confident posture and his demeanour. He was easily over six foot with short blond hair and pale blue eyes. He looked strong, fit and healthy. When he spoke, it was with an accent unfamiliar to Cissy. She had spoken to many Americans during the war, and this was nothing like their accent.

The man sat down at their table and Godfrey provided the answers she was looking for. 'Ambros is from Germany.' Cissy looked a little horrified. 'Don't worry my darling, he has been here since the late twenties, before the war started.' She looked at Ambros, inviting him to tell her more.

'I came here with my parents. We were looking for a new beginning, somewhere warm and sunny.'

'Well then you should have gone to Queensland,' interrupted Cissy rather sardonically.

Ambros laughed and she couldn't but help to notice his wide, open smile. He appeared like a nice sort of a bloke, but he was German, after everything the Nazis did in the war there was no way she was going to trust him.

'We arrived in Melbourne, and we stayed here. My father was a tailor and there was work, good tailors could always find work in the thirties. After some time, he started a little business of his own in Flinders Lane.' Cissy knew Flinders Lane well; it was the centre of Melbourne's rag trade and many famous Melbourne fashion designers had cut their first cloths in Flinders Lane. Cissy nodded at Ambros, willing him to continue.

'My father was always eager to design his own lines — and now he has. The clothing line is called Zimmerman. Many of the top menswear stores around Melbourne stock our line, and father is very well known for his women's fashions as well,' he added in that cocksure manner that only Germans had perfected. Cissy didn't mind, she was beginning to become a little fascinated by this confident European and when Godfrey excused himself from their table again, Cissy didn't notice him chatting at the bar to another young man, she was way too wrapped up in Ambros's life story. He was actually quite amusing, and Cissy was enjoying his company immensely.

Miriam finished that night after interval on the final show. Mr Cambridge had told her to get on home after serving in the kiosk and not to worry about her pay being docked, he'd look after it. She arrived to the tantalising aroma of lamb stew and baked cookies. Mrs Johnson was asleep on the couch, her knitting fallen out of her hands beside her.

'Poor woman,' thought Miriam. 'She must have been run ragged, what with looking after Mum and doing all of her cooking.' She loathed to wake her up, but as though her thoughts had reached the woman, Mrs Johnson stirred.

'Oh Miriam, there you are.'

'Mrs Johnson, how are you?'

'I'm all right love, how was work?'

'The usual, quite busy actually.'

'I've left you and your mum and a little lamb stew,' she said, checking her watch. 'You're home early.'

'Yes, Mr Cambridge let me go after interval,' Miriam noticed the expression on the woman's face. 'Said he wouldn't dock my pay.'

'Oh, he's a kind man.'

Miriam nodded towards the bedroom. 'How is she?'

'She hasn't been too bad, I've been in a couple of times, and I've just given her some more medicine, about an hour ago.'

'Thank you Mrs Johnson, you've been a godsend, and thank you for the lamb stew.' Miriam went on to explain that Miss Wright-Smith was going to help organise a roster of people to help look after her mother. Mrs Johnson said she would happily be part of that roster, and she may know some others who would be willing to give a few hours here and there.

As Mrs Johnson left, Miriam heard her mother stirring in her sleep. She went to the bedroom where the moonlight coming through the window cast a luminous glow over the sleeping woman. Miriam went over and stroked her forehead, 'Oh Mum,' she sighed as tears dampened her cheeks, her spirits falling, knowing that she was soon going to lose this woman who brought her into this world. Knowing that in many ways, she had already lost her, with her spirit gone and her will to live, Miriam's mother was just existing, and as much as Miriam wanted her around it was painful and senseless to see her suffer. She wished her mother a speedy end, she looked at the bottle of pills on the bedside table, she looked at them a long time before leaving the room and going to her own bed.

Chapter Sixteen

THE DELIVERY TRUCK was backing into the driveway under the direction of Hudson. On stopping, the driver jumped out and proceeded to unload a brand-new Kelvinator refrigerator. Hudson helped him get it into the house, where it took up its proud position, the old icebox now having been relegated to the backyard.

Hudson thanked the driver and saw him off, standing in the backyard he wondered what he was going to do with the old icebox. He wanted to get rid of the thing before the party on Saturday night. It was old and battered. It was one of the things they had saved from the farm and Hudson really had no idea why they had kept it this long. He came up with a solution.

Arriving at George's dairy, Hudson was enthused when he saw two of George's trucks sitting idle. He entered the dairy and headed towards George's office. He found George, head in his hands, the posture of a very worried man obvious. Hudson knocked.

Surprised by his visitor George looked up, 'Hudson, this is a surprise, what can I do for you?'

'A favour George, if possible.' George didn't believe he was in any position to be doing anyone any favours at the moment but was happy to hear Hudson out anyway. 'I just wondered if I could borrow one of your trucks for an hour, I have an old ice chest I need to get to the tip before Saturday night.

'It will be okay, providing you can pick it up at lunch time when the fellas are taking a break,' offered George. 'I'll need it back within the hour though.'

'Appreciate it George. I'll pick it up at twelve sharp, then have it back to you well before one.' George nodded. 'See you then.'

CC was standing on an enormous plot of land in the middle of a busy shopping strip. The side of the road he was on was yet to be developed, however across the road there were two dress shops, a menswear store, a greengrocer, a milk bar and a fish and chip shop as well as a jeweller and a shoemaker a bit further on. CC was impressed, the more he thought about the possibility of opening a cinema, a restaurant and more — right here in Cheltenham, the more he liked the idea.

He thought about calling it an entertainment precinct and was anxious to talk to Bruce about it further. He noticed Bruce pulling into a parking spot in front of the milk bar, and signalled for him to stay there, as he crossed the rather busy road to meet up with him. They entered the milk bar and CC shouted Bruce a Passiona. They wandered back over to the land, Passiona bottles in hand.

'The way I see it, we could build the hotel here, taking up this large section of land and then the theatre could go right alongside it.' Bruce was listening and following CC around as he paced out the various buildings he envisioned on the land. 'If we shape the theatre right, we can place the milk bar right here in front and then the café alongside it.'

'I can see your vision and it sounds excellent,' replied Bruce, 'but one thing puzzles me.' CC looked at him expectantly. 'Why would you want to put this milk bar right next to your theatre and take away trade from your kiosk during your intervals etc?'

'The thing is, no matter how big a kiosk we put in, it simply cannot handle the crowds at interval time.' Bruce nodded. 'The other thing is, it's all about giving the people what they want. It's all right to say you are going to make milkshakes and scoop out double ice-cream cones, but when they are ten deep at the counter and you only have twenty minutes in which to serve them, you want everything to be fast. You want everything packaged, convenient and ready to sell.' Bruce nodded again, recognising more and more that CC really knew his business. 'Let them go to the milk bar for their malted milks, we will have plenty of custom with Dixie-cup ice-creams and bottled soft drinks, we won't be left short. Besides, I believe that the more attractions there are in the one area — the more choice you give the people so the more that they will come. Think about it — a special night — you take your girl out for a meal in the hotel dining room and then off to the pictures. What better way to impress her?'

Bruce was agreeing with everything CC said, however, always the devil's advocate, 'But times are tough CC, money's tight, where are these big spenders coming from?'

'The war's over Bruce, things will start to improve. A picture show does not cost a fortune. Dinner out would be a special treat — your wife's birthday, a family celebration, we market this right and we will have people coming from everywhere.' It was hard to disagree, Bruce liked what he heard, and he liked the prospect of doing business with CC.

The two men were now standing together, finishing their Passionas. 'Well, I guess all we need to sort out now is the detail. CC patted Bruce on the shoulder, 'Why don't we go back and do that at your office.'

Seymour didn't want to be late, and he didn't want his big brother tagging along either. He was taking Loretta to lunch and she only had forty-five minutes to give him. He ordered a taxi and had arrived at Coles well ahead of time. His leg was improving day-by-day. Right now, he could walk a few steps without his crutch, but he still needed it for support if the distance was any longer. He was pacing, in a fashion, out the front of Coles when Loretta arrived. Still in uniform, she quickly pointed to a café across the road and the two hurried towards it.

As they sat down, Seymour couldn't help but notice her violet eyes and perfectly styled, rich ebony locks. Her chin came to a delicate point and her rosebud lips were crimson against her creamy skin. It was all Seymour could do to concentrate on the task at hand — buy the lady lunch.

'So, what would you like?'

'I'll have the baked beans on toast and a pineapple milkshake.' Loretta had been thinking about lunch all morning and had long ago made up her mind what she was going to order. She didn't want to have to get nervous about making decisions in front of Seymour. She didn't want him to think that she was just some airhead working behind the Coles counter. She wanted to impress him.

Seymour was so shocked at her quick decision making that he decided to have the same. Before they knew it, they were presented with baked beans and pineapple milkshakes. Loretta began to eat, kicking off the conversation, 'So, do you normally drag young women away from their work responsibilities and take them to lunch?'

Seymour was amused by her humour. 'No, I normally drag them off to dark places unknown and lock them in dungeons.'

'I see, so just how many dungeon ladies do you have at your beck and call now?' Seymour laughed as he admired her quick-witted repartee.

'I've not long got back from the war, and I have been pretty much incapacitated since then,' he offered. 'Not a lot of time for hijacking young women and locking them away for my fantasies.'

'And what are your fantasies?' Seymour laughed again, this conversation was definitely heading down a somewhat dangerous track. He changed the subject.

'Tell me about you.'

'What's to tell?' said Loretta, moving the straw around in her milkshake. 'I was born and raised in Sunshine. I have five brothers and two sisters.'

'One of eight, wow, how do your mum and dad cope with that?'

'We're battlers, we get by. Dad works at the local harvester works and Mum has taken on a bit of cleaning where she can get it. I am helping out too and my eldest brother, Tommy, he is now an apprentice at the Roberts' dairy.'

Seymour nodded, he admired this young woman more and more. He knew what it was like to battle. All of those drought years on the farm had taught him the hard way. Animals starving and dying before your eyes when there was little or nothing you could do about it. When the fire came through, they fought to save themselves, and finally, leaving their home behind they came to the city with virtually nothing, waiting for the insurance money to come through so that they could make a new start.

'But you wouldn't know what it's like, I overheard Hudson saying your father is looking to expand, I mean you are already building a new cinema at Sunshine.' Seymour's eyes crinkled gently as he smiled at her. He wanted to tell her about his past, life on the farm, the battles they'd fought, the war that he'd seen — but time had slipped by so quickly that he knew he must get Loretta back to work before she got docked.

'One day Loretta, I will tell you all about it. But right now, I need to get you back to work.' Loretta thanked Seymour for lunch. He had not asked her out again and she wondered if she had said too much. Perhaps he didn't like the way she spoke about his family — not having any money troubles and expanding their cinemas. She was sorry about that now, believing she'd blown any chance she'd had with Seymour — he had not asked to see her again. Dejectedly she went back to work.

Seymour couldn't stop thinking about Loretta. How tough life had been for her but how she has succeeded in spite of it all. She had a good position at Coles as Counter Manager, and she had been helping her family as much as she could. Funny, but it made Seymour proud of her, he was smitten and he knew it. She made him forget what he was doing or saying, he'd never been like that before. He'd even forgotten to line up another date with her. So stupid. He would think of something amazing and surprise her. A woman like Loretta was special and he planned on proving that to her.

Hudson knew he didn't have a lot of time to dump the icebox as he drove into the Sunshine tip. He was requested to go to the rear of the quarry where the road was a little lower and the quarry not so deep. As he pulled the icebox free of the truck, he noticed there, to his great amazement, stood Wilbur Maxwell. With him was one of the council tip workers, an unsavoury looking fellow in overalls and an unshaven face, unruly hair reacting badly to the wind. Flies buzzed around him.

Neither of them noticed Hudson, but the wind carried their words directly within Hudson's hearing range. 'It's not over till it's over,' Wilbur said to the worker, in a most threatening manner.

'It's right boss, it's right. But you said two hundred and fifty.'

'I said you would get the money when it's over.' Hudson was fascinated.

'But I did what you asked.'

'Yes, what I have asked so far, but it is not over yet.' The tip worker looked really annoyed. 'Look, here's a hundred quid, keep your mouth shut and wait till you hear from me, you'll get the rest later, we just need to finish the job.' This seemed to appease the tip worker and as Wilbur turned to go, Hudson quickly hopped into the dairy truck, trying as hard as he could not to be recognised.

Wilbur was shocked to see a Robert's dairy truck at the tip, just when he was dealing with Sammy. Who could have been in that truck and why were they here? Did someone know what Wilbur was up to? Things started to change in Wilbur's mind, he needed to know, he needed to find out. What did George know and how did he know it?

As they sat on the balcony of the Lansing's Beach Road home, CC listened to Bruce's proposal. 'I am eager to join you in this venture CC. It is a big one, and I am sure together we can make a success of it.' CC nodded. 'I'm willing to put in the land and seventy-five percent of the capital to get the project started. You put in your expertise, manage the project and take care of the marketing. I can help you also on the construction side of things.'

'And in return for all this Bruce, what are you expecting?'

'Fifty-fifty partners. It's only fair after all.'

'Actually Bruce, that sounds more than fair, considering as you are putting in the land and seventy-five percent of the capital.'

'I know what you're saying, but I know how valuable your input is. Your talent lies in making things work — making a success of the project. You have the skills of your family to help, with their artistic minds and mechanical know-how. That Hudson is a clever fellow and I feel very confident in his capabilities.' CC nodded proudly. 'Who knows, we may be family one day the way our youngsters are getting along with each other?'

'Stranger things have happened Bruce. What are we going to call this new-found entity?'

'CL Enterprises. What do you think? Cambridge Lansing Enterprises.'

'I like it Bruce, I like it a lot.' As the agreement was reached the two looked out to sea, envisioning their future together in the new entertainment precinct that would become famous throughout Melbourne.

Sylvia Wright-Smith was at her best when she was in charge. She liked to be in control and so when she began organising the care roster for Miriam's mother, she was in her element. She knew two war-widows who were looking to use their time by making a contribution to the needy. Miriam had given her the name of two neighbours whom she thought may be interested in helping and CC had offered to top up any extra time by hiring the person of Sylvia's choice, someone to manage the group of helpers, at two and sixpence per hour, for a maximum of forty hours per week.

Before Miriam had had time to even think about putting her mother in the hospital, Miss Wright-Smith had women knocking on the door, ready to be introduced to the sick woman and to be taken through everything that would need attending to.

Miriam didn't even know where and how to start thanking Miss Wright-Smith for her kindness. She knew that the woman supported the local cake bake at the Lion's Club, raising money for charity, so she wondered if she could scrape up enough ingredients she might be able to organise some cakes to donate to Miss Wright-Smith's cause. That would be a start.

Dr Wallace approved of Miss Wright-Smith's plan wholeheartedly, and offered to be on-call, dropping by regularly to see how Mrs Worthing was doing. He would monitor her pain medication and make sure she was as comfortable as possible. Not everyone was fortunate enough to get the level of care this woman would be receiving, and he knew how grateful her daughter must be.

He thought to himself what a good thing home care was and wondered why the government didn't put a similar scheme in place. Perhaps that was something to bring up at the next medical board meeting.

Godfrey didn't really contribute a great deal to his father's business. Most of his days were spent at the yacht club (not that he sailed that much) or the Tattersalls Club, exclusively men only. Today he was at the Royal Brighton Yacht Club, it may have been quite a distance from Sunshine, but there wasn't really much about Sunshine that Godfrey liked. He way preferred it over this side of the city and the fewer people who knew he came from Sunshine and his father ran the local garbage service, the better.

Ambros Zimmerman strode in, his confident German manner turning heads as he strolled through the club. Godfrey was waiting for him. He sat by a large window looking out over the expensive yachts, enjoying the feeling of being surrounded by wealth. 'How are you this fine day, Godfrey?'

'Couldn't be better my friend. I thought you'd be at your father's showing,' Godfrey said, referring to the first showing of his father's summer lines.

'We had the rehearsal yesterday and the actual showing isn't until this evening.'

'What about your designs? Is he featuring any?'

'Yes, matter of fact I have a complete line in evening wear. It's very exciting,' Ambrose stated proudly.

'Well then let me buy you a drink — we must celebrate.'

'No, no, that won't be necessary. I cannot afford to be inebriated, I must have my wits about me for tonight's show. Now, what did you want to talk to me about?'

'Cissy, actually.'

Ah yes, the lovely Cissy … you're a lucky man Godfrey.'

'Come on, you know me better than that. You think this is the real thing between her and I?'

'Matter of fact, you've had me puzzled since you announced your engagement.'

'Look, you know what fathers can be like.' Ambros nodded, his father was very domineering, and it was always a struggle for Ambros to express his own thoughts and creativity. Godfrey continued, 'My father wants this. He thinks that if I marry Cissy then we will be well entrenched within the Cambridge family business. I will even have control of five percent, given that is my future wife's current share. Father is working out a deal for much larger chunk at the moment. Our aim is to take control, and by marrying Cissy we are getting so much closer to that goal.'

Ambros had suspected as much. He knew Cissy was far from Godfrey's type. Ironically though, he felt incensed. It wasn't as if he didn't want the best out of life as well, but he wasn't going to step on any toes to get there. Ruining a young girl's life — to deceive her so much and lead her into a marriage that was only going to end in misery. Ambros had to get away from Godfrey. Right now, he didn't think he could spend another minute in his presence. But tactics, always tactics, you never knew what lay around the corner.

'So how can I be of service?' asked Ambros.

'Look, I am going to need a cover from time to time and Cissy does seem to have taken a shine to you. If you could just help me out, just tell her we've been to the Tattersalls Club or just caught up with some old college pals.' Ambros didn't like it one bit, he knew where Godfrey was going with this, and he wasn't sure why, but he decided to play along.

'I can do that, but you will have to let me know. Is this going to become a regular thing — part of your married life with her?'

'No, not at all, the good thing is that she has been invited to study art in Paris. Once we are married, I can pack her off and live the life I want, and still have the right to her share in the growing Cambridge Empire.'

The more Godfrey spoke the more incensed Ambros became, worse than a cad, Godfrey was a complete idiot half the time. 'Okay, well you let me know what you want to do, I've got to go.' He shook Godfrey's hand in a hearty, college pal type of manner, slamming their hands together and giving one strong shake.

As Ambros left, he breathed a sigh of relief, shook his shoulders and moved his head from side to side, stretching his neck. He felt as though he was ridding himself of something rotten, trouble was it would take more than a shrug and a stretch to rid yourself of the type of deceit and lies Godfrey Maxwell could envelop you in.

Chapter Seventeen

CC WAS out in the courtyard enjoying a cup of tea and the early sunshine of a pleasant spring morning. He looked up as Cissy came through the French doors, her own cup in one hand and a letter in the other. 'Good morning Cecilia, what do you have there?'

'Well Dad, I have been wanting to show you this for a while.' She knew her father was at his best in the morning, the freshness and hope a new morning brings before the day's burdens weigh you down. She handed him the letter.

Smiling at her, he knew what was in the letter and was happy that she had finally decided to tell him about it. Cissy was as a nervous as a calf in a tannery, she watched her father's expression change from puzzlement to disfavour, as he read the letter. 'So, when did you apply to this college? You have been going behind my back and thinking that I wouldn't find out.' His words were terse, he wasn't letting on that he already knew.

'Daddy, you'd never let me apply, I knew that, and I just wanted to see if I could get in … if I had the talent.' CC rose from his chair and began pacing as Cissy continued. 'To be honest, I never thought I stood a chance. It was quite involved the application, I had to take photos of my work …'

CC turned on her, interrupting her as she nervously spoke. 'What did you think was going to happen if you did get in?' his voice was raised now. 'That you'd just pack up and move to Paris?' Just then Hudson arrived, he had heard everything his father had said and decided it was time he stuck up for his sister.

'Be reasonable Dad. Cissy has great talent. Why not let her follow her dream?'

'What, in a war-ravaged country where her life could be in danger?'

'The war's over Dad. Europe is rebuilding.'

'That may be so — but this young lady is about to be married. Her responsibilities will lie with her husband and building a home — a family for them both.'

'There's plenty of time for that Dad,' Hudson was adamant to stick up for his sister's dreams.

'Look I haven't got time to talk about this, I have an appointment with the accountant, but you haven't heard the last of this!' CC said, heading to the garage.

Hudson looked sympathetically at his sister and went in pursuit of his father. 'Dad,' he called after him as he entered the garage where the Humber was parked.

'Don't bother me now Son, I'm in a rush.'

'Just listen Dad, it's about Wilbur.' That got CC's attention, he turned to his son, anger still apparent on his face.

'What about Wilbur?'

'I saw him at the local tip yesterday.' CC looked interested.

'What would Wilbur be doing at the tip?'

'Well, he does own the rubbish collection business,' Hudson reasoned.

'Yes, I suppose, that explains it.'

'Not really, not the way he was talking to one of the workers there, really rough looking sort of a chap.'

'Your point is?' CC was getting impatient.

'The fellow wanted money from him, but Wilbur said it wasn't over till it was over.'

'Till what was over?' asked CC.

'That's just it, I don't know. The fellow said CC had offered him two hundred and fifty pounds and Wilbur said the job wasn't finished yet.'

'Two hundred and fifty pounds, that's a hell of a lot of money. Why would Wilbur be paying a tip worker that kind of money.'

'That's what I thought. And then Wilbur gives this bloke one hundred quid, cold hard cash, and told him to await further instructions. I'm telling you Dad, something is going on there and I don't think any of it is good.'

CC had totally lost the anger stirred up by Cissy's Paris intentions and was now wondering what on earth Wilbur was up to. 'Did he see you?'

'I'm pretty sure he didn't see me. I had borrowed George Robert's dairy truck to dump the icebox, he may have seen the dairy truck.' Something stirred in CC's mind, something that didn't feel right.

'Keep an eye out Son, I think we need to get to the bottom of this.'

Hudson nodded, 'You get off to your meeting then dad, I'll be along a bit later. And yes, I will keep an eye out.'

Veronica was just finishing up for the day. She hated her job and never, ever told anyone what she did. She didn't want people to know she worked at the dairy. She looked down on people like Loretta, working at Coles, yet here she was in a dairy production line capping milk bottles. The only thing she really liked about it was the hours. Working from four in the morning till noon, gave her the afternoons free to do what she liked. Most people assumed she didn't work and had money behind her somewhere along the line — that was how she liked it.

She had taken off her uniform and was just about to leave the locker room when she noticed Godfrey entering, she ducked back, out of sight. Godfrey headed straight for the boss's office.

When George saw Godfrey approaching, he felt like hiding. Even though Godfrey was a day early, George knew he wasn't going to be able make the payment. He cursed the day he borrowed the money from Wilbur. He couldn't believe the interest rate. He had borrowed three thousand pounds and by the time he paid Wilbur back he reckoned he would have given him over seven thousand pounds.

Wilbur had given him a schedule of repayments of one hundred and eighty pounds per week. What with the staff wages, his payments on his new equipment and overheads, he was lucky to have one hundred pounds left over. Wilbur was charging him another thirty percent interest for every day George was late with payment. The hundred and eighty pounds per week alone meant that he was paying George back close to four and a half thousand pounds. With thirty percent being added to that, day after day, and compounding, that was really blowing out of all proportion. Godfrey arrived at his door.

'Hello George, just checking on payment. You'll be right next week with that will you?' George was beginning to loathe Wilbur's son as much as he was now beginning to loathe Wilbur. He was a spineless little elitist who thought he was better than everyone else.

'Come back next week and see,' was George's response. Godfrey just stood in the doorway, his shoulder resting on the door jamb. He moved his tongue around his mouth arrogantly. After one very long minute he left, George put his elbows on his desk, his face in his hands. He was a very worried man.

Veronica watched Godfrey leave, she could see that George was troubled and wondered what Godfrey had done to upset him. She waited until he was well out of sight before leaving herself.

George took out his ledger and started doing some calculations. He had a cash tin locked in his top drawer. He counted the money. One way or another he was going to make that payment to Godfrey next week. Somehow, he would do it, he just had to figure out how.

When Hudson arrived at the theatre that afternoon, he checked the deliveries. There were ten new cans of film, but he could not find *Fantasia* anywhere. It was due to be played at the kids' matinee tomorrow and the kids just loved the brilliant Disney animation. His father's door was closed but he figured this was important enough to interrupt.

His father looked at him, expression slightly annoyed, when

Hudson popped his head in. Hudson was a bit surprised to see their accountant, bank manager and Seymour in the office. It was a bit of an affront, having Seymour present and not him. His father read his expression but wasn't that perturbed about it. 'What is it Son? We're busy here.'

'I just wanted to let you know *Fantasia* hasn't arrived, it was due for delivery today.'

'Get onto the distributors and see what they've done, we've advertised that for tomorrow's matinee.'

'I know Dad, don't worry, I'll chase it up.'

As he left the office, the men got back to their business. The bank manager was looking over the accountant's figures. CC was eager to secure as much as he could from the bank in order to keep any borrowings from Wilbur to a minimum. Now that he had equal share in the land at Cheltenham, he had even more collateral to offer. The bank manager stood, he shook each of the men's hands and then, taking some of the documentation with him, he vowed to get back with an answer on Monday. Seymour and CC walked the bank manager to the door, the accountant close behind them. Hudson was in the ticket office on the phone. He could see the men as he was holding on the phone, waiting for the distributors to come on the line.

'That went pretty well I thought,' said CC to Seymour.

'Seemed to. That land in Cheltenham has helped, and he really likes your plans for expansion,' replied Seymour.

'Let's hope he can convince his colleagues,' added the accountant. Just then Hudson's phone was answered, and he missed the rest of the conversation as he got onto the matter of finding *Fantasia*. The accountant left the theatre and Seymour and CC headed back into the office, unaware that Hudson's eyes were following them.

It was still light when Eleanor called by the theatre at around 6pm. Hudson was just backing out of the projection box entrance with an armload of reels when he nearly bumped into her. 'Eleanor, sweetheart, this is a nice surprise.' She loved it when he called her sweetheart, she smiled at him.

'Hello,' she greeted, just a little nervously, her blood tingled just from being so near to him. 'I thought I'd drop by on my way home, I haven't heard from you for a couple of days, and I wondered if everything was okay?'

Hudson realised he hadn't called her and immediately felt guilty. 'I'm so sorry, what with work and the engagement party tomorrow, I just haven't stopped.' He could see she was a bit annoyed. 'How about a milkshake? We can pop across the road.' Eleanor agreed, she wanted to talk to him, and it was way too difficult in the theatre, with everyone around. Just at that minute Miss Wright-Smith walked by.

'Hello Eleanor, how are you this evening?'

'I'm very well thank you Miss Wright-Smith — and you?'

'Yes, yes, very good, but very busy, no time to stop and chat.' Eleanor looked at Hudson and they both suppressed a giggle as Miss Wright-Smith bustled off.

'Do you think that was a hint?' she said in a lowered voice to Hudson. 'Very busy? No time to chat? Am I dragging you away from your work Hudson?'

'Not at all, I couldn't think of a better reason to be dragged away.'

They sat in a booth drinking their milkshakes and Hudson told Eleanor about his day. About talking to his father regarding the weird sighting of Wilbur Maxwell and the tip worker. About Seymour attending the meeting and not him. 'I'm sure it's all quite innocent Hudson, Seymour is more of an accountant than you are, you know that.'

'Yes, but that doesn't mean I shouldn't be involved in business decisions.'

'I'm sure your father will tell you soon enough,' soothed Eleanor. 'What has he exactly told you anyway?'

'Well, I only just found out that he has struck up a deal with your father regarding the new theatre in Cheltenham.'

'I just found that out too. Apparently, they have plans for a hotel, a milk bar and a restaurant as well.'

'Quite the brave venture,' added Hudson. 'Does this mean we're family now?'

'Would you like to be family Hudson?' Eleanor asked, prodding him.

'Ha ha,' laughed Hudson, 'I don't want you for a sister, that would be too strange.'

'That's not what I meant. Just what do you want Hudson?'

'Me? I want you, I want us,' Hudson said, looking for the right words. 'I want us to be together and I want to be a big part of Cambridge Picture Theatres as the business grows. I find it all very exciting.'

'It is exciting Hudson,' Eleanor went on, 'the future is very exciting. Don't you want more though, personally, a family, a place to call your own home?'

'Of course, I want those things Eleanor, I want them for us.' Eleanor was getting more and more frustrated. Hudson had never once mentioned marriage and she was growing a little tired of it. She held her left hand up to her chin and with her right thumb and forefinger she stroked the ring finger of her left hand. Hudson noticed.

'What's wrong sweetheart — have you been bitten, mosquito?' That was it, she gave up with a huge sigh.

'Oh, Hudson you're just impossible, I'll see you at the engagement party. Did you hear that word Hudson? ENGAGEMENT party,' she said, placing huge emphasis on the word engagement as she left the hamburger café. Hudson stared after her shaking his head. Whatever had gotten into her? In fact, what was up with people today? It felt as though everyone around him was acting strange. He stood up from the table and headed back across the road to the theatre.

Chapter Eighteen

ELEANOR'S SALON was doing a roaring trade. Not only were the regular Saturday morning clients there, but Cissy had arrived with Heather, Veronica and Miriam in tow, all lining up to have their hair done for the big engagement party tonight. The place was abuzz with excited chatter. They talked about what they were going to wear and who else was coming along to the party. 'So, has Hudson popped the question yet?' Cissy asked Eleanor.

As she rolled Veronica's hair, Eleanor looked a bit pensive. 'No,' she pined, 'God knows I've dropped enough hints.' Veronica was seething. Her hopes of winning over a Cambridge man were dwindling. Godfrey was spoken for, and she really was thinking about moving on, finding the right man to give her the sort of life she wanted to become accustomed to, but then Hudson hadn't yet proposed to Eleanor, so what was stopping him, she wondered? 'He'll propose when he's ready,' said Veronica, deciding to set Eleanor's mind at rest, 'some men are just slower than others.' After all, she didn't want Eleanor panicking and proposing to him, Hudson might just accept.

As Eleanor now stood behind Cissy dressing her hair, Cissy nudged Eleanor with her elbow and said, 'Yeah, he's crazy about you. We'll be sisters in no time, you'll see.'

Eleanor laughed, 'No time, huh, that's a joke.'

'Come on, today's a day to be happy,' Miriam said. 'Cissy's getting engaged and we should all be happy for her.' Eleanor felt a bit mean then. She had dwelled too much on her own feelings and forgotten about those of her friends. Look at poor Miriam, her mother near death and yet she had really made the effort to get to Cissy's party tonight. Her hairstyle was looking fabulous too, in a softly curled updo she was looking more like Lauren Bacall than the kiosk girl at the Sunshine Picture Theatre. Eleanor wondered what she was wearing tonight and decided to ask.

'Oh, I don't know. I don't have a lot of clothes; I could never afford them.'

'Well why don't you drop by our place on the way home,' said Eleanor, knowing Heather would back her up. 'I have lots of dresses, I'm sure to have something to suit you and we are pretty much the same size.'

'I couldn't do that, you have already been so generous doing my hair.'

'That's nothing, honestly.'

Just then Heather joined in. 'Yes, come on. It will be fun. Girls together getting ready for a party.'

'Say, that's a great idea,' added Eleanor. 'Instead of coming by now, why don't you come by about an hour early for the party, and we can help you get ready.' It sounded very exciting and fun to Miriam, she decided to be a bit of daredevil.

'Okay, okay — would six o'clock be okay?'

'Perfect,' answered both Eleanor and Heather at the same time.

The weather was warming up now that November had arrived. Without shade the day was quite hot and Seymour was feeling this heat as he aimed his rifle at the target. It was a direct hit and the only thing that distracted Seymour from taking the next shot was the applause that came from behind him. He turned to see Jack Sotheby standing there, sporting his own rifle.

'Jack, I didn't know you enjoyed the sport.'

'My father taught me from a very young age. We used to go hunting all the time. I have been coming to the Braybrook rifle range since I moved to Sunshine.' Seymour reloaded his rifle, still finding it a little tricky with his injured leg. 'How's the leg?'

'Vastly improved Jack, I reckon about another couple of weeks and I'll be running marathons.'

'What's say we go hunting then?' Seymour looked at him, wondering exactly what he meant. 'Nothing too big, may be just a few rabbits until your leg is completely healed.'

'Okay mate, you're on. I haven't had a good rabbit stew in ages.'

As they re-loaded their rifles Seymour chatted to Jack. He quite liked Jack, he seemed like an honest chap. He found out that he had been raising his little brother for the last ten years, when their mother had died. Jack's father had walked out them when he was just a baby. His mother never told him who his little brother's father was, but neither of them cared really, because he wasn't around anyway.

His brother was now working at the Sunshine Harvester Works, where Jack had previously worked. It meant Jack was a little freer to be more ambitious, and hence the job at the Picture Theatres. The money wasn't quite as good because the hours weren't there, but Jack told Seymour how much he enjoyed working there and one day hoped to be promoted, particularly with this expansion, they would need more help.

Seymour listened with interest. He thought Jack was the perfect man to help them expand their business.

The kids were queued outside the theatre. *Fantasia* was playing for the matinee, and it looked as though the entire town's population of children had turned out for the event. Wilbur smiled to himself as he pulled up in front of the theatre. Not only was there money to be made now, the new picture theatre was making great progress, with the roof nearly finished. He walked down to the old grain hut theatre.

CC was surprised to see him. He was anxious to finish work for the day and get home to do what he could to help get the party organised. He had ordered crayfish and ten pounds of prawns, he had to pick those up from Victoria Market before three o'clock. That would be a surprise for Cissy and the girlfriends who were helping her. He wished Margot were here to see all this, but in many ways Cissy was becoming more like her mother every day, the way she would organise everything and have her friends pitch in and help.

When Wilbur knocked on the office door, CC was a bit annoyed. Surely the man had plenty to do himself today, business could wait, he invited him in however. 'CC, big day today.'

'Yes, for both of us. How's Godfrey?'

'Haven't seen much of him this morning, he is probably in at the Tattersalls Club or over with his yachty friends.'

'I'd have thought he'd be too busy for that.'

'I know, he's going to lend a hand later this afternoon, when Hudson's finished the intermediate session they will pick up the grog,' Wilbur explained. 'Almost family now CC. Soon we'll be business partners as well. How are the plans coming along?'

'It's all good Wilbur, everything is going according to plan.'

'I see your new theatre out the front is nearly finished; you must be anxious to get started on the others.'

'It all takes time Wilbur, I understand that.'

'It doesn't have to take too long. Why don't we finalise our deal? Haven't we waited too long now? Why don't we at least seal the bill of sale with Altona and get started on Maidstone.'

'I'm as anxious as you are Wilbur, but today's not the day.'

'No time like the present CC. How about thirty-five percent?' It was less than Wilbur wanted, but it was still a decent chuck. If you threw in Cissy's five percent that then gave them forty percent, which he knew was an equal share to CC's forty percent.

'Perhaps Wilbur, but I am in no mood to talk about it now. I have to finish up here and then run around picking up things for tonight. I take it you're all organised?'

Wilbur certainly was organised, having nothing to do at all in helping with tonight's efforts. He'd left Dorothy at home baking an assortment of cakes and had headed over to CC's. He scheming mind had though that by perhaps catching CC while his mind was on other things, it could just be the opportune moment he had been looking for.

'Organised? Why sure. Nothing much for me to do but turn up.' CC was a little peeved by the man's attitude. He bade him farewell, wanting to be free of him to finish off his work.

As Wilbur left his office CC shook his head in exacerbation. He could see that the man really didn't like pitching in to help out. What sort of a business partner would that make him? Even Bruce was helping out with the night by lending his spit roaster. The deal was done with Bruce and soon they would start construction. He didn't feel nearly as comfortable with Wilbur. Thirty-five percent, he thought — the man's got rocks in his head.

He thought back to Hudson's sighting of him at the tip, it was a strange thing and he really wanted to understand what that was all about before taking it any further. A good business partnership was crucial to the success of the company, and CC didn't want to put a foot wrong.

If the truth be known, he was a little unsure about Godfrey. He remembered when he was courting Margot, that he had a very hard time staying away from her. Godfrey, on the other hand, never seemed to be around and even Cissy now appeared to have stopped pining for him. He might have a talk to his sons, get them on the job to investigate what was going on. The last thing he wanted was for his daughter to marry the wrong man — and a Maxwell at that. Partnerships and marriage — the two don't always go together.

Fantasia was running on the big screen when Jack entered the projection box. 'Thanks Jack,' greeted Hudson, 'I'll be back to load the intermediate session and I'll let you take over for tonight.'

'That's fine Hudson,' replied Jack. 'A bit of an early finish tonight so I'll see a bit of the party at least.'

'I don't think you'll miss out on too much; these things tend to go until the early hours.'

'Sounds like a good night, you go and do what you have to, I'll see you shortly.'

On his way out, Hudson met Miriam in the foyer. 'Miriam, I thought you'd be home getting ready for the party.'

'Oh no, not a lot to do. The girls have got everything under control. I'm finishing up here after the intermediate, then heading over to Heather's to get ready there. Seymour and Roger will be here to help out at tonight's interval rush on the kiosk.'

It sounded as though everything was under control. Hudson looked at his watch. He had to hurry if he wanted to get the marquee up and get back here to load the intermediate films. He hurried out to his car, taking in the progress of the new theatre as he went.

'Where's Godfrey?' Hudson inquired as he walked through the courtyard. Cissy was in a fluster, helping Seymour with the marquee.

'Who knows?' she said testily, 'And thank heavens you're finally here.'

'Calm down, calm down. I got here as soon as I could. If they'd delivered this, this morning like they were supposed to, it'd be up by now.' Just then Bruce and Nancy walked in, with one their sons, James, Eleanor's younger brother. He was just seventeen years of age, but a fit young man, used to hard work having worked in the building industry now for over a year, with his father.

'Door was open,' greeted Bruce, 'thought you might need a hand.'

'Bruce old chap you're a godsend,' said Hudson. 'We sure could use some help.' Bruce introduced James and then they each grabbed a corner of the marquee while Nancy looked at the flustered Cissy.

'Come on Cissy, let's go see what's happening in the kitchen. Your hairdo's never going to survive at this rate.'

'I'm going to kill that Godfrey,' Cissy mumbled as she gratefully followed Nancy into the kitchen.

When they were in the kitchen Nancy asked Cissy about Godfrey. Nancy had only met him fleetingly and she was surprised that he wasn't here helping with his own engagement party. 'Oh, I don't know, he's not very hands-on,' said Cissy, 'Your husband, Mr Lansing seems so practical.'

'I never have any problems with Bruce around. He's good at so many things.'

'Seems like it. The boys were sure glad to see him turn up, he'll have that marquee up in no time,' Cissy commented as she was wrapping prunes in bacon, ready to go under the grill.

'Goodness, what are you doing with this entire pig?' Nancy said as she lifted up the lid on the enormous cooler chest.

'Well hopefully your husband can help out again. We need to get that spit going and start roasting the pig, otherwise it will never be ready tonight.' No sooner had they spoken than Bruce arrived at the kitchen door.

'The lads are finishing off the marquee, what are we doing about decorations?'

'Well Eleanor should be here any second with the balloons, I have got the streamers ready to go,' answered Cissy.

'Righto,' said Nancy. 'Cissy and I will get the boys to help us with that, why don't you set up the spit?'

Cissy was grateful to have such an organised woman to help her out. Suddenly all the stress left her, and she was ready to tackle the decorations. She did wonder where Godfrey was though. She actually wondered a lot of things about Godfrey.

Chapter Nineteen

THE BAND WAS A SENSATION, the party was in full swing. The decorations really set the mood for a successful night. Clumps of purple and lavender balloons were joined by deep plum streamers. Cissy's lavender and lily arrangements adorned every table and taking pride of place in the centre of the drinks tables was a huge cluster of lavender, lilies and greenery.

Miriam looked amazing in Eleanor's pale blue and hibiscus floral dress. It was nipped in tight at the waist, showing off her excellent figure and the bodice was princess cut highlighting her olive skin. Eleanor had loaned Miriam her sapphire necklace — that night Miriam felt like a million dollars.

All the girls were looking gorgeous. Cissy wore a sensational Dior gown she'd had on layby at George's on Collins since the announcement of the engagement. It was a deep plum in colour, tight fitting with a belted waist and plunging neckline. When Godfrey presented her with the diamond necklace as an engagement present, Cissy forgave all his 'sins'. Now sitting brilliantly against her creamy skin, Cissy certainly had all eyes on her.

'Godfrey, come and dance with me,' she urged.

'Not now, Cissy, I'm talking to the lads.' He stood by the drinks table, talking with Ambros and two other chaps Cissy had yet to be introduced to.

'Hey God,' said one of the men, 'how about introducing us to your fiancé?' Cissy didn't like the look of the guy; he was snide in the way he had spoken of her — and what was with shortening Godfrey's name to God?

'Sure,' replied Godfrey, 'Cissy, these are my chums Neal and Raymond.' Cissy greeted them and then realised she was not wanted as they continued their conversation — ignoring her. As she walked off, Neal looked her up and down, he then looked at Godfrey, raising his eyebrows and turning down the corners of his mouth. Godfrey smiled and laughed, taking another drink.

Cissy returned to her table with a disgruntled look on her face. 'Why the glum face?' asked Hudson.

'Oh, I don't know. It's our engagement party and all he wants to do is to talk to the boys.'

Hudson was very inclined to agree with Cissy. Godfrey hadn't paid her much attention all night. He would have thought they should be together, circulating among the guests who were all anxious to offer their congratulations. 'Sometimes Hudson, I have my doubts about this whole thing,' she confessed and as she did so, Ambros arrived at the table.

'Come on Cissy, I would love to dance with you,' he offered graciously. She hesitated for a second or two then thought, 'Why not?' She took Ambros's hand as he guided her onto the dance floor.

'Don't be so glum,' he said as they smoothly glided through a foxtrot, 'Godfrey can be a bit ignorant at times.'

'Seriously? I am wondering why we are getting engaged at all, he seems far more bent on hanging out with the boys than he does with me.'

'That's men for you Cissy, they like to hang out together. Funny thing is, all they're normally talking about is women, anyway.'

'I doubt that,' replied Cissy. Ambros looked at her questioningly.

'Look, if you are having doubts maybe you should have a talk to Godfrey, find out what he's all about.'

'What do you mean — what he's all about?'

'Well, people aren't always what they seem on the surface. Sometimes it is a good idea to delve a little deeper. That way you won't find any nasty surprises when you are married.' Cissy thought about Ambros's words, it made sense really, but she did wonder why he was encouraging her to investigate her fiancé's behaviour. It felt like a warning, and Cissy was definitely thinking about heeding that warning.

CC was feeling on top of the world. He'd sealed the deal with Bruce earlier in the evening and now he was enjoying his daughter's engagement party. There were a lot of people CC had never met, mostly friends of the Maxwells, but now he watched his daughter dance with the stranger and this fellow really stood out. He was about six foot two, with short blond hair and pale blue eyes. CC hadn't seen him around anywhere before and wondered who he was.

His thoughts were interrupted when Sylvia Wright-Smith arrived. 'Hello CC,' she greeted him and then before he could say anything, 'Well I have been run off my feet tonight, but I still have enough energy left for a dance.' As she looked at CC expectantly, he realised she was asking for a dance.

'You've picked the wrong man here Sylvia, I gave up dancing many years back, two left feet.' Sylvia could see she was not going to get anywhere and settled for a drink instead, seating herself next to CC.

As she did so CC noticed George on the other side of the room, with a tilt of his head, CC invited him over. 'How are you enjoying the party, George?'

'You've put on a fine show here, CC.'

'Not my doing, the kids have done it all George, been working their tails off all day. How's everything going for you?' CC asked, implying a deeper meaning into his problems with the blackmailer.

George glanced at Sylvia, wondering how much he should say in front of her. 'Not good CC. The interest rate is killing me.'

'Interest rate? Is the bank involved?'

'Not the bank CC, my private lender.'

'Hmmm, that doesn't sound good George, tell me more.' Just then

George's body jolted forward from the severe slap on the back given to him by Wilbur, who had conveniently arrived at their table.

'Well, if it isn't father of the groom to be,' announced CC, sensing something very wrong between the two.

'CC, Sylvia, George,' Wilbur greeted. 'How's the dairy going George?'

'At the moment Wilbur, I stand to lose everything.'

'Goodness gracious me, we don't want to hear things like that.' George looked at Wilbur tight-lipped and CC could almost cut the tension with a knife.

'Gentlemen, tonight is not a night for talking business. Let's all put our problems aside for a little and enjoy the evening, shall we?' Just then George spotted his wife through the crowd. She was sitting all alone on the other side of the marquee. George excused himself to go and join her. As George left, CC looked at Wilbur, he was becoming more uncomfortable around this man the more time he spent with him.

Loretta and Seymour were in the courtyard. She had taken Seymour's breath away when he first saw her that evening. She was already at the party, Seymour being a late arrival having come in after interval of the Saturday night pictures. She was by the bandstand, wearing a dress of pastel florals, low in the neckline where a perfectly placed spray of violets brought out the intense colour of her eyes and accentuated her creamy skin. Pinched tight at the waist, emphasising the delicate voile of the full skirt. Her jet-black hair was held back by the finest tiara of violets and sapphire earrings completed the stunning vision.

Now as Seymour sat here in the courtyard, he wanted more of her, he wanted this woman for his own, he had never been surer of anything. Seymour took Loretta in his arms and they kissed, long and deep and passionately. It was too soon to ask for her hand in marriage. He was a cautious man and heeded temptation, but he would ask her soon, he knew that, he just wanted to give her a little time.

Godfrey was well and truly under the weather. With his left arm draped around Cissy's shoulders, he swayed back and forth with a drink in his right. The men he was with earlier were still gathered around him. The party was starting to thin out now, at one o'clock in the morning. CC thought his daughter was looking a little vexed. He decided to investigate.

Godfrey's friends were smirking as Godfrey virtually paraded Cissy before their eyes. 'And so my friends, Cecelia Cambridge is to be my wife, my little woman, my better half, my old lady, my…'

'Are we all enjoying ourselves?' CC cut in with a strong hint of authority in his tone. Godfrey staggered again, still using Cissy as a prop.

'CC,' he almost shouted, 'Father of the future. Come and join us.' Tears were welling in Cissy's eyes, she'd really had enough of Godfrey's treatment.

'Son,' warned CC, 'I think you've all had enough for one night.' Godfrey looked offended. 'How are you all getting home?'

'Home?' Godfrey's voice was rising again. 'No, no, no! The night's only just beginning.' Then he gestured with a wide sweep of his arm, glass still in hand, spilling most of the remaining contents, 'Let's all have another drink.' As CC glared at him Godfrey's friends were taking the hint. Cissy became exacerbated and burst into tears, running for the sanctum of her bedroom.

'Well how do you like that?' slurred Godfrey, still swaying, 'You show a girl a good time and what does she do?'

CC had had enough, 'Okay, okay, pack it up, let's pack it up fellas.' Sensing trouble, Hudson and Seymour arrived to offer back-up.

'All right, all right, I'm going,' said Godfrey, seeing the reinforcements arrive. Reluctantly he left the party, an arm draped over the shoulders of a friend on either side, who supported him to the car. Mouth pursed tight, Wilbur's eyes followed his son as he exited, he would have something to say to him in the morning, why couldn't his son have played the part, just for one night? A very important night, his engagement. He'd already had one disappointment for the day with CC holding off on the deal, he didn't need his son ruining everything.

Hudson and Seymour remained talking to CC when Eleanor arrived. 'Where's Cissy?' asked Eleanor of Hudson.

'In her room I should imagine, she dashed off, very upset.'

'I'll go to her,' offered Eleanor, and she left the three men standing there with the remaining party stragglers scattered around them. Wilbur decided it was probably time for he and Dorothy to take their leave.

In her room Cissy was sitting in front of her mirror, wiping her eyes. 'Oh Cissy, I'm so sorry for you. Men can be completely stupid at times,' Eleanor said, entering Cissy's room.

'He's always hanging around with his mates. He practically spent the whole night with them, didn't even want to dance with me,' sobbed Cissy.

'It was a big night for him. He was proud of you; I saw him showing you off to his mates.'

'Showing me off? Making fun of me would be more to the point. He even had the nerve to call me his old lady!'

'Well, that's not on, but look cheer up now. Don't let this ruin your whole night. It's been a lovely night and I am sure he just had too much to drink,' Eleanor soothed. 'Come on down now and let's have a cup of tea, your dad and brothers are still there, and a few other people. What do you say?... it's your party.'

Cissy agreed and together they went downstairs, both women doubting the strength of the engagement. Cissy wondering where she was going from here and Eleanor thinking that Cissy should take her time before marrying Godfrey.

Chapter Twenty

THE MARQUEE WAS testament to a party enjoyed by all. Streamers and balloons were lying on the ground, bottles lay like corpses and glasses that were clung to the previous evening now lay abandoned, many half-empty and bearing the insult of extinguished cigarette butts floating in them like sodden relics. Hudson and Seymour moved laconically through the remnants of the previous evening's revelry.

'The morning after the night before,' said Hudson, 'Not my favourite pastime.'

'Still, it was a good night though,' said Seymour, now getting around without the crutches, just a slight limp.

'Except for Godfrey, of course,' replied Hudson. 'He was a bit of jerk, wasn't he?'

'Yeah, I don't get it. Here he's got a beautiful woman he has just become engaged to and all he wants to do is to hang with his mates.'

'I know, I mean have you really seen Godfrey and Cissy being affectionate towards each other?'

'Come to think of it, no. Not since those early days at the Palais, anyway.'

To interrupt their conversation Eleanor arrived. 'Why don't you talk even louder so that the whole neighbourhood can hear you, instead of just Cissy in her bedroom.'

'That's all right,' said Cissy, walking into the marquee and surprising everyone by her appearance. 'I'm starting to agree anyway. He was a such a swine last night I really am having a bit of a think about the whole thing.'

'Good for you, you want to be sure,' said Hudson, 'marriage is a big commitment.' Eleanor looked at him and huffed out her breath, when would the penny drop with Hudson?

'What's that other guy all about — that Ambros, the one you were dancing with?' asked Seymour trying to divert the subject and brighten Cissy up.

'He's just a nice guy,' said Cissy. 'A friend of Godfrey's — although he doesn't seem anything like his other mates.'

'But he is German though,' added Hudson.

'Yes, but he's not a Nazi,' retorted Eleanor. Hudson glared at her.

'No, she's right,' defended Cissy. 'He came out here in the late twenties with his parents, before the war even started.'

'He's still a German,' said Seymour.

'Well, I quite like him,' said Cissy, 'and he said he was going to pop around this afternoon, to see how I was after Godfrey's performance last night.'

'Just watch him, okay?' said Seymour protectively.

'Who are we watching?' questioned CC, entering the marquee.

'That man Cissy was dancing with last night, the German,' put in Seymour.

'German? Damn it Cissy what are you doing with a German?'

'He's not a Nazi dad,' she shot back, 'he's a nice guy.'

'Just don't be spending time with any Germans Cissy, I will not have it.' With that Cissy turned on her heel and stormed out of the marquee. Had the world gone mad? First of all, her fiancé treated her like a complete jerk and now her father was banning her from seeing someone because he was German. She was furious, frustrated and wondering what to do next.

George was in his office. The letter in front of him would not change no matter how many times he looked at it. Grimly he reread the words from the State Bank of Victoria:

Third and final notice. Please bring loan payments up to date within the seven days, otherwise the bank regrets having to take action over your business and your property.'

As he rested his elbows on the desk, head in his hands, there was a tap on his door. He looked up to see CC. 'Hello George, I hope you don't mind me dropping in on a Sunday, I thought I'd find you in here today.'

'Not at all CC, take a seat.' CC got straight to the point.

'Look, I can tell you have some problems George, it is obvious in everything you are doing lately.' George looked at CC, mouth firmly shut. CC decided to push it.

'I don't know what's going on George, but I do know about you being blackmailed — you came to me first, remember? Now Wilbur has loaned you the money I thought things would start to improve for you, but from what I can gather they have gone from bad to worse.'

Still nothing from George.

'Hudson borrowed one of your trucks the other day to take our old icebox to the tip,' said CC, not giving up. George gave CC a nod of acknowledgement. 'When he came back, he told me he had seen Wilbur talking to some degenerate tip worker and not only that, he handed him a wad of cash,' CC really had George's attention now. 'Hudson clearly heard the words, one hundred quid. Apparently, there is more to come, the total payment being two hundred and fifty pounds. Whatever would that be for George?'

George could barely believe it, but now it all made sense. Wilbur had set this whole thing up. What was his end game? Perhaps CC could help him to figure that out. 'It all makes sense now CC.'

'What? Tell me George.'

'That man Hudson saw — that was the fellow who is blackmailing me. Sammy.'

CC was shocked. 'Oh my God, you mean ...'

'That's exactly what I mean. Wilbur's behind this whole thing.'

'Why?' CC was confounded, 'Why would Wilbur do such a thing?'

'Well, he is charging me an enormous amount of interest, that much I know.' CC looked interested. 'I borrowed three thousand, by the time I get it paid back I reckon I'll have given him over seven.'

CC sent a long breath of air out through his gritted teeth, making a whistling noise. 'That's criminal, surely, charging that amount of interest.'

'Exactly, but who is there to stop him?'

'I know what you're saying, but one way or another he has to be stopped. We can't have him going around playing dirty tricks on the town's good businessmen.'

'The rate I'm going I am at risk of losing my entire dairy.' George showed CC the letter.

'You're six weeks behind in repayments with the bank.'

'I'm struggling to pay Wilbur and fearful of what he'll do if I don't, he has taken a lien over the dairy.'

'Good God, you can't be serious.' George nodded that he was, indeed, very serious. 'The man's a complete swine.'

'Oh, I know that now. So, you can see why my payments to him have taken priority over the bank repayments and now they're threatening to foreclose.'

'There must be something we can do George, I can't see you lose your business over some lousy shyster like Wilbur Maxwell.'

'They're strong words CC, does that mean you will not be going into partnership with him?'

'This has really made up my mind, no, I won't; but let's keep that under wraps for now. I would like to do a little investigating into Wilbur … and his son too, if the truth be known.' CC stood to leave. 'Look, stop worrying now and get on with your business. Make the payment to Wilbur, we don't want to arouse suspicion. You have got seven days with the bank, we'll have something sorted out by then.'

The relief on George's face was obvious, he shook CC's hand and thanked him, glad to have a friend like him. With renewed hope he went back to his paperwork.

CC was back in his office when Sylvia Wright-Smith walked in. 'Wilbur Maxwell has been ringing you all morning, CC.'

'Oh, damn the man,' said CC, 'and what are you doing in on a Sunday anyway?'

'I left early last night to get to the party, so I have just been in here tying up loose ends.'

'What did he say anyway?'

'Who? Oh, Wilbur you mean? He said he'd drop by around about lunch time.'

'Hmmmm, we'll see about that.'

'You sound perplexed CC, whatever's the matter?'

'Never mind Sylvia, nothing I can't sort out.'

'Well, if you want my opinion, Wilbur Maxwell is the wrong partner for you. I don't trust him ... or his useless son. I would be steering clear of the Maxwells completely, and I'd be letting Cissy know that too.' Not waiting for a response Sylvia Wright-Smith bustled off, her nose in the air, happy to have voiced the opinion she had been wanting to give out for so long.

CC watched her go, a baffled look on his face. She was right of course, the more he had thought about it the more concerned he became about becoming involved with the Maxwells. But how to tell Cissy? A young girl's heart is a tender thing, and he wasn't ready to shatter his daughter's. He sat back into his large leather office chair and thought pensively. Maybe Paris wasn't such a bad idea after all? It would certainly get her away from Godfrey and into a new way of thinking. He would mull it over, some things are sent to us for a reason, and Paris could be one of those things.

Cissy didn't want to meet Ambros at the hamburger shop, the place was too close to the theatre, and she didn't want her father seeing her with 'the German'. He was looking smartly casual in his light blue sweater and casual trousers. He was sitting on a park bench, under a spreading oak tree, when Cissy arrived at the Footscray Gardens. She had enjoyed the train trip in and was happy that she was far enough away from prying eyes.

She greeted Ambros. 'What did you want to see me about?'

'I like you Cissy, you are a lovely girl, and I don't want to see you hurt.'

'Why would I be hurt?'

'How much do you know about Godfrey?'

'Well, we have been going steady now for nearly five months.'

'Exactly, not long at all. In that time how much do you really know him?'

'Sometimes I wonder. He doesn't really tell me a lot about himself, and he spends so much time doing his own thing — there are times when I wonder if I know him at all.'

'I don't want to burst your bubble Cissy, but maybe it's time you found out a little more about your fiancé. You deserve to know who it is you are really marrying.'

'How can I do that when he won't include me in things?'

'You know what I'd do?'

'What?'

'Enlist the help of your brothers. There is nothing like a brother to get to the bottom of his sister's affairs — especially when a man is involved.'

Cissy sat there thinking about it. A lot of what Ambros said made sense. She wondered why he had gone to all this trouble to bring her this caution. He was a good-looking man and Cissy liked him very much, she really did appreciate his concern for her. 'Now that we have that sorted out,' she suddenly said, 'why don't we have a stroll through the gardens, I have never been here before.'

Ambros agreed, he could think of nothing better to do on a Sunday than to stroll through the gardens with this interesting woman. What a fool Godfrey was, but then Ambros knew what Godfrey was all about. He had come here to save her from Godfrey, and he was hoping that's exactly what he had done. They chatted easily as they walked through the beautiful canopy of trees, immaculate lawns and serene swans swimming peacefully on the little lake, centrepiece of the Footscray Gardens.

Wilbur was ready to clinch the deal. He was tired of CC's constant delays and would get him to agree to the deal today. The kids were almost married now so they were practically family, that had to make a big difference to the security of the partnership. He strolled confidently into the theatre to find Sylvia Wright-Smith coming out of CC's office, 'Speak of the devil and he shall appear,' she said, referring to Wilbur of course.

'How dare she?' Wilbur thought, referring to him as the devil. He didn't much like the woman, he thought she was a busy body, always interfering in CC's business. After all, she was just a secretary, what right did she have to go sticking her nose in everywhere? He looked at her with disdain, 'Is he in?'

'Yes, you can go through.' As if he needed her permission. He strolled into CC's office as though it was his own.

'Morning CC, it is still morning, just. How have you pulled up after the big night?'

'I'm getting there Wilbur, and yourself?'

'All good CC. Have you had a chance to think about our situation?'

'I have Wilbur, and I'm reluctant to do anything at this stage.'

'What do you mean, reluctant? You've wanted to get the Maidstone theatre built and purchase the Altona theatre now for a while. What has changed your mind?'

'As you can see, the new Sunshine Theatre is nearly finished. What I have decided to do is to concentrate all of our efforts on that, consolidate our borrowings and then expand. I have had a talk to Martin down at the bank, it makes sense to him too.' CC wasn't telling Wilbur anything about the deal with Bruce Lansing, the less he knew about things the better.

'I can see you wanting to get things in the right order CC, but where does that leave me. I thought we had a good thing going here?'

'I'm not saying I'm leaving you out of anything at this stage Wilbur,' CC didn't want Wilbur getting suspicious. 'I am just putting the brakes on for a while.'

'I don't see why you want to wait CC, it doesn't make sense at all to me. I am not going to give up. I have got a little something in the pipeline that might sweeten the deal for you. Leave it with me. I'll get back to you in the next few days.'

'Whatever you think Wilbur,' CC said rising, indicating that this conversation was over. Wilbur took the hint and left CC's office. CC watched him go, wondering what on earth Wilbur could be up to now?

Chapter Twenty-One

WITH SPRING COMING to an end and summer settling over Melbourne, more and more people were taking advantage of the balmy evenings. Cissy was busy helping Hudson hang the posters they had just completed. CC had decided on re-running *Gone with the Wind*. The classic always drew great crowds, it seemed that people just couldn't get enough of Clark Gable, Vivien Leigh and the drama that surrounded the plantation, Tara.

The poster was magnificent, definitely one of their best. Cissy had painted Clark Gable carrying Vivien Leigh away from the fire that destroyed Tara. Hudson had done the lettering and the result was astounding. Cissy handed the glue bucket to Hudson as he stood on a ladder, pasting the poster to the billboard he had erected especially for this purpose. Behind him stood proudly, the almost finished building of the new Sunshine Picture Theatre.

The roof was under construction and the place looked enormous compared to the humble army hut that housed the current picture theatre. 'Congratulations,' said Eleanor as she approached them from behind, surprising both Cissy and Hudson. 'The poster looks outstanding, who's the brilliant artist on this one?'

'All credit goes to Cissy,' replied Hudson.

'Hudson did a great job on the lettering, I am just no good at that.'

'Well, it looks sensational, bound to pack the house out. I would just love to see it.'

'Well then of course you shall, my Dear,' said Hudson in his best Clark Gable voice.

Eleanor laughed, 'When's the opening planned for the grand new theatre by the way?'

'We are having it just before Christmas — a sort of Christmas celebration,' explained Hudson.

'Saturday December 8, 1945,' added Cissy.

'Gee wizz, you haven't got long to get things organised — that's only a few weeks away,' commented Eleanor.

'Panic will set in as soon as the roof is finished,' joked Hudson, 'which should be next week.' He then addressed Eleanor more seriously, 'Sweetheart, I have a couple of things to finish up inside, can you give me about thirty minutes?'

'I wanted to talk to you anyway Eleanor,' said Cissy, 'why don't we shoot across the road for a milkshake?' Eleanor agreed, and the girls left Hudson to take in the ladder and glue bucket, as they headed over to Peter the Greek's hamburger shop.

With the evening in its early stages, the hamburger shop was busy. Eleanor found the last remaining empty booth while Cissy ordered the milkshakes. Returning to the table she wondered how to tell Eleanor her problems, she decided to cut to the chase.

'Do you still get excited when Hudson touches you?' Eleanor was a little taken aback by Cissy's directness. She had never been this personal before and wondered why now?

'What do you mean?'

'You know, when he touches you do you feel anything, like a tingle or a bolt of lightning? What do you feel?' Eleanor looked at Cissy curiously, wondering why she suddenly needed to know all this. She then decided to share her feelings, she'd told Heather all about how Hudson made her feel, and she was sure she could trust Cissy with her innermost thoughts.

'When he touches me, it is like a livewire of electricity. And when he kisses me, well yes, it is like a bolt of lightning, but then it settles into something deeper — a longing, a need deep inside me and I want him so much.' She looked at Cissy's downcast face and knew something was wrong. 'Why do you ask, Cissy?'

'I needed to know what it was like,' Cissy explained as the milkshakes arrived. 'You see I felt that way with Godfrey at first, the electricity and all that, but it's not there anymore. It's gone, and I just wondered if everyone felt that way after a little while.'

'Oh Cissy, if you are not feeling any passion then why are you marrying this guy?' It was out, Eleanor had been wondering about Godfrey for so long and now this was her opportunity to make sure Cissy was moving in the right direction.

'I'm really beginning to wonder. Ambros said I should find out more about Godfrey. He suggested getting my brothers to do a bit of investigating.'

'Maybe that's not such a bad idea. I will have a talk to Hudson.'

'Will you?

'Yes, I will do it tonight. At least that will stop me worrying about my silly problems for a while.'

'What problems?'

'Oh, it's nothing really,' replied Eleanor, wondering if Hudson was ever going to pop the question, did he really want to marry her? She was beginning to wonder. 'Anyway, tell me a bit more about Ambros, he seems very interesting.'

'I quite like him actually,' confessed Cissy. 'He has asked me to sketch some of his designs.'

'Designs?'

'Yes, he is a fashion designer. His father has a business in Flinders Lane, I am going in there on Thursday for a look around.'

'Well, that is exciting, you will be so good at that,' Eleanor encouraged as she moved her straw around her milkshake, and then looking up, she saw Hudson approaching.

'I have a very special night planned for you tonight,' said Hudson, jiggling his eyebrows up and down at Eleanor. 'Come with me to the Casbah,' he said in a husky, amusing voice mimicking Charles Boyer in the famous film, *Algiers*.

Eleanor giggled and took Hudson's hand. Cissy wished Godfrey was even half as romantic as her brother was, she said goodnight and remained at the hamburger shop. She had arranged to meet Veronica, who should be along any minute. As she finished her milkshake, she wondered what Eleanor would say to her brother and where things would go from here.

Veronica was just passing the dairy on her way to meet Eleanor, when she noticed an unsavoury looking chap sneaking down the cobblestone drive. He was heading towards the stables, and she wondered what he could possibly want with the horses. She decided to follow him. She noticed that he'd dropped something into the feeding bin, she hid in the tack room as the miscreant found his way out of the stable. Veronica knew the horses would be fed from that bin and wanted to make sure it wouldn't happen before it was found out exactly what he had put in that bin.

She found a pencil and a note pad in the tack room and quickly scribbled a note: *Do not feed to horses, could be poison.* She left the stables, wondering who the man was and why he would want to bring harm to George's horses.

When she reached the hamburger shop, she was anxious to tell Cissy everything. Cissy adored animals and loved the big, strong draft horses with their long manes and hairy hooves. Why would anyone want to hurt these hard-working creatures? 'We'll tell Hudson, he's just across the road with Eleanor, he'll know what to do.'

Within minutes Veronica and Cissy burst into the picture theatre, not seeing Hudson anywhere they dashed into the auditorium. They were stunned to see the credits rolling for *Gone with the Wind* and the theme music filling the almost empty theatre, but for Eleanor and Hudson, who sat in the middle of the theatre, arm-in-arm. 'I hate to break up this private viewing, but I really need to speak with you urgently,' blurted Cissy. As unintentional as it was, Veronica was delighted she'd broken up their little tryst, while Cissy led her brother out of the auditorium to explain what had happened, Veronica decided to watch the film with Eleanor.

'*Gone with the Wind*? How come you're watching it now?'

'Hudson surprised me, I said I wanted to see it and so he put on this private show for me.'

'How very romantic,' Veronica sneered sarcastically. Eleanor let the remark wash over her, she had thought it very romantic too, and thought that just maybe tonight was the night that Hudson would propose.

Veronica was seething with jealousy. She was going to end this relationship between Hudson and Eleanor, one way or another. Cissy came back in, telling Veronica that Hudson wanted to talk to her. Veronica smiled as she left Eleanor with Cissy. 'I say, it's not everyone he puts on a private screening for, in fact I would have to say that this is a first,' said Cissy, excited for Eleanor.

Eleanor was chuffed by Cissy's candour. The show was beginning, and she was settling in to watch the drama unfold. 'It would have been romantic if he were still here.'

'He told me to stay with you until he gets back, he won't be too long, about twenty minutes.' Eleanor nodded, she wanted to watch the show with or without Hudson and as Vivien Leigh took centre stage, the girls watched, mesmerised.

When Hudson arrived home with Veronica, CC was surprised. 'Where's Eleanor?' he asked, a little indignant at this new lady's presence.

'She's fine Dad, she's at the theatre with Cissy. Veronica here has some very important information I thought you might like to hear.'

'Go on,' encouraged CC. Veronica explained what had happened, CC was incensed that George seemed to be everyone's victim at the moment.

'This good-for-nothing sounds like the very same person I saw Wilbur talking to down at the dump,' added Hudson.

'Wilbur Maxwell you mean?' asked Veronica.

'That's right,' answered Hudson.

'Now that's strange, because I saw Godfrey hanging around Mr Roberts' office the other morning, and it looked as though he was really upsetting Mr Roberts.'

'What were you doing at the dairy at that time of the morning?' asked Hudson.

'Look, don't worry about any of that now, obviously there is something underhanded going on and we need to get to George and let him know before those horses start dropping on him,' said CC, unknowingly rescuing Veronica from revealing her secret job at the dairy.

'Can you handle that Dad? I've got a date with Eleanor and I'm sure Veronica has other plans for the evening.'

'Yes, yes, of course. I have all the information I need now.'

Veronica felt as though she had earned a lot of kudos with the Cambridges, all she needed to do now was to put it to good use. Hudson drove her back to the theatre. She loved being in his car next to him, she felt as though it was where she belonged, however when they arrived, he went back in to be with Eleanor.

Clark Gable's handsome face filled the screen as the roguish *Rhett Butler*. Eleanor was glued to the screen and, putting his pointing finger to his pursed lips, Hudson shushed his sister, ushering her away from his seat and slipping in beside his sweetheart. Eleanor looked at him momentarily and smiled, then slipping her arm through his they settled in to watch the rest of the show together.

Cissy led Veronica out of the theatre, they had planned to spend the night sewing. Veronica had a new dress that needed altering and Cissy had offered to help her with that. With the Cambridge home being close to the theatre, the girls took off on foot in that direction.

The draft horses were unsettled when CC arrived at the stables. He noticed how easy it would be for anyone to access the outbuilding and thought that George should install some better security, especially given the circumstances. He had found George in his office doing some after-hours bookkeeping, worrying over the future of the dairy.

George was alarmed at the idea of anyone messing with his horses and immediately both men hurried to examine the feed. Mixed in with the oats and barley he noticed a smattering of crushed berries which he identified as deadly nightshade.

'How could anyone be so cruel?' asked George.

'Money can make some men do anything — and obviously Wilbur is one of those men.'

'I should never have got mixed up with that man.'

'Come now, I am the fool, I introduced you to him. We can all see his true colours now.'

The two men looked long and hard at each other. 'Look, I'm going to have a talk to Bruce Lansing. He has got a team of builders working all the time. I would like to see this dairy of yours a little more secure than it is, especially out here at the stables, given this latest happening. I'm sure he can have someone around in the morning.'

'I can't afford to ...'

'Did I mention money? No, I did not. You let Bruce and I sort this out. In the meantime, let's get rid of this feed and replace it with something these big beasts can eat safely.'

The two men proceeded to do just that, and George felt endeared to CC. He knew he had a friend he could trust, and he felt as though somehow, everything was going to be all right.

Miriam enjoyed the nights she could spend at home with her mother. The days were long at the clinic and working on Friday nights at the picture theatre meant she was on her feet for from eight o'clock in the morning until eleven o'clock at night. Monday to Thursday nights however were her nights at home, as well as all day Sunday. Her mother was holding her own at the moment and Miriam had her propped up in an armchair surrounded by pillows.

Mrs Worthing still enjoyed knitting and Miriam always loved to see the little baby clothes that were her specialty. Miriam wondered what in heaven's name they were going to do with all of these baby things, currently they had two trunk loads of them. She knew her mum was pining for grandchildren, but courtship and marriage were the furthest things from Miriam's mind.

When not tending to her mother, Miriam loved to bake. She was currently whipping up an orange cake, then later she planned on doing a batch of fresh Anzac cookies. Miss Wright-Smith had been most grateful for the cakes Miriam donated to the Lion's cake stand, but last week she told Miriam the cakes were getting too much for the Lion's Club, they weren't selling all the cakes and she hated to see them go to waste.

Miss Wright-Smith had been an absolute angel the way she had organised all of the caring people to look after her mum. She'd even now suggested to Miriam that if she wanted to bake, perhaps she should think about selling her cakes through some of the local food shops, like Peter the Greek's hamburger shop.

Now Miriam's baked delights were literally selling like hotcakes in little shops throughout Sunshine, Eleanor even had some at her hairdressers and supplied the busy café next door. Some of Miriam's mother's carers had wanted to get in on the action. Miriam supplied the ingredients and when the carers visited to look after her mother, they would also bake as her mother slept. It was a good arrangement, it gave the ladies something to do in the time they weren't tending to Mrs Worthing, and it put a bit of spare cash into their pockets. Extra income was hard to come by and the ladies liked to have this bit of money to call their own, saving it to spend on something special.

Miriam placed her orange cake into the oven. Her mother had dropped her knitting and fallen asleep. Miriam fussed around her, making sure she was comfortable. The doctor was due tomorrow, she wondered what his latest report would be.

THE END slowly dissolved onto the screen. Eleanor was in tears and dabbed at her eyes with her handkerchief, feeling so silly in front of Hudson. 'You must think I'm such a fool.'

'Not at all,' said Hudson, 'that's the absolute last thing I think you are.'

Eleanor looked at Hudson, eyes still glistening from tears. 'What *do* you think of me Hudson?'

Hudson stumbled for the right words, 'I-I think you're just sensational Eleanor, I love everything about you.'

'So, are you telling me that you love me Hudson?'

'Of course I love you, how can you not know that?'

'How can I know it if you don't tell me?'

'I love you, Eleanor Lansing. I love every little bit of you, and I can't get enough of you.' Eleanor looked at Hudson in anticipation, she thought that perhaps this was the moment, but she could see Hudson's questioning eyes, she knew he didn't have a clue that all she wanted was a proposal.

Letting out a breath and sagging her shoulders, she gave up. 'Well, I guess the show's over, we should go home.' Hudson thought Eleanor was behaving strangely and for the life of him he couldn't figure out why. He had professed his love to her, and she seemed to dismiss it fairly quickly. She had not said that she loved him, and Hudson was starting to wonder if there was something else on her mind. Women? Who could figure them out. Hudson led her out of the theatre, locking up as he left.

In the dining room of the Derrimut Hotel, the other Cambridge brother was romancing his sweetheart. Loretta and Seymour sat in the candlelit corner, dessert sitting on the starched white tablecloth, the waiter bringing them a cognac to complete their meal. 'I think the ideas Dad has for Cheltenham are going to be fantastic.'

Seymour had been telling Loretta all about CC's plans for expansion. The new Sunshine Picture Theatre was about ready to open, and Altona wouldn't be too far away, given the theatre was already there, CC just had to finalise the contract. The plans for Maidstone were truly magnificent and he knew his dad even had his eye on a little theatre down in the glen that was Bacchus Marsh.

Loretta loved to hear about the plans. She thought the theatre business was so exciting and she would dearly love to be a part of it. 'It all sounds so amazing Seymour, you must love being part of this incredible journey.'

'It is so different from where we used to be, on the land, battling to make a living during those years of drought, then of course I was off at the war. This life I lead now is charmed, at least I feel as though it is. Yet in lots of ways I feel as though I am doing something really important. Bringing the people pleasure in entertainment, a chance to escape from the drudgery of day-to-day life.'

'Exactly Seymour, that's definitely what you are doing — I'd just love to be a part of it too.'

'Well of course you can, when the new theatre opens up we are going to need more help. Besides, when we get married you are going to be a very big part of it then.'

Loretta put down her cognac, staring at Seymour open-mouthed. 'Did you say married?'

'Sure, I did, what did you think?' he asked, looking at her dumbfounded expression. 'What, don't you want to marry me, Loretta?'

'Of course, I do Seymour, of course I do. But this is so sudden.'

'Well, it's something I've been thinking about, but I have just been putting off asking you until poor dad sorts out Cissy, she really is in a bit of a mess.'

'Why is that?'

'Hmmm,' ruminated Seymour, 'he's not at all happy with Wilbur Maxwell and he thinks very little of Godfrey. In fact, I would like to take a bit of a closer look at Godfrey myself, see what he's up to.'

'Yes, you don't want your sister marrying him if he's not right for her.'

'Exactly. Then you can understand why I don't really want to announce our engagement just yet. I want to see Cissy sorted out. I think it would break her heart if we were shouting about our happiness while hers was falling into tatters.'

'See, that's what I love about you Seymour,' she said taking his hand across the table, 'you are so thoughtful.' Smiling, they looked into each other's eyes and Seymour thought his world would blow apart with happiness. Loretta was on cloud nine, she felt safe and was glad she was marrying a man with such thought for his sister. She knew she would have a very happy life being part of the Cambridge family.

Chapter Twenty-Two

CISSY LOVED GOING into the city. Flinders Street station was always abuzz with people going here and going there. City shoppers, workers, professionals — all striding purposefully to their destinations or anxiously heading home after a long day's work. Flinders Lane was a quick walk from the station and Cissy cut through one of the many glamorous arcades that joined Flinders Street to Flinders Lane.

She loved all the little shops, the curios, the cobblers and the patisseries. When she reached Flinders Lane, she turned left and headed towards Elizabeth Street, knowing Zimmerman designs was just down from the corner.

Ambros was delighted to see her, and Cissy was impressed with the beautiful dresses and coats that were displayed in the reception area. When Ambros took her out the back, where the sewing machines buzzed and the designers sat at drawing tables striving to come up with the next big thing, Cissy was very excited.

Ambros showed her his latest designs and she thought they were just beautiful. There were shimmering floor length gowns, there were striking tailored suits and stunning day dresses that finished just below the knee. Ambros was pleased with her reaction and explained how he needed someone to really capture his range and show it off in its best light. When Cissy agreed to the challenge, Ambros went in search of his father, leaving Cissy at his drawing desk to await his return.

The studio was quite messy in an arty sort of a way. Cissy was no stranger to that, often scattering her paints and brushes around her own studio, she felt quite at home. She was a little surprised however, when she was approached by a young man. At first, she wasn't sure whether he was a man or a lady, and when he spoke, he did so in the most feminine of tones.

'So, are you the latest squeeze?'

'What … what do you mean?'

'Ambros honey, are you his latest love doll?' he said, flapping his right hand about in an extremely unusual manner.

'Goodness me no, Ambros and I are just good friends.'

'That's what they all say honey.' She wished he would stop calling her honey. The way he talked and the way he behaved reminded her a little of some of Godfrey's friends, only he was more pronounced in everything he did. Just then Ambros returned.

'Norman, I see you've met the lovely Miss Cissy. She is going to be sketching the designs for our winter range.'

'Oooh how exciting,' exclaimed Norman, clapping his hands together quite gleefully. Cissy was a little overwhelmed by the man's exuberant manner, but the mood was broken when a tall man radiating confidence, strode over to investigate the young lady his son had brought into the studio.

Hans Zimmerman was a tall and confident man. His greying hair was very distinguished as were the grey tints in his moustache. He held himself erect and offered his hand to Cissy upon being introduced. To her surprise he took her hand and placed a gentle kiss, just on the top of her knuckles. Cissy had never had anyone kiss her hand before and didn't know quite how to respond.

Ambros sang the praises of Cissy, her wonderful drawings and artwork, and that she had been invited to study in Paris. 'Of course, you will go my dear, when will that be?' Mr Zimmerman asked.

'Oh, I don't know yet whether my father will allow me.'

'But he must. It is such an honour and Paris is the place for artists. It will change your whole perspective on life.' Cissy smiled, not knowing what to say to this imposing man. 'But enough of my drivel. When will you be starting with us?'

Ambros answered for her, 'Next week sometime, we have yet to fix a date.'

'Very good, I'll leave you to do that Son.' Hans Zimmerman left Cissy with a slight bow and Cissy noticed his impeccably tailored shirt, definitely silk, and sleek trousers. Everyone at Zimmerman Designs was superbly dressed, and she thought it little wonder seeing as that was their stock in trade.

As Ambros escorted Cissy from the building, Cissy inquired about Norman.

'Oh, don't worry about Norman,' said Ambros, 'he's as queer as they come.'

'What do you mean by that?' asked Cissy innocently.

'Goodness me my sweetness, don't you know what it means?'

'What what means?'

'Queer, homosexual, pansy.'

'You don't mean that he …' she trailed off, unable to voice what she was thinking.

'Does it with men, my sweetie, he likes men.'

'Oh my God that's disgusting,' said Cissy grimacing.

'Get used to it darling because you are going to meet a lot of it in this industry, half our staff are a little queer.' Cissy was lost for words, the visions flashing through her mind were things she was unable to cope with. 'Come on, be a big girl now, we're all grown-ups and these people aren't hurting us. As long as they are not chasing me down, I don't mind what they do.'

Cissy looked at Ambros, in a way he was right. What did it matter what people did as long as they didn't intentionally hurt others? 'Besides Cissy, if you go to Paris you'll be encountering a lot of homos over there — women too, watch out for them — they'll be after your pretty little body.' Cissy's cheeks flushed.

'Say, did you get your brother to investigate that fiancé of yours?' With the swift change of subject Cissy's mood changed.

'Eleanor was going to mention something to Hudson last night, I'll ask her if she did when I next see her.'

'Yes, well don't leave it for too long.' Cissy wondered what the urgency was but didn't follow through on the comment. As she left Ambros, she thought a little trip to Georges on Collins might be in order.

Wilbur left Bruce Lansing's home just after lunch, with the deed to the Balcombe Road land in his hand and a smile on his face. This was just the ammunition he needed to secure that share of Cambridge Theatres. As he left, Bruce walked back into his home to find his wife in the kitchen cleaning up the lunch dishes.

'I don't like that man, there is something about him,' Bruce said to her.

'Yes, well you don't have to like everyone you sell land to Bruce, otherwise we might not sell any.' He laughed.

'That's true Dear, but I do worry about Carleton Cambridge starting up a partnership with him.'

'Hmmm, well he hasn't finalised it yet, has he?'

'No, he seems a bit hesitant,' commented Bruce.

'A bit like his son.'

'What do you mean by that?'

'Oh you know, I thought he might have stated his intentions towards Eleanor by now,' explained Nancy, 'no mention at all of marriage.'

'Some men are a little slow at these things Dear.'

'Certainly not like you, it only took you a month and you were pleading with me to marry you,' laughed Nancy.

'Come on … I wouldn't actually call it pleading.'

'Oh phooey, all those flowers and chocolates.' Bruce approached his wife, clutching her around the waist and giving her the biggest hug, swinging her from side to side.

'Yes, you were irresistible then and you are still irresistible now.' Nancy squealed with delight at Bruce's antics, just as their youngest son came in from the garden.

'What's going on in here? What are you two up to?'

'Nothing Son,' said Bruce, releasing his grip on Nancy.

'We were just saying that it was high time Hudson either proposed to your sister or at least stated his intentions.'

'What? I always thought they would be getting married,' said young James.

'Well as far as we know nothing has been said along those lines. James pursed his lips, he was about to speak when the front doorbell chimed. 'I'll see who it is,' said Bruce, and left his son there talking to his wife.

Hudson was very worried about Eleanor's behaviour the previous night. He had given her that private screening on *Gone with the Wind* and even told her he loved her, yet something seemed to have crawled under her skin and stayed there. His father had always said there was nothing like flowers and chocolates to melt a girl's heart and he thought it was about time he delivered these very same gifts to his true love.

As he walked towards his car, he was peeved to see Veronica prancing vampily up the sidewalk towards him. She waved. 'Hi Hudson, where are you off to?'

He wasn't telling her because it was none of her business. 'Just running a couple of errands.'

'Need some company?' Damn the woman, it was the last thing he needed.

'No really, I'll be fine.'

'Have you done any more about that business with Wilbur Maxwell and Mr Roberts?' Hudson sighed, he really wished she wasn't involved in any of this, but she had seen what she had seen, and her report had hopefully stopped a disaster occurring for George and his horses, not to mention his dairy.

'I believe my father is taking care of things, that's all I know.'

'Say, I don't suppose you're going anywhere near Footscray, I really must pop in and see Eleanor, my hair's a mess.' Blast it. He didn't want to turn up at Eleanor's with Veronica in tow. 'Pleeeeez,' she pleaded, 'I'm running late, and the next train is not for twenty-five minutes.' What could he do? He was going to the salon and knowing his luck she would find him there anyway.

'Okay, hop in, but I need to pick something up on the way.'

When CC told Bruce all about George's plight and Wilbur's hand in it, Bruce was furious. 'I knew that man was up to no good,' Bruce said as he poured CC a Scotch. They were on his balcony, taking in the view while they discussed the situation. 'I just didn't like him from the word go.'

'And to think I nearly went into business with him.'

'You're not doing that now?'

'No, I am most absolutely not.' The two men looked at each other, establishing an understanding.

'What are we going to do to help George?' asked Bruce, 'And hopefully bring down that charlatan at the same time.'

'Well, I think first of all we need to devise a plot that is going to put Wilbur right in it, we demand back the money that George has paid to him, seeing as the three thousand pounds went back to Wilbur anyway.' Bruce nodded. 'Exactly. So, George gets back the three thousand quid he gave to Sammy, that tip worker, plus the interest he has been paying Wilbur.'

Unbelievable interest at that. Add to the fact that George stands to lose his entire dairy to Wilbur.'

'I say we snare Wilbur, tell him that if he ever does anything like that again, we will go to the police, and he will end up right where he belongs.'

'And what about your girl CC? Surely you can't let her marry into that family?'

'Hudson and Seymour are doing a bit of investigative work on Godfrey, and I'm pretty sure I know what they are going to find.' Bruce raised his eyebrows quizzically. 'Let's just wait and see on that one,' CC explained. 'What about this tip worker character ... this so-called Sammy?'

'I reckon my boys could take care of him; you develop some pretty big muscles in the building industry.' Bruce leaned forward to refill CC's glass, they toasted to the success of their mission.

Hudson glared at Veronica. The exquisite bouquet of roses he had bought for Eleanor was now marred. One perfect bloom of twelve, sagging sadly, twisted out of shape, its stem broken. 'Sorry Hudson, it must have snapped when I was getting out of the car.' For some reason Hudson didn't believe her. She had insisted on nursing the flowers when he had bought them. He had wanted to place them gently in the back seat, but Veronica had said they would be much safer with her. And now look what had happened.

He walked into the salon with the dozen red roses and a large box of Cadbury Roses Chocolates, Veronica swiftly on his tail. Eleanor's face lit up when she saw Hudson walking in with the romantic gifts, but then her face dropped a little when she saw Veronica's smug face, following Hudson like some conquering queen. 'Hudson,' she exclaimed trying to ignore Veronica and not being too gushy in front of her clients. One lady was seated under the dryer, and another was in the middle of a perm.

'I won't keep you my love,' greeted Hudson, 'I just thought that a beautiful lady deserved beautiful gifts.' Eleanor's clients were swooning over the romantic gesture as Eleanor accepted the flowers. The corners of her mouth downturned when she noticed the broken bloom. Hudson moved his eyes to the right, in the direction of Veronica. Eleanor was quick to pick up on the inference and immediately understood.

'What can I do for you Veronica?'

'Oh, nothing really. I just came over for a drive with Hudson.' Hudson was mortified that she would tell such a blatant lie.

'That's not true,' he blurted out, 'you told me you wanted Eleanor to look after your hair.' Veronica laughed at Hudson which made him all the more incensed.

'Come now Hudson, can't you take a joke?' She stroked his arm as she said it and then turned to Eleanor, 'Can you do my hair darling? I'm such a mess.' Eleanor was beginning to think that 'mess' wasn't exactly the right descriptive word for Veronica.

'You'll have to come back in an hour. I have to finish off with these ladies and then I am taking a thirty-minute break.'

'Mind if I join you on that break?' asked Hudson. Eleanor rose up on her tiptoes to whisper in Hudson's ear,

'Only if you are alone.' She then gently kissed his cheek. The colour was rising in Veronica's face.

'OK, I'll be back in thirty, I'll go and do a bit of browsing in Barkly Street.'

'Mind if I tag along?' said Veronica following Hudson out of the door, Eleanor's eyes followed her with a furious stare. Her clients had been witness to everything.

'I'd be watching that hussy if I were you love,' said one of them.

'She's after that handsome man of yours, nothing surer,' responded the other, and they went on to chat about the evil ways of jealous women. Eleanor told them how Hudson believed she had broken one of the roses as the evidence lay in the bouquet on Eleanor's reception desk.

CC was sporting his bowler hat as usual when he returned to the Sunshine Picture Theatre. Sylvia Wright-Smith was there to greet him, bringing a tray of tea into his office. 'Did you sort the situation out with George?'

'I think Bruce and I have a solution. I will get Wilbur in here tomorrow and tell him the way things really are, then I will go and have a talk to Martin at the bank. But once I get George's repayments back off Wilbur there shouldn't be too many problems.'

'Good CC, good. And have you thought any more about Cissy.' CC let out a sigh,

'I'm wondering if I shouldn't just let her go to Paris. I certainly don't want her marrying that Godfrey, not after all this. Paris would get her well away from him.'

Even Sylvia was beginning to soften on the idea of Paris, with Cissy so far away perhaps she could hope for more of CC's attention, she could look after him and the boys more without Cissy there to cook, clean and run after them, however she didn't want to appear too anxious. 'There's no rush is there? You don't need to make a decision yet, let's just see what happens with Godfrey.'

'I think that's a good idea. Hudson and Seymour are going to follow him around for a couple of days and nights, just to see what he's up to. All of us are getting the feeling that he is not what he appears to be.'

'Yes, I get that feeling too,' agreed Sylvia, nodding.

It was all Hudson could do to shake Veronica. Why wouldn't the woman leave him alone? She had tagged along with him all the way down Barkly Street and when he entered the motorbike shop for a browse, she was right behind him. 'Veronica, I need a bit of space. Please go and do whatever it is ladies do and leave me to admire these bikes on my own.'

'Oh, but I love motorbikes Hudson,' she purred.

'Well go and love them somewhere else, I just want to be on my own.'

Dejected, Veronica turned and left, but she hadn't given up, not by a long shot. Now, as Hudson walked back into the salon, Eleanor was in the middle of arranging the blooms, she removed the broken one. 'Such a pity,' she pined, looking at it.

'Yes, and I'm pretty sure I know how that pity happened.'

'Watch out for her Hudson, she's after you, nothing surer.'

'No … she knows we are together.'

'That doesn't seem to be stopping her.'

'You know I'm not interested in her, you are all any man could ever want.'

'And right now, I want some food,' she said, stopping Hudson mid-speech, 'there's a cheap little place on the corner. And by the way, the gifts are beautiful, but you do really need to start being a bit more sensible with your money — we might need it one day. Those roses must have cost a small fortune.'

'Worth every penny,' Hudson said as he opened the door for his true love.

Chapter Twenty-Three

LORETTA WAS ecstatic when she received the promotion at Coles. She was now manager of the entire cosmetics department. She couldn't wait to tell Seymour, but she wondered how he would feel about it. He had told her that she could become more involved in the theatres once they expanded. Now she wasn't so sure that was what she wanted. She had achieved this success all on her own and was very proud of that. It helped her family too, which was important. When she married Seymour how would that affect her family? There were things she needed to talk to him about.

So when he walked into Coles that morning, it seemed as though he was right on cue. 'Have you been reading my mind or something?' Loretta asked, standing behind the cash register.

'What do you mean?' he answered with a question.

'I was just thinking about you.'

'Well that is nothing — I am always thinking about you.' Loretta blushed.

'I have some news.'

'And I have some news,' responded Seymour. 'You first.'

'I have been promoted, I am now manager of the cosmetics department,' Loretta almost squealed with delight.

'Oh my sweet I am so proud of you.'

'So, what's your news?'

'I have bought a block of land.' Loretta was taken aback; this was a major purchase.

'You have? Where? Why?'

'Why? For us of course, we can build our dream home.' The thought of owning her own home had never even occurred to Loretta, she was overwhelmed with the power of it all — her new position, her own home, marriage. Seymour continued, 'It's just near Dad's, in Watt Street and very close to the theatre as well.'

'Seymour that's wonderful, it really is.'

'It's all wonderful darling,' said Seymour, taking Loretta's hands and pulling her towards him. Just then the store manager walked up, coughing behind his hand. Loretta quickly took the hint and dropped Seymour's hands, returning to her cash register. Seymour nodded his head at the manager and then quickly addressed Loretta before leaving. 'I cannot see you tonight my love, I am on a mission. I will tell all later.'

As Seymour left Loretta standing behind the cash register, the store manager gave her a pinched expression of annoyance, before getting on his way to the front of the store. Loretta watched him go, trying hard not to giggle at his self-importance, smothering her smirk with her hand, turning then to check on some of the stock.

Hudson found his father in the courtyard, reading the Melbourne Age while enjoying his breakfast of scrambled eggs and orange juice. 'Good morning Dad, lovely day.'

'Yes Son, have a seat.'

'How's the expansion going?'

'It's all good m'boy. With the new Sunshine Theatre nearly finished, I'm just about to secure Altona and then get started on Maidstone.'

'What about this new venture with Eleanor's father?'

'I'm off to see Vincenzo later in the week, get started on the plans.'

'Well, it's all very exciting. Where do I stand in all of this Dad?'

'What do you mean Son?'

'Well, we've never really spoken about it, and I notice you are including Seymour in your business discussions, and yet I am left in the dark,' Hudson was getting a little heated.

'Son, you have nothing to worry about — nothing at all. Your talents are very much needed. You are going to have to start on the new projection room soon, in fact I think you can get started now, a lot of the equipment has already arrived, you should be going through and checking it all.'

'I was going to do that today actually. But that still doesn't answer my question.'

'You have absolutely nothing to worry about. You're as much a part of this business as Seymour is. You each hold an equal share of ten percent, and with all that has been happening I am actually planning to put that up to fifteen percent.'

'So how are you funding the expansion now?'

'I am just slowing it down a little. I can secure Altona and I have the land at Maidstone, with Sunshine opening, our revenue will increase quickly, we can re-invest that and not have to worry about the likes of Wilbur. Sunshine and Altona will also give us more collateral, and Martin at the bank will like that.'

CC could see that his son still had his worries, he wanted to put his mind at rest. 'Look, how much do you still owe on that car of yours?'

'Not a lot actually, just over three hundred quid, but the repayments have been holding me back a bit, there's something I would really like to buy.'

Thinking that his son might be considering an engagement ring for Eleanor, he smiled, 'Let me take care of that for you Son, free you up financially and stop you worrying so much.' Hudson was pleased with this decision, he smiled and thanked his father. He knew Eleanor was getting a bit anxious about saving money, but there was really no need to worry, his father would always be around to help them out of a hole.

'Well, I need to get into the office, let me know if you need anything else.' CC picked up his bowler hat and headed towards the garage. Hudson saw *The Age* newspaper on the table and relaxed into his morning's read.

When CC arrived at the theatre, Wilbur was there to greet him. 'So, you must be nearly ready to open?' he commented as he stood watching the last of the roof being constructed.

'Yes,' replied CC. 'The fittings are arriving today, so they need to finish that roof. We have rows of six hundred seats coming through, plus ice-cream freezers and refrigerators for the kiosk.'

'Impressive CC, very impressive. Makes a man anxious to become part of it. Let's talk turkey shall we.'

'I thought we had settled that the other day, put the brakes on for a while.' CC was a bit annoyed, but he saw it as an opportunity to fix things up for George. 'However, I wouldn't mind a chat.' Wilbur chuckled to himself; he would have CC eating out of his hand in no time.

Sitting down in CC's office Wilbur began, 'Look CC, maybe we can go a little slower on the Maidstone deal, but I do know about your plans to build at Cheltenham.' CC nodded cautiously. 'And it's not as though I am trying to usurp you or anything, but I have acquired that land from Bruce.' CC was amused, he already had the deed to the land on which he planned to build the Cheltenham theatre complex, in his filing cabinet. What was Wilbur up to now?

'Is that so Wilbur, is that what you have there?'

'Yes,' said Wilbur, handing over the document. CC was struggling to keep the inquisitive smile off his face, what on earth could this be and what had Bruce sold him?

CC opened the deed. 'I see this is a very valuable piece of land,' said CC, as he rose to go to the filing cabinet. He opened the drawer and took out the deed to the land he and Bruce had agreed on, 'but you see Wilbur it is not my land.' The satisfied expression on Wilbur's face began to change. 'This land of yours, sure it's in Balcombe Road — but it's right down near Reserve Road, a long way from the throng of the shopping strip. This land would be useless for me, I don't know what you have planned for it.'

He threw his deed onto the desk and pointed out the address to Wilbur, 'This land here however, that belongs to CL Enterprises is a going to be a little gold mine.' Wilbur's face had dropped dramatically.

'But I am glad you dropped by Wilbur, because there is something I want to talk to you about.' Wilbur suddenly looked interested again.

'Old George Roberts is doing it tough.' Wilbur nodded, wondering where this was going. 'You loaned him the money to get him out of a hole.' Wilbur agreed. 'But now he's in a worse hole than ever because your interest rate is too high, and your demands are unreasonable.'

'Demands? What demands?' Wilbur said defending himself.

'You know exactly what I am talking about Wilbur,' CC's anger was rising. 'You set the whole thing up, paid some slimy little bastard down at the council works to blackmail George. What are you planning on doing Wilbur, taking over the dairy when the bank forecloses?'

Wilbur was exasperated, how did CC figure this whole thing out? As if reading his mind CC said, 'Hudson saw you down at the tip with that council worker,' Wilbur's mind flashed back to the dairy van he'd seen there the other day. 'I went to George, and he told me everything, it didn't take a lot to figure it out from there.'

'Look CC,' said Wilbur in a desperate attempt to redeem himself, 'George did the wrong thing. He shouldn't go putting it around where it doesn't belong.'

'More like you hired some tramp to get George totally drunk and have those photos taken. It's absolutely despicable Wilbur.' Wilbur was silent, CC continued, 'So I'll tell you what is going to happen now. You are going to pay back George all of the money he has given you in repayments and I have a couple of lads who are going to be paying a visit on Sammy. I want all and every photo and negative destroyed and I never, ever want to hear anything about this again. You think your little blackmail scheme was brilliant — well wait until you see the sorts of schemes that we can cook up.'

'Are you threatening me CC?'

'Bloody oath I am. Now get out of my office and get that money back to George. My business with you is over.'

Wilbur was furious, never one to be defeated he picked up his deed and left with the final parting words, 'You're going to regret this.' CC ignored him as he watched him storm away, glad to be rid of such abhorrence, and then, picking up the deed to the Cheltenham land, he chuckled at Bruce's wisdom of selling Wilbur the wrong parcel of land.

Miriam's home was one of many built along the side of the railway tracks. Cissy thought of how noisy it must be as she approached the small fibro home. It was painted in a pale blue and the front yard featured the burnt brown remains of what was once grass, with a few surviving weeds here and there. Cissy thought of her own garden and how depressing this one was, she would like to do more to help Miriam if she could.

Being a Wednesday evening Miriam was in for the night. When she answered the door and saw Cissy standing there with a huge basket of fruit, she was delighted. Cissy entered the house to the glorious aromas of Miriam's baking. 'My you are so clever, what are you cooking?'

'Just a few cakes, it is nothing, you are the clever one with your beautiful artwork.'

Cissy didn't want to talk about herself. 'No seriously, your cakes are delicious, Peter the Greek can't get enough of them.'

'Well, he does have me run off my feet a bit, and I am now supplying two other shops as well as Eleanor selling my cupcakes. Mrs Johnson has now offered to pitch in — she makes the best cream sponges ... and her lamingtons — yum. With three of the other ladies helping as well, we are really churning out the cakes.'

'You know you could really get yourself a little business going here,' as she spoke those words Cissy noticed a collection of baby clothes in a basket on the couch. 'My goodness, look at these gorgeous little things.' Then thinking more about what she was seeing, 'Is there something you're not telling me?'

'Don't be ridiculous,' said Miriam taking the baby booties Cissy was holding up, 'this is just my mother's hobby. I suppose she is ever-hopeful as well.'

'They're just beautiful, you two should go into business. The Bake 'n' Booty. Your cakes and your mothers cute little baby things.'

Miriam laughed at the thought of her in her own business, 'That's crazy, The Bake 'n' Booty.'

'No it's not … anything is possible. Say, how's your mum doing anyway? That's what I came to find out.'

'I was just about to check on her when you arrived, won't be a minute.' When Miriam left the room Cissy remained, looking through the gorgeous little baby things Mrs Worthing had created.

Suddenly she heard the most mournful scream from Mrs Worthing's bedroom, then Miriam's voice crying out, 'Mum!' Cissy rushed to her aid. Miriam was there, hand to her mouth, tears in her eyes, looking down at the still body of her mother. Cissy tried to comfort her, then, thinking it best to leave her alone to grieve over her mother, she telephoned the only person she knew who could help.

Miss Wright-Smith told Cissy that she would be there right away. Poor Mrs Worthing had passed away and Sylvia Wright-Smith would know how to handle things and help the distraught Miriam.

Seymour wondered what Godfrey was doing in Melbourne's red-light district. Fitzroy Street St. Kilda was becoming increasingly known for prostitution, strip clubs and sleazy bars. Seymour sat across the road, keeping an eye on Godfrey as he strolled past various bars. The sidewalk was thronging with people from all backgrounds. Young and old, white, black, Asian. What really stood out to Seymour was the female impersonators, strutting boldly in their hideously outrageous clothes and make-up, the scene was enough to make Seymour sick, but Godfrey didn't seem to mind. Many of them pawed at him when he went by, beckoning him to give them a little something, but he just laughed and kept going.

Seymour got up from his seat and began walking, as he was losing his line of sight on Godfrey. He noticed him talking to a young man and the two of them then walked into an alleyway between two bars. It was about as seedy as you could get and Seymour hated the idea of following, but the war had showed him worse, and he was determined to keep going.

His leg just about healed now so he had no trouble keeping up, especially as the two seemed in no hurry at all. Godfrey's new friend seemed quite drunk, staggering a little from time to time. They reached a recessed doorway and decided to stop there. Moving into the doorway Seymour almost lost sight of them. Carefully he crept along the wall, wanting to get a closer look at what they were up to.

Shock struck Seymour when he saw Godfrey passionately kissing this young man. The young man held Godfrey's hands to his own chest, revealed now through his open shirt. The man was moving Godfrey's hands up and down, caressing his own breasts as he passionately kissed Godfrey back.

Seymour was momentarily spellbound, he had never seen two men in such an embrace, and he had seen a lot during the war. Godfrey opened his eyes to look at his lover, when the first thing he saw was a man standing in the shadows watching them. He smiled at the man, in a come-on sort of way, almost inviting the man to join them, until he noticed who it was.

Godfrey froze when he made out the person to be Seymour. Seymour gave him one last look, and then, with a slight shake of his head, turned on his heel to leave. He'd seen enough. The young man was tampering with Godfrey's trouser belt, Godfrey laughed and got back to business, what did he care what Seymour had seen? With his father now not entering into business with CC, he believed it was all over with Cissy anyway — he'd never felt more relief in his life actually, except maybe for what this young man was doing to him right now.

Chapter Twenty-Four

THE NEW SUNSHINE Picture Theatre was now standing in all its brand-new glory. Peter the Greek was outside his hamburger shop admiring it when CC pulled up in the Humber Super Snipe. Peter gave him a wave as CC got out of his car, bowler hat in place, he went into his grand new theatre.

Hudson had erected scaffolding in the foyer and, clad in his paint splattered white overalls, was busy painting the decorative ceiling plaster mould. It was the framing piece for the theatre's huge chandelier. An elegant dome housed the chandelier, which was surrounded by a decorative rose and leaf pattern that Hudson was painstakingly painting — every tiny leaf and rosebud in a hue of reds and pastel greens. It was a work of art and his father stopped to admire it.

'Magnificent Hudson, you are doing a magnificent job.' Hudson smiled at the acknowledgement. 'How's the projection room coming along?'

'The rest of the equipment should be arriving this afternoon; I will continue on in there then.'

'Excellent,' replied CC, and headed towards his new office.

It was just off the foyer and far more spacious than his previous office in the grain shed. He ran his hand over his sizeable new leather topped desk, then tested out his new leather desk chair. Everything was to his liking. He moved the telephone a little to the right and slid the Teledex to its correct spot. He leant back in his chair, looking around like a very contented and satisfied man, letting out an agreeable sigh, only to have his thoughts interrupted by Seymour.

'Hudson's doing a fine job with that ceiling,' were his younger son's first words to him that day. CC agreed, wondering what Seymour was doing here when he should be organising the stock for the kiosk. 'I wanted to talk to you, it's about Godfrey.' Hudson had come down from the scaffolding and had heard his brother's words, he rushed into his father's office before Seymour could close the door.

'Hang on brother, I don't want to miss out on this. I have been wondering what happened last night.'

As Seymour described the unsavoury scene, CC, while finding the entire thing extremely distasteful, was not surprised. 'I had a feeling all along, I didn't want to believe it. I didn't want to believe my sweet, innocent daughter could fall for such a cad.'

'But isn't it a good thing we found out when we did?' commented Hudson. 'Does Cissy know yet?'

'No, I haven't had a chance to tell her, she took off early this morning, apparently going into the city to sketch for the German.'

'Hmmm,' mumbled CC, 'there's another problem, the German.' The brothers looked at each other, they could see that CC wasn't happy about Cissy's growing relationship with Ambros, but right at this point in time they let it ride. They had already sorted out one of their sister's problems, perhaps this other pending issue would never develop into anything.

'Well, let's get on and get things organised for our opening shall we,' said CC, escorting his two sons from his office. 'Everyone will be here you know. The mayor, the councillors, even old James McCall's coming along.' The family was happy. Part of their dream was about to come true, and the town was ready to celebrate with them.

It was all foreign to Cissy, but it was very exciting. People were chattering while frantically getting models prepared to parade the gowns. Cissy was there ready, pencil in hand, eager to sketch these wonderful creations as they fell sinuously over the lovely female bodies. It was a big responsibility and Cissy was taking it seriously. She would do her very best to make these creations shine. She would sketch them now, and then, taking the sketches to her home studio, she would use water-colour to complete their texture and tone.

She remembered a particular grade of pencil she had left in the back room, it seemed as though the models wouldn't be ready for ages yet, so she believed she had plenty of time to duck out the back to get it. She hadn't noticed at first, her fiancé standing by Norman's desk. Norman was just returning from the stationery cupboard when he saw him, 'Godfrey darling what brings you here?'

Cissy stood stock still, disappearing behind a high pile of fabric. 'I was in the area; just thought I'd pop in.' The two kissed, European style, each cheek. Cissy thought it was very odd behaviour for two men.

'So, how's it all going with your engagement? What are doing marrying a woman darling, you should be down on your knees proposing to me,' said Norman, signalling with three fingers for Godfrey to get down on his knees.

Godfrey laughed. 'Don't worry about the ridiculous engagement. After Cissy's old man threw a pile of the proverbial in my father's face, I doubt I want anything more to do with her and with her family.' On hearing that Cissy burst out from behind the pile of fabric. Ripping her ring off her finger she thrust it at him.

'Well guess what Godfrey? You won't have to, you …. you queer!' Godfrey was shocked, but arrogance got the better of him.

'Come, come now poppet, don't go getting your knickers in a twist,' he said derogatorily.

'Oh, I wish I'd never met you!' Cissy explained, becoming more and more upset.

As Norman and Godfrey gave each other a stunned look of amazement, Ambros had, on hearing the commotion, come out to the back room. 'What is it?' He then saw Cissy in tears. 'What is it Cissy?'

'I've just broken it off with that ...' she pointed at Godfrey, 'that queer.'

'Don't worry angel,' he said, taking her in his arms, 'I am sure you've done the right thing.'

'Well, a great friend you turned out to be,' retorted Godfrey.

'I was never your friend Godfrey,' replied Ambros. 'You just always wanted to hang around here because there so many lovely little boys for you to play with.' Godfrey was shocked. 'Well guess what mate?' Ambros said angrily. 'Game's over. You take your weird and sick pansy tendencies elsewhere, we've got a business to run here.'

Norman was horrified but stood where he was as Godfrey left in a huff. Norman valued his job and realised that he needed to toe the line and not let the likes of Godfrey come into his workplace upsetting the flow of things. Ambros turned his attention back to Cissy who was still in his arms, he stroked her back, gently comforting her.

Cissy felt oddly comfortable in Ambros's arms but knew she must now pull herself together. 'Thank you Ambros, I'll be all right now.'

'Ready to face the challenge of my creations?'

'Most definitely,' replied Cissy, and accepting Ambros's handkerchief, she wiped her eyes and shook off her blues. She was glad she had ridded herself of Godfrey, he had caused her nothing but grief and worry, and she was now ready to face the world with her talent and her new-found direction. As she left the back room to sketch the creations, Norman scurried over to pocket the discarded ring.

Hudson finished up early at the new theatre. He had to wait for more equipment to arrive and had a very important mission in Footscray. He had phoned Eleanor to say he would pick her up at five, and it was now getting onto four o'clock. Leaving his car in the garage, he hurried to the station to catch the train to Footscray.

On the trip in he wondered about Eleanor, something was bothering her, he knew it and he would love to know what it was. He would pick her up tonight and take her for a spin. With the wind in her hair and her arms wrapped around him how could she help but be happy.

Perhaps they would go over to Altona, check out the picture theatre there and have a stroll on the beach. That would be romantic. He reached his destination and alighted the train, hurrying to the shop before it closed.

The salesman was delighted to see Hudson return, he had his bike all ready for him and Hudson had his cheque book and pen poised. He couldn't believe he was now the proud owner of a gleaming new motor bike, he hopped on board and headed straight for the salon.

Eleanor wondered whoever it could be, having the cheek to park a motor bike right on the pavement outside her shop, and the thing was he looked as though he was headed right inside. Then as he turned around, she realised who it was. What was Hudson doing on a motorbike? She loathed the things.

He entered the shop with a grin from ear to ear. 'Don't you think she's a beauty?' he asked.

'Who does it belong to?' asked Eleanor.

'It's mine, all mine. I just bought it.' Eleanor was horrified.

'What do you mean you just bought it?'

'At Mitchell's Motorbikes, down in Barkly Street.'

'What do you need a motorbike for Hudson, you have a car?'

'I thought we could have a bit of fun, go for a ride.'

'I'm not going anywhere with you on that thing.' Hudson was beginning to see that she was serious. 'No Hudson, just go, please. I don't know why you are wasting all of your money on these stupid things when you should be saving for our future.'

Hudson didn't know what to say, and when he started to, she stopped him. 'Just go Hudson,' she said again. 'Please just go.' Hudson did as he was told, his bubble completely burst as he dejectedly got onto his motor bike and headed back to Sunshine. He really couldn't understand why she was so upset. Women — who knew?

Sylvia Wright-Smith had done everything she could for Miriam. She had called the undertakers and consoled Miriam as much as possible. She had called Dr Wallace who immediately came to pronounce

Miriam's mother dead and then Miss Wright-Smith had insisted that Miriam take the week off with full pay.

The funeral was to take place on the following Monday, Miriam had said there would not be a lot of people attending, only those who had been caring for her as well as her sister from Preston. Miss Wright-Smith suggested that they have a small afternoon tea at the Worthing home, and for her not to worry about anything as she would take care of everything. Miriam however, insisted on baking some cakes, to keep her mind off things.

Being impressed with Miriam's baking, Miss Wright-Smith thought that yes, it probably would keep her occupied. She would take care of the savouries and refreshments. Miriam had a little put aside for the funeral and Miss Wright-Smith had helped her come to a payment arrangement with the funeral parlour. She felt sure CC would foot the bill for the few refreshments they would be serving.

She left Miriam alone, giving her time for mourning. She felt sorry for the girl, who was now all alone in the world. Still, she had a roof over her head, some very good friends and solid employment. She was sure that Miriam would come out of her sorrow eventually and make a success of her life. Now without her mother to look after, the only way was forward. Having no children of her own, Miss Wright-Smith vowed to keep an eye on her to make sure she was coming along well.

Hudson hung up the telephone in the hallway of their home. He wore the face of a beaten man as he made his way into the kitchen. 'What's happened to you?' asked Seymour. 'I thought you'd be on top of the world with that new bike of yours.'

'To be honest brother, I'm not really sure.'

'Oh boy, you'd better tell me all, obviously woman trouble.'

Hudson explained what had happened with Eleanor. How she was furious that he had bought the bike and told him to just leave. How she was upset the other night, even though he told her he loved her. How she was always going on about the future and then going all quiet on him, he was befuddled — didn't know what she wanted him to say.

'How stupid can my brother be?' asked Seymour. Hudson looked at him, miffed. 'Listen Huddo, isn't it about time you bought the girl a ring?'

'What do you mean? Marry her?'

'Why not? And an engagement ring would be a start.' Hudson just stared at him, shell-shocked. 'Well you do want to marry her, don't you?'

'Yes of course I do, but ...'

'Then let her know. I mean no wonder she's upset with you. You tell her you have a big surprise for her and then turn up on the stupid motorbike. Girls don't like motorbikes Huddo, they like diamonds.'

Hudson shook his head; he was beginning to see the error of his ways. 'What am I going to do now, she's gone home to her parents?'

'Don't do anything tonight Huddo, let her settle down. Then tomorrow I suggest you go and call on her, ring in hand, and ask the fair maiden to be your wife.'

Hudson agreed, he would take the bike back tomorrow and then go shopping for a diamond ring. He'd bought the bike on the guarantee that he could return it within seven days if he cooled off, he was silly to think Eleanor would love it as much as he did. He decided to go down to the Derrimut for a drink, drown his sorrows and prepare himself for a big day tomorrow. 'You up for a drink?' he asked his brother.

'Don't mind if I do.'

And so, the brothers left for a pot or two at the Derrimut Hotel, while Eleanor was at home revealing all to her family.

Chapter Twenty-Five

IN FRONT of the brand-spanking new Sunshine Picture Theatre, a truck was unloading the rows and rows of seating, ready to be installed in the cinema. The seats for the front stalls were dark blue in colour, of a leathery-vinyl type material and slightly less padded than the more deluxe red velvet versions reserved for the higher paying lounge customers.

It was Saturday morning when Hudson pulled his motorbike up to the kerb, in front of the delivery truck, he didn't notice Veronica in the hamburger shop across the way. Miss Wright-Smith was walking towards the picture theatre when she noticed the motorbike. 'Goodness gracious me Hudson, what have you gone and done now — and what do you think you are going to do with this contraption?'

'Panic ye not, Miss Wright-Smith, it is going back today. I am replacing it with something far more useful.' As they entered the theatre together, Veronica approached the motorbike. Hudson was only in the theatre for a minute or two before he came back outside to see Veronica sitting on his bike, he was incensed with her boldness.

'Veronica, what do you think you are doing?'

'Nice bike Hudson, I'd love a ride.'

'Come on, off you get. I have important business to get on with.'

'Oooh, important business,' she said invidiously. Hudson's ire was up. He wanted to get this woman away from his bike and get on with his mission.

'As a matter of fact, I am going to buy a ring for Eleanor,' he blurted out and was sorry as soon as the words left his mouth. The shocked look on Veronica's face was hard to hide, but she regained her composure quickly as her meddling mind ticked over.

'A ring hey? I could help you with that, show you the sort of ring that a woman like Eleanor would love.' Hudson thought about it and did think that the idea made a lot of sense. He really wouldn't have the first clue of what type of ring to buy Eleanor.

'Well okay, why not? You probably would know what she would like better than I would.' Veronica remained on the back of the bike while Hudson managed to get on around her. As they took off, she was extremely contented, her arms wrapped firmly around his waist and her cheek pressing into his back. That was the picture that Cissy got as she came around the corner, watching the bike disappear into the far distance along Hampshire Road.

Bruce and Nancy sat in the sitting room listening to their daughter's woes. They didn't notice their youngest son, James, in the kitchen, listening to every word. Bruce was upset with Hudson for being such a thoughtless idiot. What did he want with a motorbike? He decided to give CC a call and get his thoughts on the matter. As he left the room to use the phone, James left by the back door, in search of his brothers.

'Well, yes I heard about it,' said CC as he listened to Bruce almost exploding over the phone. 'The boy can be a bit rash at times Bruce, I know. I'm a bit annoyed.'

'Is he ever going to state his intentions to my daughter?'

'I think you might be surprised there Bruce, I think the penny may have dropped.'

'Yes, but do I want him? An impulsive spendthrift!'

'Give the lad a chance Bruce, don't you remember when you were twenty-two?'

Bruce calmed down a bit, seeing CC's side of things. CC changed the subject, 'So I spoke to Martin at the bank.'

'About?'

'The situation with George. George got the money he'd paid Wilbur on loan repayments and was able to bring the bank loan almost up to date. Martin is happy to let him pay a little extra each fortnight until he catches up.'

'That's great news CC, and that swine Wilbur?'

'Oh, I don't think he'll be bothering us now Bruce, except you may have him bothering you over there in Cheltenham with that land that you sold him.'

'He'll have a hard time finding builders over this side of town CC, my boys have seen to that.'

'And what happened with that snivelling little coward of a council worker?'

'Well let's just say I don't think he'll be doing any more blackmailing for a while, and I don't think he'll have anything to do with Wilbur or Godfrey again.'

'That's good news Bruce. And look, try not to worry about your daughter. I am sure Hudson has seen the error of his ways and I think he'll be along before you know it to try to make amends with Eleanor. Just wait and see what he comes up with.'

'If you say so CC, I suppose we should leave our kids to sort out their own differences.'

'Quite right Bruce, I'll see you next week to review stage one of the plans for Cheltenham.'

'You got it CC.'

The jewellery shop was quiet when Hudson and Veronica arrived. The shop attendant was all over them. Desperate for a customer and a sale he immediately assumed that the two were a couple. While fussing all over Veronica, Hudson clearly pointed out that they were not getting engaged. 'No, no. This girl has just come to help me choose, she is not my fiancé.'

As they browsed through the rings, Veronica kept leading Hudson in the direction of rubies, while the shop attendant keeping guiding him in the direction of diamonds. Hudson remembered Seymour's words about ladies preferring diamonds to motorbikes and decided to take the shop attendant's advice, he was never that keen on Veronica's ideas anyway and wondered why he had brought her along in the first place.

The ring was quite spectacular, featuring a two-carat brilliant cut diamond superbly set in platinum and surrounded by clusters of smaller diamonds on an eighteen-carat gold band. Hudson had a slight conniption at the price when he first heard it, but the return of the motorbike had topped up his wallet and he could afford it, the fact that he hadn't yet paid off the car was of no concern to Hudson. The shop attendant placed the ring on Veronica's finger, that didn't bode well with Hudson, but he didn't make a scene. While Veronica admired it, imagining the true meaning of the ring, Hudson politely asked the shop attendant to remove the ring and wrap it. Veronica could see that Hudson was annoyed, she was annoyed herself.

As Hudson placed the ring in his jacket pocket, Veronica was green with envy, if only someone would spend that much money on a ring for her. They left the jewellery shop and walked to the train station. Hudson was anxious to get back to the theatre and work on the new projection set-up but at the same time he couldn't wait to see Eleanor. He would surprise her tonight by dropping in unannounced. He couldn't wait to see the look on her face when she saw that incredible engagement ring.

When Veronica sat next to Hudson on the train, he moved along the black vinyl bench seat a little further to make some space between them, he then placed his jacket in the space to define the boundaries, he didn't really want his leg rubbing on hers. Veronica noticed the jacket and remembered which pocket Hudson had placed the ring in at the jewellers. She placed her handbag onto her lap and decided to leave Hudson to his thoughts for a little while.

As the train rocked gently on the tracks, Hudson found himself dreamily looking out of the window. He was lost in his thoughts of

Eleanor and their engagement and did not notice at all when Veronica slipped her hand into his jacket pocket and removed the ring. Quickly placing it into her handbag, she smiled surreptitiously and closed her hands over her bag. When they arrived at Sunshine Station, Hudson was none the wiser, he had bought Eleanor an engagement ring and he was about to present it to her tonight.

Wilbur walked into his billiard room and firmly shut the door behind him. Godfrey was just pouring their drinks and offered his father a glass as he approached him. 'So, the engagement's all over then?'

'I'm afraid so dad.'

'Not your fault Son, if the little whore sees more value in someone like that fairy German bloke, then she deserves what's coming to her.' Godfrey had of course lied to his father. He lived in fear of his father finding out he was homosexual. The very fact that his father accused Ambros of being a pooftah said it all. The only thing different about Ambros was his beautifully designed clothes, he was as straight as they came, and Godfrey had been wondering whether Cissy had actually been seeing him on the side, the entire time of their courtship. Godfrey was confident that his father had no idea about his sexuality, and he preferred to keep it that way.

'So, what was the real reason for calling me in Dad?'

'Well to be honest Son, I'm very upset with the whole thing.'

'Look Dad I tried,' said Godfrey leaping to his own defence, believing his father was going to continue on about his broken engagement.

'That's not what I mean, the engagement's over. It was never going to work out anyway given my current situation with CC, but I've got to tell you I am not happy about it.'

'What, you mean with the way CC treated you?'

'Exactly Son, exactly.'

'Well, I couldn't agree more, but there's not much we can do about it now.'

'You're always a bit slow off the mark Godfrey. There's plenty that can be done, and we'll make sure it is.' Godfrey looked at him quizzically. 'Revenge my lad, revenge. If you can't have your way, then you can have revenge.' He lifted his glass, 'And believe me lad, revenge is very sweet, very sweet indeed.'

The afternoon sun was filtering an amber glow through the windows of the design studio when Cissy was finishing for the day, 'I won't be in tomorrow,' she said, 'in fact I can't really make it in until Monday now. I have to help with the drapes at the theatre as well as a thousand other things that will need doing before the opening. Will that be all right?' she asked Ambros.

'Of course, Cissy, you have outlined all of the sketches now and they are looking magnificent, so you will have them completed by the end of next week without any problem?'

'Yes of course, and thank you for your support, Ambros, I couldn't have got through all of this without you.'

'I care about you Cissy; I care about your happiness.'

Cissy looked at the genuine concern in Ambros's eyes. The more she got to know him the more she liked him. 'Cissy, will you go out with me?' he asked, taking her hand. Cissy felt that familiar jolt of electricity that had stopped what seemed so long ago with Godfrey. She knew it was too early to think about another romance, but she was finding it harder and harder to resist this good-looking German with the caring nature.

'When?' was her simple answer.

'Sunday, let's do it Sunday. I know how busy you are on Fridays and Saturdays. What about a nice picnic on Sunday? We can go to the Lerderderg Gorge.'

'Lerder-what?' asked Cissy with a bit of a laugh.

'Lerderderg Gorge. It's a pleasant drive from Sunshine. You will love it.'

'So, what can I bring?'

'Don't you lift a finger, I will pick you up at ten thirty and I will have everything organised.' Cissy smiled. Godfrey never did anything like this for her. She reached up to Ambros and gave him a little peck on the cheek before turning and heading for Flinders Street Station. In spite of her recent break up, Cissy had never felt happier.

Strangely enough Hudson felt very nervous as he approached the door of the Lansing home. Upon knocking he was a bit peeved to be greeted by Eleanor's older brother, Edward, and Edward didn't look that pleased to see him. 'Ah, if it isn't the Cambridge chap, what can I do for you?'

'I am here for Eleanor.'

'Is that right? Well, I can tell you you're the last person she wishes to see.' Suddenly Edward was joined by younger brother James and middle brother, Clive. Hudson was starting to feel a little uncomfortable.

'What do you mean by upsetting our sister?' asked James, who felt he had the right to lead this vendetta since he was the one who overheard his parents discussing Eleanor's woes regarding Hudson. He stepped out of the front door, followed by his brothers, forcing Hudson back into the garden.

'Look, I'm sorry, I know I was an idiot, but I am here to make amends.' Eleanor had heard her brothers out in the front garden and wondered what they were up to now, always getting into a spot of bother. She went to the front door to see Hudson standing there surrounded by them.

Her brothers were big fellows, and leering over Hudson with threatening looks that would be enough to frighten anyone. She was just about to interrupt when she heard Hudson say, 'I am going to ask her to marry me.'

Eleanor caught her breath.

'Like hell you are,' said James.

'Yeah, she's our sister,' said Clive, 'and we'll decide who she marries.' By this time Eleanor was incensed. How dare her brothers!

'Stop it you idiots,' she said, bursting through front door. Eight male eyes turned to her. 'What did you say Hudson? Tell me what you just said.'

'I said I want you to marry me ... please.' He was looking at her with those gentle eyes and she was melting by the moment.

'So, where's the ring then?' asked Edward smartly. Hudson reached into his pocket. Realising it wasn't there he frantically began patting his other pockets, he couldn't believe this was happening.

'Yeah, it's all a big joke to you isn't it. You'd say anything to have your way with her again.'

'Hudson?' Eleanor questioned, looking for an answer.

'I ... I ... it must have been Veronica.'

'Veronica, what is it with you and Veronica?' Eleanor said, her voice rising. 'Oh Hudson, and I really believed you wanted to marry me.' She turned, in tears, running into the house in tears, yelling to her brothers as she went, 'And he hasn't had his way with me either.'

Hudson was shattered, he just knew Veronica had stolen the ring and he was furious. He turned sharply and headed back to the car. 'And don't come back again,' the brothers called after him as he drove off in a puff of dust, he would wring that Veronica's neck if it was the last thing he did.

Chapter Twenty-Six

IT WAS JUST one week to the opening and there was so much to be done. People were walking by and popping their head in the door, looking at the magnificent new theatre excitedly. Cissy was heading into the auditorium and noticed Seymour stocking the bar. 'Have you seen Hudson?' she asked him.

'No, but the last time I did see him he was pretty riled up, said he was heading over to Veronica Pritchard's, something about a ring.'

'Mmmm, I spoke to Eleanor last night. What a disaster the whole thing has been for him.' Cissy explained everything to Seymour and as she was doing so who should walk in but Veronica Pritchard.

'Well you've got a nerve,' said Cissy. 'Waltzing in here like you haven't caused World War Three.'

'I came to return this,' she said, handing Cissy the ring. Cissy opened the box to reveal the stunning engagement ring. She gasped at the sight of it.

'You do know the trouble you've caused,' said Cissy.

'Come on, it was just a joke,' said the vacuous Veronica.

'A joke? You call it a joke when my brother nearly gets beaten up by Eleanor's brothers and Eleanor is refusing to marry him.'

Cissy noticed the slight smirk on Veronica's face. 'Come on, it was a joke I'm telling you, it was just a joke.' That was when Hudson walked in the door and spun Veronica forcefully around to face him, the look on his face was enough to wilt the toughest man.

'What do you think you're playing at?' he roared, 'Give me back Eleanor's ring.' He held Veronica firmly by the arm.

'Gee-whiz, let me go,' she moaned. 'It was only a joke.'

'Some joke,' shouted Hudson, 'you have more than likely ruined my life!'

Cissy stepped in, 'It's all right Hudson, I have the ring. Here it is. It's beautiful.'

'But everything's not all right, Eleanor refuses to marry me and her brothers think I am some sort of philanderer.'

'It'll be all right Hudson, I am sure of it. Go to her and explain it. She'll listen to you.'

Hudson gave a sigh of defeat and taking his sister's advice headed to his car, only to hear the pathetic pleading of Veronica, 'It was only a joke Hudson, I was never going to keep the ring.'

'Oh, for God's sake get out of here,' said Cissy, 'and don't come back again.'

Veronica left. She'd blown it big time. She didn't really know what her next move was. Perhaps it was time to look for fresh hunting grounds.

The salon was busy when Hudson arrived. Ladies' heads turned as he walked in, eyes directed at Eleanor.

'I'm busy, I don't have time for you Hudson and I don't want to talk to you.' Ladies being ladies, immediately tuned into the mini-drama that was unfolding before them. Eleanor stood with her hands on her hips, tail comb in one hand. Hudson got down on one knee. He reached into his pocket and this time successfully came out with the ring, 'Make me the happiest man in the world Eleanor and marry me, please?'

Eleanor caught her breath at the sight of the ring, speechless. She looked at him, lips sealed, not knowing what to say. 'Eleanor, I love you with all of my heart and I am sorry for all my stupidity. Please say you'll marry me?' The clients held their collective breaths.

'All right, all right I'll marry you.'

'Good for you,' yelled one patron and they all burst into applause as Hudson stood and swept Eleanor into his arms.

'Just one thing,' said Eleanor, 'what happened to the ring?'

'That was Veronica.' Eleanor glared at him, but not so much so that she was going to go back on her word to marry him.

'Who's Veronica?' asked a lady sitting under the dryer.

'You don't want to know,' said Hudson, as he looked into his future wife's eyes and planted the biggest kiss on her lips to the further applause of their little audience.

'Now go on, get out of here,' she ordered her fiancé.

As Hudson left, unable to hide his glee, he turned and gave her a little wave, all of the women's eyes on him.

'I'd look out for that Veronica if I were you love,' commented one of the women.

'Yes, she sounds like a piece of work,' added another.

Eleanor couldn't agree more, but she wasn't going to get into it with her clients. As she accompanied one woman over to the basin, she thought about Veronica, she would keep an eye on her, a very close eye.

The Saturday night show in the little grain shed picture theatre was over. Seymour locked up the front door as he walked his sister down the poplar tree-lined lane past the stunning new theatre, now lit-up in all its glory, on their short walk home. 'Got anything planned for tomorrow?' he asked.

'Matter of fact, Ambros has asked me on a picnic to Lerderderg Gorge.'

'Are you sure you're not jumping from the frying pan into the fire Cissy? First a pansy and now a German.'

'Look, I know I made a mistake with Godfrey — a hideous mistake, but Ambros is different. He is such a gentleman, and he is definitely not one of those.'

'How do you know?'

'I just do, I can just tell.'

'Hmmm, well you be careful little sister. Your choice in men has not been the best so far.' They reached the gate and Cissy walked in ahead of her brother, not wanting to discuss her personal life anymore.'

The sun was shining the next morning and Cissy was up early. She was so excited about the picnic with Ambros. It was quite strange really, because she had never really felt this way about a date before in her life. She wore a pretty yellow cotton dress that had a scooped neckline with covered buttons down the front, short sleeves and a sash tie at the waist. The pattern was delicate with sprays of tiny purple and white snowdrops.

Cissy so hoped Ambros would like it. She was becoming very conscious of the fact that he was a fashion designer. Perhaps everything she wore was ugly. Maybe she should change. Just then the doorbell rang, and she heard her father go to the door. She hadn't told him about the picnic and her heart sank.

He might not even let her go. He might throw the German out on his ear. Cissy was in a mild panic, she hurried downstairs to meet Ambros. He was in the den with her father. CC had offered him a cup of tea and the two were now sitting, having a man to man. 'And here she is,' said CC when his daughter entered the room. Ambros stood and bowed slightly when she entered the room.

'Good morning Cissy. You are looking very fresh and summery.' CC couldn't help but be impressed with his manners.

'Ambros and I have been talking,' said CC. 'You didn't tell me that his father was the famous Hans Zimmerman.'

Cissy was surprised, she didn't know that her father knew anything about the world of fashion, let alone know of Ambros's father. Her father saw the surprise in her face and explained, 'Your mother was a great fan of his work. As a matter of fact, her wedding dress was designed by Mr Zimmerman. Such a pity we lost it in the fire, but I do have a photo.'

Cissy was stunned that her mother had worn a dress designed by Ambros's father. 'Is that the dress that I have always loved? The one in your wedding photo?' Cissy turned to look at the beautiful wedding photo of her mother and her father that took prime position on the mantle above the fireplace, the sight of her mother in that spectacular wedding gown always took her breath away.

'Your father designed this dress?' she asked Ambros, showing him the photo.

'I probably wasn't even born then, but we would have an archive of it somewhere, dad keeps all of his designs on record.'

'It's simply beautiful.'

'As is your mother, I can see where you get your beauty from.'

CC was warming to this young man. He seemed to have a very good attitude, but it was more than that. He sensed a kindness, a caring nature that had certainly been absent in Godfrey. 'You didn't tell me anything about this picnic, Cissy.' Cissy suddenly felt herself colouring from embarrassment. What if her father wouldn't let her go?

'I'm sorry Dad, things have just been so hectic.' CC thought about Margot. Just looking at their wedding photo had brought out a flood of memories again. She would tell him to stop being so over-protective, to let the girl have her fun. She was grown-up now and he needed to trust her.

'It's okay sweetheart, it's fine. You two go along now and have a good time.'

As they left the house, CC wondered how serious Cissy was about this young man. He knew a little more about him now, so he felt far more comfortable, but there was still more investigating to be done. If Cissy was going to be seeing this German chap, CC wanted to know everything about him.

Sammy may have been frightened by the visit the Lansing boys paid him, but nothing could stop him from taking a risk for a good quid.

They were sitting in Godfrey's car, well out of the view of anyone, parked on the banks of Kororoit Creek. The factories nearby were closed on a Sunday, but you could still see their effluent running into the creek and the place smelt of waste. Godfrey wanted to get away from there as quickly as he could.

'So, you have everything you need?' he asked the reprobate.

'Yes, but I am going to need money in advance,' warned Sammy.

'Here's a hundred quid, you'll get the rest when the job's done.'

'No deal, you said the same on the blackmail job and I never did get the balance of payment. I did my bit and all I got for it was a lousy hundred quid and a bit of a bruising from those Cheltenham boys. I want two hundred up front and another two when the job's done, otherwise you can do it yourself.'

Sammy was driving a hard bargain, but secretly Godfrey thought he would be a fool not to. This was a big risk he was taking, and Godfrey would have paid him another two hundred on top of that, but he wasn't letting on. 'All right, all right. As long as the job's done tomorrow morning, on the dot of ten o'clock, when the funeral is on.'

Sammy took the money and got out of the car. He was going to clear out of town after this. Things were getting too hot. A new place, a new start. Maybe he'd even go straight.

The birds were chirping merrily as Cissy and Ambros sat by the bank of the river that ran through the gorge. Ambros had brought a bottle of champagne and Cissy was a bit heady with all the bubbles. The picnic he had packed was superb, with some European meats she had never tried before, like prosciutto and salami. The biscuits were also unusual — quite savoury and the cheeses ripe and pungent, but she loved it all and felt pampered like a queen. No one had gone to this much trouble over her before.

She lay down on the picnic rug on her back, staring up at the clouds slowly moving by. 'I often wonder where those clouds are going and what it would be like to be up among them.'

'Have you ever been up in a plane?' asked Ambros.

'Goodness me no, I couldn't possibly get into one of those things. Have you?'

'Oh yes, several times. A friend of dad's has an airstrip on his property and has a Tiger Moth. It's quite good fun, you should try it one day.'

'Is that an invitation?'

'If you want it to be?'

'Okay,' said Cissy, surprising Ambros. He lay down beside her, on his stomach, staring into her blue eyes.

'That was a sudden turn-around.'

'I know, I'm impulsive. I don't want to miss out on things in life, if you don't stick your neck out a bit, how are you going to experience all of the exciting things the world has to offer?'

'That's what I like to hear. Take a risk, live dangerously and enjoy life to its fullest.' Cissy was laughing at Ambros's gaiety. He stared down into her face and impulse overwhelmed him, he lowered his face to hers and kissed her tenderly.

Cissy felt every nerve in her body electrify. The feelings consumed her, and she gently placed her arms around Ambros's neck, kissing him back. He stopped momentarily, looking into her eyes. He asked her, 'Are you sure about this?'

Cissy nodded, 'Yes Ambros, oh yes.' Suddenly he was on top of her, and their embrace was inflamed with passion. His hand travelled down her body and Cissy bent one knee up, her body rising into his. He caressed her bare leg, and she felt his heat. Cissy couldn't get enough of him, nor he of her. He removed his hand from her leg to find the buttons of her bodice. Gently he undid them until he revealed her breasts.

If passion could become any more intense Cissy was sure she didn't know how. Ambros's tongue brushed her nipples and she thought she would go wild with desire. She wanted all of him and she loosened his shirt from his trousers and found his bare skin.

It was enough for Ambros. He wanted her completely, and fired with passion but filled with tenderness, he made love to her. Cissy could never have imagined such feeling, such depth of emotion, and her tears were testament to that. But they were tears of joy, tears of discovery, tears of knowing when something felt utterly pure and right, more so than anything she had every experienced in her life. She succumbed to her feelings and on the banks of Lerderderg River, Cissy knew what it was like to truly give yourself in the name of love.

Chapter Twenty-Seven

THE BURIAL WAS A SIMPLE AFFAIR. More of the townsfolk than Miriam had anticipated turned out. Those women who had cared for Mrs Worthing in her final days had come along. Sylvia Wright-Smith was unusually calm and solemn. The Cambridge family was showing support as was everyone in attendance. George Roberts had taken time off from the dairy and Peter the Greek had donned his best suit to show respect for the mother of Miriam, a young woman for whom he had great admiration.

After the burial Sylvia bustled around, organising people to come to Miriam's home for a cup of tea and some refreshments. Miriam, finding it hard to control her tears, was glad Cissy was there by her side, consoling her friend and doing all she could to help.

Not terribly interested in a cup of tea, and feeling as though they had paid their respects, Hudson and Seymour gave their condolences once again to Miriam and said they must head into the theatre to continue on with the final arrangements for the opening. The brothers left in Hudson's car while Cissy escorted Miriam over to CC's Humber.

As Cissy watched Hudson drive away, she had a feeling of foreboding and could not define it. She shook it off as she hopped into her father's car, ready to help Miriam through the wake, knowing that her friend could begin to rebuild her life once all of these affairs were in order.

Hampshire Road was unusually quiet for a Monday. Peter the Greek had closed his hamburger café to attend Mrs Worthing's funeral. With the entire Cambridge family also in attendance, the new picture theatre was locked up tight and there was no one working in the old grain shed picture theatre at the back. Sammy acted quickly. He had surrounded the border with kerosene and was now at the back of the theatre where he had piled up as much litter and fallen tree branches and other dried leaves that he could find.

He was grateful for the fact that not all of the debris had been cleared away from the construction works, it all made nice kindling and would add great fuel to the fire.

He lit the match.

He then ran like the devil, straight across the railway lines at the back of the theatre and well out of sight. The theatre was engulfed in flames in seconds, but not before Hudson and Seymour pulled up and saw the horrific result of Sammy's work. Hudson ran for the hose located at the old picture theatre at the back of the property.

There was a fire alarm directly across the road and Seymour raced over to it. Surrounding houses saw the flames and rushed to the Cambridge's aid. The house next door hooked a hose to their front garden tap and Seymour was frantically using it on the front of the theatre while Hudson was hosing the back.

Hudson was concentrating on the pile of debris someone had built up against the back wall and he cursed the builders for not clearing up properly but was relieved to see the fire diminishing the more he hosed the pile of rubble. Brick was a wonderful building material, and this solid structure was not giving in quickly to any man-made fire.

Neighbours were carting buckets and throwing them onto the north side of the building, where, if the line of poplars caught fire, then the threat of flames could spread rapidly.

Finally, the bell of the fire truck arrived. The station was only a block away and a team of horses was always harnessed during the day and ready to go. The firemen acted quickly, they brought out their big hoses and a team of two men charged to the rear of the building.

Hudson had done a great job of controlling the flames, but it looked like there was a bit of activity going on in the roofing area. 'We are going to need access to the building,' shouted the fireman. Hudson dropped his hose and immediately ran to the front door, but his brother was ahead of him. Seymour had opened up the building and a team of firemen was rushing in.

The foyer was largely undamaged. They rushed through to the auditorium and right down to the front of the stalls. Flames were flaring up around the screen area and the fireman acted quickly to bring this under control.

CC had heard the bad news and was quickly on the scene. He walked in to join his two sons, Sylvia Wright-Smith following right behind. 'I know who has done this,' he said.

'How can you be sure?' said Seymour. They all knew who he was talking about.

'Oh, I am sure,' said Hudson. 'The back of the theatre was piled up with debris, someone put that there, it certainly didn't get there on its own.'

The three men looked at each other. They would give the culprits what they deserved, but right now there was damage to assess and decisions to be made. The fire having been brought under control; CC led the family to the front of the theatre.

The neighbours were there, and other folks had come from further afield originally to see the spectacle, but now they wanted to see what they could do to help. They were gathered, some in the smoky foyer and some on the steps of what was the grand entrance to the theatre. 'What can we do?' spoke up old Timothy Murphy. 'This is an outrage. We understand what you have lost, but it is our loss too, we were all looking forward to this great new picture theatre. The town was excited and now someone — and I must say it would be someone who has a grudge against you and your family,' he said to CC, 'has tried to ruin this for all of us. Well, I say to hell with them and let's get in and fix it.'

A roar of approval went up from the crowd. CC quieted them by patting his hands in the air. 'I appreciate everyone's concern and offers of help. Heaven knows we could use it and we will. I am going to put Seymour and Hudson in charge of righting the wrong that has been done to us today. All those who would like to help please give your name and address, as well as what you believe you could do to help, to one of my boys. The picture theatre will open, a little bit later than we expected but by God if we can't have it open early in the New Year then I will bare my bum in Bourke Street!'

The crowd roared laughing at CC's humour in the face of adversity. They bustled forward, jostling for position to put their names on the list. CC nodded to Sylvia Wright-Smith, and they entered his office, sitting down like the two weary folk that they were, and pouring a glass of Scotch each.

'To the future,' said CC, raising his glass.

'To our future,' was the comeback from Miss Wright-Smith. And they chinked glasses, savouring the golden liquid.

Epilogue

FINALLY, it was time to open the grand new theatre. Cissy was run off her feet that morning. They were screening a double feature of *Yankee Doodle Dandy* and *Going My Way*. CC thought the musicals appropriate for the opening, he wanted this to be a real celebration. He had ordered in a buffet spread for the extra-long interval and everyone who had helped restore the theatre after the fire, was invited to attend at no charge.

Cissy and Hudson's poster looked amazing. They had painted extra sheets and hung them on the back wall of the kiosk. Everything was coming together when that sudden nauseous feeling overcame Cissy once more. She had been feeling it now for going on a week and couldn't understand why. She was never normally sick and had no change in her diet. She went to the kiosk for a soda water to settle her stomach.

Miss Wright-Smith arrived and began to go through some of the details just as Cissy thought she might really be sick, she excused herself, she was never sick, but when she finally made it to the toilet, she found herself violently retching.

She left the toilet and headed to the basin, splashing cold water on her face and wrists. Perhaps it was the January heat getting to her. As she left the toilet she noticed Miss Wright-Smith's eyes following her.

Sylvia Wright-Smith thought it very odd that Cissy was rushing to the toilet like that. Obviously the girl was sick. 'Why don't you go home, relax. We'll be able to handle this.'

'No, I'm all right, really.'

Miss Wright-Smith looked at her strangely. Cissy was never sick.

THE END OF BOOK ONE

IN MEMORY OF NOLA

Don't Miss Book Two

Read how the Cambridge family went on to open the Sunshine Picture Theatre and expand their empire. Learn the outcome of Cissy's relationship with Ambros and Sylvia Wright-Smith's determination to ensnare CC in a contract of marriage. It is a year of weddings for the Cambridge family. Will Miriam take up Cissy on her idea of the Bake 'n' Booty? How is Peter the Greek affected by the new Sunshine Picture Theatre and how is George coping now that he has ridded himself of the terrible stress of Wilbur's blackmail? What of the Maxwells? Are they still plotting against CC and his family? Where did Sammy disappear to? These and other mysteries are awaiting you in Book Two of The Cambridge Empire.

Acknowledgments

Where do I start? I owe this story to my family, to my wonderful childhood growing up in the picture theatres, particularly, the Sunshine Picture Theatre. Thanks go to my grandfather, George Kirby, for inspiring the Carleton Cambridge character. To my father, Kingsley Kirby, for the Hudson character, to my Uncle Roc for the Seymour character, to my mother for the Eleanor character, to my Aunty Lucy for the Cissy character and my Aunty Beatrice for the Loretta character. Thanks to Aunty Wanda and Uncle Lloyd too, for just being part of it all. Unfortunately, all these wonderful people are no longer with us.

I'd like to thank all my cousins, John, Robert, Geoffrey, the late Jennifer and Alfred, Wendy, Rick, Helen and Trish. Thanks for all the fun we had at the theatres and for creating memories that inspired this book and will become more apparent in future books about the Cambridge Empire.

I am grateful to my sisters Nola, Cheryl and Denise for their ongoing support. Cheryl's input into our background was of enormous help.

There are many others who worked for the theatres who have given me great inspiration into creating further characters. There are people who lived in the community of Sunshine with whom I grew up, many have been fashioned into characters and others will find their voice in future books. Kay Taylor, if you ever get to read this, take note that your bakery is going to be a big feature in my next book in the Cambridge series.

If I have left anyone out I sincerely apologise, just put it down to a
dodgy memory.

About the Author

CHRIS KIRBY-RYAN

Chris's love of writing was triggered from an early age, being brought up in a family that owned several cinemas, when she was growing up back in the fifties and sixties. Chris would watch the movies over and over again, inspiring her to create stories of her own.

She entered advertising at the age of eighteen and became a copywriter, working in many large, multi-national advertising agencies at senior writer and creative director level. She has had hundreds of articles and editorials published and has written across a broad spectrum of media. Chris opened her own advertising agency in the eighties, then later became a full-time freelance writer, helping others tell their stories and completing several novels of her own.

Chris currently lives in the Brisbane seaside suburb of Redcliffe, Queensland, with her husband, John.

Memorabilia

Let me share a little of the history of the
Kirby picture theatres and our family.

Location: **128 Hampshire Road**   **Sunshine**

                                                                    Map Reference: 40 H1

Recommended Level of Significa *City*   **Other listings:**

2000 Study Site N *126*   **Heritage Overlav:** *127*   **Reg No:**

PAHT: *8 Developing Australia's cultural life*   **HO status:**

SUBTHEME *8.1 Organising recreation*

AHC Criteria: *A4, E1, G1*

Statement of Significance

The former Sunshine Picture Theatre is of historical, architectural and social significance to the City of Brimbank as a relatively well-preserved pre-World War Two cinema which represents the expansion of the cinema to suburban centres around Melbourne and the 'Golden Years' of cinema- going and popular entertainment in Australia. The cinema was the focus of both common and sophisticated entertainment and recreation in Sunshine from the 1930s to the 1970s. It is the only near -original cinema exterior in the City of Brimbank. It is also a major building in what was the social and civic centre of Sunshine in the inter-war period. Architecturally, it compares with the Moderne styling seen in a more articulated manner at Sunshine Technical School but there are few other buildings of comparable size and style in the municipality.

Description

This is a Moderne style, one and two-storey, former theatre, sited opposite the Masonic Hall in the former civic and social centre of Sunshine. The street facade has a streamlined tiered treatment with curved corners and projecting fins, all executed in moulded cement. The projection booth, set back in the upper level, sits forward of the auditorium and so is expressed externally. Originally, banding at the plinth and a string course at the top of the entrance created a strong horizontal effect. This was accentuated by the curve-edged cantilevered verandah over the set-back entrance. The multiple sets of glass doors sat at the top of a small flight of three steps. Internally, the building was decorated with Moderne style geometric patterns executed in plaster, with timber panelling in the foyer. Much of this has been removed in the conversion to first a furniture shop, and then to offices. However, the ceiling panels and proscenium arch remain intact.

History   **Architect:**   **Date** 1925, altered 1936

Cinema came to Sunshine in 1918 when the Johnstone Brothers of Lyric Pictures set up weekly shows in the Mechanics Institute. Later N.J. Vernon showed pictures at the Sunshine Town Hall for a brief period before C.H. Meddesdorffer took over late in 1925. In the 1920s, Melbourne accountant Jack O'Brien formed Sunshine Pictures Pty. Ltd and purchased a grain store in Hampshire Road, opening it as a cinema on 21 March 1925, with The Hummingbird, starring Gloria Swanson. The then -silent movies were accompanied by a theatre pianist. The competition from the cinema brought an end to pictures at the town hall before the end of the decade. This grain store is believed to have been on the site of the present Sunshine Theatre, and may have been subsequently incorporated in the redeveloped cinema. The next development of cinema entertainment came when Benz 'all-Australian talkie equipment' was installed at the Sunshine Picture Theatre in 1930. In the following year George Kirby arrived in Sunshine and took over the cinema. He was responsible for extensive alterations around January 1936, renaming it 'The New Sunshine Theatre' in 1938. The impact of the cinema in Sunshine extended to amateur cinematographers such as John H. Jackson, who was president of the Sunshine Movie Society in 1935. The cinema had mixed fortunes in the post-war period, operating profitably into the 1960s, but then suffering a decline in the '70s, eventually closing and being converted to a furniture store in around 1975. It is now used as offices by the Smith Family.

Condition/Integrity

In fair condition. Much of the original art deco decoration has been removed, both inside and out. The conversion to commercial use has meant the foyer has been stripped and the entrance remodelled in modern glazing.

Context/Comparative analysis

One of a diminishing number of suburban cinemas of the pre-World War Two period, for example, the demolished Padua Theatre in Brunswick.

References

C.G. Carlton (ed.), Sunshine Cavalcade, 1951, p.50. Prue McGoldrick, When the Whistle Blew, 1989, pp 119, 143-4, Sunshine Advocate, January 1936.

Recommendations

Recommended for inclusion in the Heritage Overlay of the City of Brimbank Planning Scheme.

SUDDEN DEATH OF LEADING CITIZEN

George Kirby's Great Public Service

Citizens of Sunshine were shocked on Saturday to learn of the sudden death of Mr. George A. Kirby, of the Sunshine Theatre. He collapsed while getting into his car in Durham Road.

Mr. Kirby was in his late seventies and was a most estimable public citizen. His passing will be mourned by a large circle of friends.

After a boyhood in the Preston district he went to a farm near Leongatha which his father had bought, and George became a man on the land.

In the 1920's he sold his interest in the property and entered the motor industry at Geelong and equipped the most up-to-date garage and motor car agency in that city.

With the depression at its highest peak Mr. Kirby like many others, received the full impact of low values and general unemployment, and lost practically everything he had.

Seeking an avenue of business to start afresh, and having a liking for entertainment, he was given a chance in 1932 to secure a lease of the moribund Sunshine Theatre. He took it over and a new era in his life commenced.

With perseverance and attention to detail he placed the theatre once more on a paying basis, and as the years have gone by he and his family have acquired interests in other theatres in suburbs and

country. He was regarded as the biggest independent theatre director in Victoria.

BENEFACTOR

Sunshine people knew him better for his interest in the public welfare. Every local organisation has at some time or other come under his beneficial and benevolent influence.

Commencing with sporting activities, he was a vice-president of Sunshine Cricket Association, president of Druids Cricket Club (30 years), Baseball Club (25 years), and for a period was on the committee of Sunshine Football Club.

For the past 15 years he has been the president of Sunshine City Band and was prominent in the building of the present bandroom. He served two years as president of the Dads Association and was a foundation member of the Lodge of St. Mark.

Mr. Kirby was a member of Sunshine Lions and was probably the oldest member in Victoria of that organisation.

The funeral was one of the largest in Sunshine's history and the services at the St. Mark's Church of England and at the crematorium were conducted by the Rev. J. L. McAuley. Sunshine Band played

hymns and then marched at the head of the funeral cortege from the church and at the Fawkner Cemetery.

At Sunshine city council meeting on Monday reference was made by Cr. F. Grundy to Mr. Kirby's record of citizenship and council was adjourned for a few minutes out of respect to his memory and to the memory of others whose death occurred during the last few days.

Mr. Kirby's wife died some years ago. He is survived by Kingsley, Wanda (Mrs. White), Roscoe and Lucy (Mrs. Ogilvie), and 13 grandchildren.

The Roxy Theatre in Maidstone

Mr. KIRBY'S ENTERPRISE.

Mr. George Kirby, proprietor of the Sunshine Theatre, completed arrangements this week for the purchase of the Bacchus Marsh Theatre. The acquisition of this theatre completes a circuit of three that Mr. Kirby has been hopeful of securing, the Altona Theatre being under the control of Mr. Kirby for some time. It is expected that Mr. Kirby will now be able to compete for the early suburban release of the latest feature films, and thus Sunshine people will benefit through his enterprise.

★ OBITUARY

Mrs. Rosa June Kirby

THE death occurred on Friday last of Mrs. Rosa June Kirby, well-known to Sunshine people through her association with her husband (Mr. George Kirby) and sons (Kingsley and Roscoe) in the management of the Sunshine Picture Theatre.

The late Mrs. Kirby, who was born at Bairnsdale, came to Sunshine with her husband and family from Geelong about 20 years ago, and resided in the district ever since.

In her own quiet way she assisted many charitable causes and was highly esteemed throughout Sunshine.

She leaves her husband, two sons and two daughters (Mrs L. White and Mrs. C. Ogilvie) and thirteen grand children to mourn their sad loss.

The funeral, which was largely attended, took place to the Fawkner Crematorium on Monday last, and there were many beautiful floral tributes.

The pall bearers were Councillors Parsons, Green and Beachley, J's.P., Ex-Cr. G. E. Dobson, J.P., Mr. E. Hargreaves (town clerk), Mr P. J. White (Sunshine City Band), Mr. C. G. Carlton, J.P., Mr. T. Houghton of Sorrento, and Mr. R. Wanklyn (manager RKO Radio Pictures).

Mr E. W. Jackson of Williamstown was the funeral director.

Complimentary Social to Mr. G. Kirby

Organised by the Sunshine Old Boys' Association a complimentary social evening was tendered to Mr George Kirby in the Masonic Hall, Sunshine, on Tuesday evening last.

There were about 150 present and the toast of the "Guest of the Evening", proposed by Mr. T. Hyde (President, Old Boys Assoc.) was supported by Mr. H. Weeding (Vice President), Mr. T. Laffan (Baseball Club), Mr. P. J. White (Sun. Dist. Band), Mr. J. Parten (Cricket Assoc.), Mr. R. Butlimer (Druids C.C.) and Mr. N. Green (Sunshine C.C.).

Each of the speakers referred in generous terms to the interest Mr. Kirby had displayed in local activities, particularly in relation to sport and the district brass band.

On behalf of the organisations named, Mr. E. Shepherd, M.L.A., presented Mr. Kirby with a wristlet watch and asked him to accept a china tea service for Mrs. Kirby.

In reply, Mr. Kirby referred to the immense pleasure he had derived through his association with a wonderful band of fellows, and anything he had done or tried to do was at all times a labor of love.

Mr. R. K. McDonald proposed the toast of the Braybrook Shire Council and the response was given by Cr. T. R. Barclay. The toast of the "Old Boys Assoc." was given by Cr. A. G. Penn It and responded to by Mr. Reg Hand and Mr. W. Hallahan.

Mr. C. G. Carlton, J.P., compered the entertainment and an excellent musical program was rendered by Mr. Herbert Browne (baritone), Mr. Ken Mountain (comedian), Marlo (magician and escapologist), Mr. Arch Noble (hypnotist) and Mr. A. Olarenshaw (pianist).

KIRBY'S THEATRES EXTEND

Mr. George Kirby, the enterprising head of Kirby's Theatres, has added another link to his chain of picture theatres; by the acquisition of the theatre in one of Victoria's most popular seaside holiday resorts.

It is understood that the purchase embraces a very large estate. This will bring the circuit up to five theatres, the others being Sunshine, Roxy (Maidstone), Bacchus Marsh and Altona.

Wedding Bells

KIRBY — WHITE

A wedding, with an Air Force flavour, was celebrated on Saturday last at St. Luke's Church of England, Yarraville, when Miss Wanda Lulea Kirby, eldest daughter of Mr. and Mrs. G. Kirby, of the Sunshine Theatre, was united to Aircraftman Lloyd George White, only son of Mr. and Mrs. George White, of Barkly Street, Footscray, by the Rev. S. H. Smith. The bridesmaids were Miss Lucie Kirby, sister of the bride, and Miss Patricia White, sister of the bridegroom.

The bride looked charming in a white moire taffeta gown with a heart shaped neckline, with shirred bodice and very full skirt. A hand-worked veil was held with a spray of azaleas, and she carried a bouquet of azaleas and delphiniums.

The bridesmaids wore Love-in-the-Mist crinckled georgette, with heart shaped neckline and sunray pleated skirts.

Flying Officer R. Winter was best man and Sergeant W. Newington, R.A.A.F., groomsman.

The reception was held at the residence of Mr. and Mrs. Kirby, at 127 Durham Road, Sunshine, at which there were 60 relatives and friends present. Mrs. Kirby wore a gown of beaded dusty pink and carried a bouquet of Cecil Brunner roses, whilst Mrs. White's frock was of rose beige and brown velvet, and her bouquet contained miniature roses and gladioli.

Flying-Officer Winter had charge of proceedings and his humor was infectious. The usual toasts were honoured and the responses were made by the bridegroom, the best man, and Messrs G. Kirby and G. White.

My Father's paintings and drawings

Some of my Father's paintings and charcoal drawings
of movie stars of the time. Most of these were done as he wiled
away the hours in the projection box at Sunshine Picture Theatre.

Ronald Colman

Victor Maclachlan.

An old movie advertising sign hand-done by my father,
shown here at the Sunshine railway crossing,
circa 1948.

Other Books by Chris Kirby-Ryan

RAINBOW HOUSE

When two 13-year-old girls become foster sisters, their lives seem worlds apart. Rachel is the daughter of the town's rich Mayor, while Summer — due to tragic circumstances — has been a victim of the foster system and all the pitfalls that can go with it.

Having escaped from an abusive foster home, Summer lives in fear of her former foster father catching up with her. Rachel simply lives in fear. When the girls get together, they realise their lives aren't really that different after all, and together with the town's new policewoman, they begin an investigation which leads them to one of the country's, if not the world's, biggest paedophile rings.

From the involving and tragic stories of the suffering children in Part 1, to the revelations and high-profile court trial in Part 2, Rainbow House will keep the reader intrigued from start to finish and thinking about the story long after they have turned the final page.

MARRIED IN MACEDONIA

Choosing Sasa's remote hometown on the other side of the world was meant to keep their wedding small and intimate, it's gone way past that. Jacki may be Miss Popularity, but she has no idea how her unassuming and placid fiancé will cope.

With the cat out of the bag, and the wedding no longer a secret, who'd have thought so many Australians would go above and beyond to get to Macedonia for a wedding? Not Jacki and Sasa — that's for sure. Now with one hundred and fifty Australians heading for Macedonia, the wedding is heading for disaster. The hire equipment is hijacked, the catering is falling in a heap and the bride is falling apart. Her gown is far from ready, her dream wedding is rapidly declining into a nightmare and calling it off would solve everything.

Can Sasa rescue this mess? Can he put aside his insecurities and pull this wedding back into line? Will the wedding even proceed? It's time for Shirley to step up and take action. With the big day about to dawn, guests arrive, gowns are finally readied and the little town is abuzz with excitement.

Married is Macedonia is a rollicking ride of hilarity and sometimes tears as we share the marital journey of the lovable Sasa and Jacki. With guests virtually walking over hot coals to get there, and in spite of all the hurdles only a Macedonian village can throw up, a beautiful wedding takes place — family feuds are forgotten and even the wedding crashers are welcomed.

SHE'S MY BABY

Grace Draper comes out of emergency surgery to find an empty crib. Now the police are looking for little Ella-Louise, the precious daughter she gave birth to just three days ago. Known baby-brokers are under investigation but the detectives just can't get a break.

This is a romance thriller set in the beautiful Southern Highlands of New South Wales, but the high-tension chase for the missing baby leads us through the gritty underworld of Sydney's inner fringe. Charlie Draper is an accomplished detective, however when it's his own daughter who's missing, Charlie is doing all he can not to fall apart. His wife walked out on him two weeks before the baby was due and his life has been on a downward spiral ever since. Still madly in love with Grace he is doing everything within his power to convince her to come home, and to find their daughter; but no matter how hard he tries he just can't seem to win Grace back.

She hadn't left him unthinkingly. They had been married for three years but had been together for five. As he progressed through the ranks of the police force his time became more and more taxed. He kept telling her it would change. Once he'd made Senior Sergeant he would have more time on his hands.

But right now all she wanted was her baby back.

Martha O'Reilly had wanted a baby since she was a little girl playing with dress-up dolls. At thirty-eight her biological clock was ticking and when she was about to give birth to her first child there wasn't a happier mother-to-be. But the euphoria was short lived. Due to birth complications her baby was stillborn. But Martha would have her baby — no matter what.

The search for Ella-Louise uncovers a ring of baby-brokers, murderers and extortionists. Can a doctor be involved in this web of deceit, what is his motive? Little does Martha know, but her desperate actions will help many grieving mothers to recover their long-lost infants by creating a trail of evidence that goes way beyond one baby — one kidnapping.

Come back Charlie. Come back Ella Louise.

She's My Baby will have you enthralled from cover to cover as the police turn up dead end after dead end — but in the end it's love that will win and it's a mother who truly knows her child.

SHADOWS OF YESTERDAY

This is story is based on Georgina Thompson's horrific childhood. From the age of just two, Georgina experienced some of the most horrendous abuse and cruelty, unimaginable to the average person. Whilst evil seemed to dominate her life, help came to her and her siblings from beyond the natural. A mystical being, an outer-universal authority who took Georgina, Dolly and Tommy on some fascinating and often frightening, learning journeys.

But it wasn't enough. The days were still filled with cruelty, it seemed as though the children would never escape this web of abuse. A mother who suffered a long history of violence, uncles cursed with evil, a gangster for a father and later a stepfather whose evil outtrumped all others. Georgina survived her battles, she overcame the generational curse, escaped death and lived to tell this story.

CHRIS KIRBY-RYAN

For more about Chris Kirby-Ryan, visit her website:
www.chriskirbyryan.com.au